Sylvia's Marriage

Upton Sinclair

Contents

SYLVIA'S MARRIAGE

BY

Upton Sinclair

SYLVIA'S MARRIAGE
SOME PRESS NOTICES

"The importance of the theme cannot be doubted, and no one hitherto ignorant of the ravages of the evil and therefore, by implication, in need of being convinced can refuse general agreement with Mr. Sinclair upon the question as he argues it. The character that matters most is very much alive and most entertaining."-- *The Times.*

"Very severe and courageous. It would, indeed, be difficult to deny or extenuate the appalling truth of Mr. Sinclair's indictment."-- *The Nation.*

"There is not a man nor a grown woman who would not be better for reading Sylvia's Marriage."-- *The Globe*

"Those who found Sylvia charming on her first appearance will find her as beautiful and fascinating as ever."-- The Pall Mall.

"A novel that frankly is devoted to the illustration of the dangers that society runs through the marriage of unsound men with unsuspecting women. The time has gone by when any objection was likely to be taken to a perfectly clean discussion of a nasty subject."-- *T.P.'s Weekly.*

BOOK I
SYLVIA AS WIFE

1. I am telling the story of Sylvia Castleman. I should prefer to tell it without mention of myself; but it was written in the book of fate that I should be a decisive factor in her life, and so her story pre-supposes mine. I imagine the impatience of a reader, who is promised a heroine out of a romantic and picturesque "society" world, and finds himself beginning with the autobiography of a farmer's wife on a solitary homestead in Manitoba. But then I remember that Sylvia found me interesting. Putting myself in her place, remembering her eager questions and her exclamations, I am able to see myself as a heroine of fiction.

I was to Sylvia a new and miraculous thing, a self-made woman. I must have been the first "common" person she had ever known intimately. She had seen us afar off, and wondered vaguely about us, consoling herself with the reflection that we probably did not know enough to be unhappy over our sad lot in life. But here I was, actually a soul like herself; and it happened that I knew more than she did, and of things she desperately needed to know. So all the luxury, power and prestige that had been given to Sylvia Castleman seemed as nothing beside Mary Abbott, with her modern attitude and her common-sense.

My girlhood was spent upon a farm in Iowa. My father had eight children, and he drank. Sometimes he struck me; and so it came about that at the age of seventeen I ran away with a boy of twenty who worked upon a neighbour's farm. I wanted a home of my own, and Tom had some money saved up. We journeyed to Manitoba, and took out a homestead, where I spent the next twenty years of my life in a hand-to-hand struggle with Nature which seemed simply incredible to Sylvia when I told her of it.

The man I married turned out to be a petty tyrant. In the first five years of our life he succeeded in killing the love I had for him; but meantime I had borne him three children, and there was nothing to do but make the best of my bargain. I became to outward view a beaten drudge; yet it was the truth that never for an hour did I give up. When I lost what would have been my fourth child, and the doctor told me that I could never have another, I took this for my charter of freedom, and made up my mind to my course; I would raise the children I had, and grow up with them, and move out into life when they did.

This was when I was working eighteen hours a day, more than half of it by lamp-light, in the darkness of our Northern winters. When the accident came, I had been doing the cooking for half a dozen men, who were getting in the wheat upon which our future depended. I fell in my tracks, and lost my child; yet I sat still and white while the men ate supper, and afterwards I washed up the dishes. Such was my life in those days; and I can see before me the face of horror with which Sylvia listened to the story. But these things are common in the experience of women who live upon pioneer farms, and toil as the slave-woman has toiled since civilization began.

We won out, and my husband made money. I centred my energies upon getting school-time for my children; and because I had resolved that they should not grow ahead of me, I sat up at night, and studied their books. When the oldest boy was ready for high-school, we moved to a town, where my husband had bought a granary business. By that time I had become a physical wreck, with a list of ailments too painful to describe. But I still had my craving for knowledge, and my illness was my salvation, in a way--it got me a hired girl, and time to patronize the free library.

I had never had any sort of superstition or prejudice, and when I got into the world of books, I began quickly to find my way. I travelled into by-paths, of course; I got Christian Science badly, and New Thought in a mild attack. I still have in my mind what the sober reader would doubtless consider queer kinks; for instance, I still practice "mental healing," in a form, and I don't always tell my secret thoughts about Theosophy and Spiritualism. But almost at once I worked myself out of the religion I had been taught, and away from my husband's politics, and the drugs of my doctors. One of the first subjects I read about was health; I came upon a book on fasting, and went away upon a visit and tried it, and came back home a new woman, with a new life before me.

In all of these matters my husband fought me at every step. He wished to rule, not merely my body, but my mind, and it seemed as if every new thing that I learned was an additional affront to him. I don't think I was rendered disagreeable by my culture; my only obstinacy was in maintaining the right of the children to do their own thinking. But during this time my husband was making money, and filling his life with that. He remained in his every idea the money-man, an active and bitter leader of the forces of greed in our community; and when my studies took me to the inevitable end, and I joined the local of the Socialist party in our town, it was to him like a blow in the face. He never got over it, and I think that if the children had not been on my side, he would have claimed the Englishman's privilege of beating me with a stick not thicker than his thumb. As it was, he retired into a sullen hypochondria, which was so pitiful that in the end I came to regard him as not responsible.

I went to a college town with my three children, and when they were graduated, having meantime made sure that I could never do anything but torment my husband, I set about getting a divorce. I had helped to lay the foundation of his fortune, cementing it with my blood, I might say, and I could fairly have laid claim to half what he had brought from the farm; but my horror of the parasitic woman had come to be such that rather than even seem to be one, I gave up everything, and went out into the world at the age of forty-five to earn my own living. My children soon married, and I would not be a burden to them; so I came East for a while, and settled down quite unexpectedly into a place as a field-worker for a child-labour committee.

You may think that a woman so situated would not have been apt to meet Mrs. Douglas van Tuiver, née Castleman, and to be chosen for her bosom friend; but that would only be because you do not know the modern world. We have managed to get upon the consciences of the rich, and they invite us to attend their tea-parties and disturb their peace of mind. And then, too, I had a peculiar hold upon Sylvia; when I met her I possessed the key to the great mystery of her life. How that had come about is a story in itself, the thing I have next to tell.

2. It happened that my arrival in New York from the far West coincided with Sylvia's from the far South; and that both fell at a time when there were no wars or

earthquakes or football games to compete for the front page of the newspapers. So everybody was talking about the prospective wedding. The fact that the Southern belle had caught the biggest prize among the city's young millionaires was enough to establish precedence with the city's subservient newspapers, which had pro-ceeded to robe the grave and punctilious figure of the bridegroom in the garments of King Cophetua. The fact that the bride's father was the richest man in his own section did not interfere with this--for how could metropolitan editors be expected to have heard of the glories of Castleman Hall, or to imagine that there existed a section of America so self-absorbed that its local favourite would not feel herself exalted in becoming Mrs. Douglas van Tuiver?

What the editors knew about Castleman Hall was that they wired for pictures, and a man was sent from the nearest city to "snap" this unknown beauty; where-upon her father chased the presumptuous photographer and smashed his camera with a cane. So, of course, when Sylvia stepped out of the train in New York, there was a whole battery of cameras awaiting her, and all the city beheld her image the next day.

The beginning of my interest in this "belle" from far South was when I picked up the paper at my breakfast table, and found her gazing at me, with the wide-open, innocent eyes of a child; a child who had come from some fairer, more gracious world, and brought the memory of it with her, trailing her clouds of glory. She had stepped from the train into the confusion of the roaring city, and she stood, startled and frightened, yet, I thought, having no more real idea of its wickedness and horror than a babe in arms. I read her soul in that heavenly countenance, and sat looking at it, enraptured, dumb. There must have been thousands, even in that metropolis of Mammon, who loved her from that picture, and whispered a prayer for her happiness.

I can hear her laugh as I write this. For she would have it that I was only one more of her infatuated lovers, and that her clouds of glory were purely stage illu-sion. She knew exactly what she was doing with those wide-open, innocent eyes! Had not old Lady Dee, most cynical of worldlings, taught her how to use them when she was a child in pig-tails? To be sure she had been scared when she stepped off the train, and strange men had shoved cameras under her nose. It was almost as bad as being assassinated! But as to her heavenly soul--alas, for the blindness of men, and of sentimental old women, who could believe in a modern "society" girl!

I had supposed that I was an emancipated woman when I came to New York. But one who has renounced the world, the flesh and the devil, knowing them only from pictures in magazines and Sunday supplements; such a one may find that he has still some need of fasting and praying. The particular temptation which overcame me was this picture of the bride-to-be. I wanted to see her, and I went and stood for hours in a crowd of curious women, and saw the wedding party enter the great Fifth Avenue Church, and discovered that my Sylvia's hair was golden, and her eyes a strange and wonderful red-brown. And this was the moment that fate had chosen to throw Claire Lepage into my arms, and give me the key to the future of Sylvia's life.

3. I am uncertain how much I should tell about Claire Lepage. It is a story which is popular in a certain sort of novel, but I have no wish for that easy success. Towards Claire herself I had no trace of the conventional attitude, whether of contempt or of curiosity. She was to me the product of a social system, of the great New Nineveh which I was investigating. And later on, when I knew her, she was a weak sister whom I tried to help.

It happened that I knew much more about such matters than the average woman--owing to a tragedy in my life. When I was about twenty-five years old, my brother-in-law had moved his family to our part of the world, and one of his boys had become very dear to me. This boy later on had got into trouble, and rather than tell anyone about it, had shot himself. So my eyes had been opened to things that are usually hidden from my sex; for the sake of my own sons, I had set out to study the underground ways of the male creature. I developed the curious custom of digging out every man I met, and making him lay bare his inmost life to me; so you may understand that it was no ordinary pair of woman's arms into which Claire Lepage was thrown.

At first I attributed her vices to her environment, but soon I realized that this was a mistake; the women of her world do not as a rule go to pieces. Many of them I met were free and independent women, one or two of them intellectual and worth knowing. For the most part such women marry well, in the worldly sense, and live as contented lives as the average lady who secures her life-contract at the outset. If you had met Claire at an earlier period of her career, and if she had been concerned to impress you, you might have thought her a charming hostess. She had come of good family, and been educated in a convent--much better educated than many society girls in America. She spoke English as well as she did French, and she had read some poetry, and could use the language of idealism whenever necessary. She had even a certain religious streak, and could voice the most generous sentiments, and really believe that she believed them. So it might have been some time before you discovered the springs of her weakness.

In the beginning I blamed van Tuiver; but in the end I concluded that for most of her troubles she had herself to thank--or perhaps the ancestors who had begotten her. She could talk more nobly and act more abjectly than any other woman I have ever known. She wanted pleasant sensations, and she expected life to furnish them continuously. Instinctively she studied the psychology of the person she was dealing with, and chose a reason which would impress that person.

At this time, you understand, I knew nothing about Sylvia Castleman or her fiancé, except what the public knew. But now I got an inside view--and what a view! I had read some reference to Douglas van Tuiver's Harvard career: how he had met the peerless Southern beauty, and had given up college and pursued her to her home. I had pictured the wooing in the rosy lights of romance, with all the glamour of worldly greatness. But now, suddenly, what a glimpse into the soul of the princely lover! "He had a good scare, let me tell you," said Claire. "He never knew what I was going to do from one minute to the next."

"Did he see you in the crowd before the church door?" I inquired.

"No," she replied, "but he thought of me, I can promise you."

"He knew you were coming?"

She answered, "I told him I had got an admission card, just to make sure he'd keep me in mind!"

4. I did not have to hear much more of Claire's story before making up my mind that the wealthiest and most fashionable of New York's young bachelors was a rather self-centred person. He had fallen desperately in love with the peerless Southern beauty, and when she had refused to have anything to do with him, he had come back to the other woman for consolation, and had compelled her to pretend to sympathize with his agonies of soul. And this when he knew that she loved him with the intensity of a jealous nature.

Claire had her own view of Sylvia Castleman, a view for which I naturally made due reservations. Sylvia was a schemer, who had known from the first what she wanted, and had played her part with masterly skill. As for Claire, she had striven to match her moves, plotting in the darkness against her, and fighting desperately with such weak weapons as she possessed. It was characteristic that she did not blame herself for her failure; it was the baseness of van Tuiver, his inability to appreciate sincere devotion, his unworthiness of her love. And this, just after she had been naively telling me of her efforts to poison his mind against Sylvia while pretending to admire her! But I made allowances for Claire at this moment--realizing that the situation had been one to overstrain any woman's altruism.

She had failed in her subtleties, and there had followed scenes of bitter strife between the two. Sylvia, the cunning huntress, having pretended to relent, van Tuiver had gone South to his wooing again, while Claire had stayed at home and read a book about the poisoners of the Italian renaissance. And then had come the announcement of the engagement, after which the royal conqueror had come back in a panic, and sent embassies of his male friends to plead with Claire, alternately promising her wealth and threatening her with destitution, appealing to her fear, her cupidity, and even to her love. To all of which I listened, thinking of the wide-open, innocent eyes of the picture, and shedding tears within my soul. So must the gods feel as they look down upon the affairs of mortals, seeing how they destroy themselves by ignorance and folly, seeing how they walk into the future as a blind man into a yawning abyss.

I gave, of course, due weight to the sneers of Claire. Perhaps the innocent one really had set a trap--had picked van Tuiver out and married him for his money. But even so, I could hope that she had not known what she was doing. Surely it had never occurred to her that through all the days of her triumph she would have to eat and sleep with the shade of another woman at her side!

Claire said to me, not once, but a dozen times, "He'll come back to me. She'll never be able to make him happy." And so I pictured Sylvia upon her honeymoon, followed by an invisible ghost whose voice she would never hear, whose name she would never know. All that van Tuiver had learned from Claire, the sensuality, the *ennin*, the contempt for woman--it would rise to torment and terrify his bride, and turn her life to bitterness. And then beyond this, deeps upon deeps, to which my imagination did not go--and of which the Frenchwoman, with all her freedom of tongue, gave me no more than a hint which I could not comprehend.

5. Claire Lepage at this time was desperately lonely and unhappy. Having made the discovery that my arms were sturdy, used to doing a man's work, she clung to them. She begged me to go home with her, to visit her--finally to come and live with her. Until recently an elderly companion, had posed as her aunt, and kept her respectable while she was upon van Tuiver's yacht, and at his castle in Scotland. But this companion had died, and now Claire had no one with whom to discuss her soul-states.

She occupied a beautiful house on the West Side, not far from Riverside Drive; and in addition to the use of this she had an income of eight thousand a year--which was not enough to make possible a chauffeur, nor even to dress decently, but only enough to keep in debt upon. Such as the income was, however, she was willing to share it with me. So there opened before me a new profession-- and a new insight into the complications of parasitism.

I went to see her frequently at first, partly because I was interested in her and her associates, and partly because I really thought I could help her. But I soon came to realize that influencing Claire was like moulding water; it flowed back round your hands, even while you worked. I would argue with her about the physiological effects of alcohol, and when I had convinced her, she would promise caution; but soon I would discover that my arguments had gone over her head. I was at this time feeling my way towards my work in the East. I tried to interest her in such things as social reform, but realized that they had no meaning for her. She was living the life of the pleasure-seeking idlers of the great metropolis, and every time I met her it seemed to me that her character and her appearance had deteriorated.

Meantime I picked up scraps of information concerning the van Tuivers. There were occasional items in the papers, their yacht, the "Triton," had reached the Azores; it had run into a tender in the harbour of Gibraltar; Mr. and Mrs. van Tuiver had received the honour of presentation at the Vatican; they were spending the season in London, and had been presented at court; they had been royal guests at the German army-manoeuvres. The million wage-slaves of the metropolis, packed morning and night into the roaring subways and whirled to and from their tasks, read items such as these and were thrilled by the triumphs of their fellow-countrymen.

At Claire's house I learned to be interested in "society" news. From a week-ly paper of gossip about the rich and great she would read paragraphs, explaining subtle allusions and laying bare veiled scandals. Some of the men she knew well, referring to them for my benefit as Bertie and Reggie and Vivie and Algie. She also knew not a little about the women of that super-world--information sometimes of an intimate nature, which these ladies would have been startled to hear was going the rounds.

This insight I got into Claire's world I found useful, needless to say, in my oc-casional forays as a soap-box orator of Socialism. I would go from the super-heated luxury of her home to visit tenement-dens where little children made paper-flow-ers twelve and fourteen hours a day for a trifle over one cent an hour. I would spend the afternoon floating about in the park in the automobile of one of her expensive friends, and then take the subway and visit one of the settlements, to hear a discus-sion of conditions which doomed a certain number of working-girls to be burned alive every year in factory fires.

As time went on, I became savage concerning such contrasts, and the speeches I was making for the party began to attract attention. During the summer, I recol-lect, I had begun to feel hostile even towards the lovely image of Sylvia, which I had framed in my room. While she was being presented at St. James's, I was study-ing the glass-factories in South Jersey, where I found little boys of ten working in front of glowing furnaces until they dropped of exhaustion and sometimes had their eyes burned out. While she and her husband were guests of the German Emperor, I was playing the part of a Polish working-woman, penetrating the carefully guarded secrets of the sugar-trust's domain in Brooklyn, where human lives are snuffed out almost every day in noxious fumes.

And then in the early fall Sylvia came home, her honeymoon over. She came in one of the costly suites in the newest of the *de luxe* steamers; and the next morning I saw a new picture of her, and read a few words her husband had condescended to say to a fellow traveller about the courtesy of Europe to visiting Americans. Then for a couple of months I heard no more of them. I was busy with my child-labour work, and I doubt if a thought of Sylvia crossed my mind, until that never-to-be-forgotten afternoon at Mrs. Allison's when she came up to me and took my hand in hers.

6. Mrs. Roland Allison was one of the comfortable in body who had begun to feel uncomfortable in mind. I had happened to meet her at the settlement, and tell her what I had seen in the glass factories; whereupon she made up her mind that everybody she knew must hear me talk, and to that end gave a reception at her Madison Avenue home.

I don't remember much of what I said, but if I may take the evidence of Sylvia, who remembered everything, I spoke effectively. I told them, for one thing, the story of little Angelo Patri. Little Angelo was of that indeterminate Italian age where he helped to support a drunken father without regard to the child-labour laws of the State of New Jersey. His people were tenants upon a fruit-farm a couple of miles from the glass-factory, and little Angelo walked to and from his work along the railroad-track. It is a peculiarity of the glass-factory that it has to eat its children both by day and by night; and after working six hours before midnight and six more after midnight, little Angelo was tired. He had no eye for the birds and flowers on a beautiful spring morning, but as he was walking home, he dropped in his tracks and fell asleep. The driver of the first morning train on that branch-line saw what he took to be an old coat lying on the track ahead, and did not stop to investigate.

All this had been narrated to me by the child's mother, who had worked as a packer of "beers," and who had loved little Angelo. As I repeated her broken words about the little mangled body, I saw some of my auditors wipe away a surreptitious tear.

After I had stopped, several women came up to talk with me at the last, when most of the company was departing, there came one more, who had waited her turn. The first thing I saw was her loveliness, the thing about her that dazzled and stunned people, and then came the strange sense of familiarity. Where had I met this girl before?

She said what everybody always says; she had been so much interested, she had never dreamed that such conditions existed in the world. I, applying the acid test, responded, "So many people have said that to me that I have begun to believe it."

"It is so in my case," she replied, quickly. "You see, I have lived all my life in the South, and we have no such conditions there."

"Are you sure?" I asked.

"Our negroes at least can steal enough to eat," she said.

I smiled. Then--since one has but a moment or two to get in one's work in these social affairs, and so has to learn to thrust quickly: "You have timber-workers in Louisiana, steel-workers in Alabama. You have tobacco-factories, canning-factories, cotton-mills--have you been to any of them to see how the people live?"

All this I said automatically, it being the routine of the agitator. But meantime in my mind was an excitement, spreading like a flame. The loveliness of this young girl; the eagerness, the intensity of feeling written upon her countenance; and above all, the strange sense of familiarity! Surely, if I had met her before, I should never have forgotten her; surely it could not be--not possibly--

My hostess came, and ended my bewilderment. "You ought to get Mrs. van Tuiver on your child-labour committee," she said.

A kind of panic seized me. I wanted to say, "Oh, it is Sylvia Castleman!" But then, how could I explain? I couldn't say, "I have your picture in my room, cut out of a newspaper." Still less could I say, "I know a friend of your husband."

Fortunately Sylvia did not heed my excitement. (She had learned by this time to pretend not to notice.) "Please don't misunderstand me," she was saying. "I really *don't* know about these things. And I would do something to help if I could." As she said this she looked with the red-brown eyes straight into mine--a gaze so clear and frank and honest, it was as if an angel had come suddenly to earth, and learned of the horrible tangle into which we mortals have got our affairs.

"Be careful what you're saying," put in our hostess, with a laugh. "You're in dangerous hands."

But Sylvia would not be warned. "I want to know more about it," she said. "You must tell me what I can do."

"Take her at her word," said Mrs. Allison, to me. "Strike while the iron is hot!" I detected a note of triumph in her voice; if she could say that she had got Mrs. van Tuiver to take up child-labour--that indeed would be a feather to wear!

"I will tell you all I can," I said. "That's my work in the world."

"Take Mrs. Abbott away with you," said the energetic hostess, to Sylvia; and before I quite understood what was happening, I had received and accepted an invitation to drive in the park with Mrs. Douglas van Tuiver. In her role of *dea ex machina* the hostess extricated me from the other guests, and soon I was established in a big new motor, gliding up Madison Avenue as swiftly and silently as a cloud-shadow over the fields. As I write the words there lies upon my table a Socialist paper with one of Will Dyson's vivid cartoons, representing two ladies of the great world at a reception. Says the first, "These social movements are becoming *quite* worth while!" "Yes, indeed," says the other. "One meets such good society!"

7. Sylvia's part in this adventure was a nobler one than mine, Seated as I was in a regal motor-car, and in company with one favoured of all the gods in the world, I must have had an intense conviction of my own saintliness not to distrust my excitement. But Sylvia, for her part, had nothing to get from me but pain. I talked of the factory-fires and the horrors of the sugar-refineries, and I saw shadow after shadow of suffering cross her face. You may say it was cruel of me to tear the veil from those lovely eyes, but in such a matter I felt myself the angel of the Lord and His vengeance.

"I didn't know about these things!" she cried again. And I found it was true. It would have been hard for me to imagine anyone so ignorant of the realities of modern life. The men and women she had met she understood quite miraculously, but they were only two kinds, the "best people" and their negro servants. There had been a whole regiment of relatives on guard to keep her from knowing anybody else, or anything else, and if by chance a dangerous fact broke into the family stock-ade, they had formulas ready with which to kill it.

"But now," Sylvia went on, "I've got some money, and I can help, so I dare not be ignorant any longer. You must show me the way, and my husband too. I'm sure he doesn't know what can be done."

I said that I would do anything in my power. Her help would be invaluable, not merely because of the money she might give, but because of the influence of her name; the attention she could draw to any cause she chose. I explained to her the aims and the methods of our child-labour committee. We lobbied to get new legislation; we watched officials to compel them to enforce the laws already existing; above all, we worked for publicity, to make people realise what it meant that the new generation was growing up without education, and stunted by premature toil. And that was where she could help us most--if she would go and see the conditions with her own eyes, and then appear before the legislative committee this winter, in favour of our new bill!

She turned her startled eyes upon me at this. Her ideas of doing good in the world were the old-fashioned ones of visiting and almsgiving; she had no more conception of modern remedies than she had of modern diseases. "Oh, I couldn't possibly make a speech!" she exclaimed.

"Why not?" I asked.

"I never thought of such a thing. I don't know enough."

"But you can learn."

"I know, but that kind of work ought to be done by men."

"We've given men a chance, and they have made the evils. Whose business is it to protect the children if not the women's?"

She hesitated a moment, and then said: "I suppose you'll laugh at me."

"No, no," I promised; then as I looked at her I guessed. "Are you going to tell me that woman's place is the home?"

"That is what we think in Castleman County," she said, smiling in spite of herself.

"The children have got out of the home," I replied. "If they are ever to get back, we women must go and fetch them."

Suddenly she laughed--that merry laugh that was the April sunshine of my life for many years. "Somebody made a Suffrage speech in our State a couple of years ago, and I wish you could have seen the horror of my people! My Aunt Nannie--she's Bishop Chilton's wife--thought it was the most dreadful thing that had happened since Jefferson Davis was put in irons. She talked about it for days, and at last she went upstairs and shut herself in the attic. The younger children came home from school, and wanted to know where mamma was. Nobody knew. Bye and bye, the cook came. 'Marse Basil, what we gwine have fo' dinner? I done been up to Mis' Nannie, an' she say g'way an' not pester her--she busy.' Company came, and there was dreadful confusion--nobody knew what to do about anything--and still Aunt Nannie was locked in! At last came dinner-time, and everybody else came. At last up went the butler, and came down with the message that they were to eat whatever they had, and take care of the company somehow, and go to prayer-meeting, and let her alone--she was writing a letter to the Castleman County *Register* on the subject of 'The Duty of Woman as a Homemaker'!"

8. This was the beginning of my introduction to Castleman County. It was a

long time before I went there, but I learned to know its inhabitants from Sylvia's stories of them. Funny stories, tragic stories, wild and incredible stories out of a half-barbaric age! She would tell them and we would laugh together; but then a wistful look would come into her eyes, and a silence would fall. So very soon I made the discovery that my Sylvia was homesick. In all the years that I knew her she never ceased to speak of Castleman Hall as "home". All her standards came from there, her new ideas were referred there.

We talked of Suffrage for a while, and I spoke about the lives of women on lonely farms--how they give their youth and health to their husband's struggle, yet have no money partnership which they can enforce in case of necessity. "But surely," cried Sylvia, "you don't want to make divorce more easy!"

"I want to make the conditions of it fair to women," I said.

"But then more women will get it! And there are so many divorced women now! Papa says that divorce is a greater menace than Socialism!"

She spoke of Suffrage in England, where women were just beginning to make public disturbances. Surely I did not approve of their leaving their homes for such purposes as that! As tactfully as I could, I suggested that conditions in England were peculiar. There was, for example, the quaint old law which permitted a husband to beat his wife subject to certain restrictions. Would an American woman submit to such a law? There was the law which made it impossible for a woman to divorce her husband for infidelity, unless accompanied by desertion or cruelty. Surely not even her father would consider that a decent arrangement! I mentioned a recent decision of the highest court in the land, that a man who brought his mistress to live in his home, and compelled his wife to wait upon her, was not committing cruelty within the meaning of the English law. I heard Sylvia's exclamation of horror, and met her stare of incredulity; and then suddenly I thought of Claire, and a little chill ran over me. It was a difficult hour, in more ways than one, that of my first talk with Mrs. Douglas van Tuiver!

I soon made the discovery that, childish as her ignorance was, there was no prejudice in it. If you brought her a fact, she did not say that it was too terrible to be true, or that the Bible said otherwise, or that it was indecent to know about it. Nor, when you met her next, did you discover that she had forgotten it. On the contrary, you discovered that she had followed it to its remote consequences, and was ready with a score of questions as to these. I remember saying to myself, that first auto-mobile ride: "If this girl goes on thinking, she will get into trouble! She will have to stop, for the sake of others!"

"You must meet my husband some time," she said; and added, "I'll have to see my engagement-book. I have so much to do, I never know when I have a moment free."

"You must find it interesting," I ventured.

"I did, for a while; but I've begun to get tired of so much going about. For the most part I meet the same people, and I've found out what they have to say."

I laughed. "You have caught the society complaint already-- *ennui*!"

"I had it years ago, at home. It's true I never would have gone out at all if it hadn't been for the sake of my family. That's why I envy a woman like you--"

I could not help laughing. It was too funny, Mrs. Douglas van Tuiver envying me!

"What's the matter?" she asked.

"Just the irony of life. Do you know, I cut you out of the newspaper, and put you in a little frame on my bureau. I thought, here is the loveliest face I've ever seen, and here is the most-to-be-envied of women."

She smiled, but quickly became serious. "I learned very early in life that I was beautiful; and I suppose if I were suddenly to cease being beautiful, I'd miss it; yet I often think it's a nuisance. It makes one dependent on externals. Most of the beautiful women I've known make a sort of profession of it--they live to shine and be looked at.

"And you don't enjoy that?" I asked.

"It restricts one's life. Men expect it of you, they resent your having any other interest."

"So," I responded, gravely, "with all your beauty and wealth, you aren't per-fectly happy?"

"Oh, yes!" she cried--not having meant to confess so much. "I told myself I would be happy, because I would be able to do so much good in the world. There must be some way to do good with money! But now I'm not sure; there seem to be so many things in the way. Just when you have your mind made up that you have a way to help, someone comes and points out to you that you may be really doing harm."

She hesitated again, and I said, "That means you have been looking into the matter of charity."

She gave me a bright glance. "How you understand things!" she exclaimed.

"It is possible," I replied, "to know modern society so well that when you meet certain causes you know what results to look for."

"I wish you'd explain to me why charity doesn't do any good!"

"It would mean a lecture on the competitive wage-system," I laughed--" too serious a matter for a drive!"

This may have seemed shirking on my part. But here I was, wrapped in luxurious furs, rolling gloriously through the park at twilight on a brilliant autumn evening; and the confiscation of property seems so much more startling a proposition when you are in immediate contact with it! This principle, which explains the "opportunism" of Socialist cabinet-ministers and Labour M.P.s may be used to account for the sudden resolve which I had taken, that for this afternoon at least Mrs. Douglas van Tuiver should not discover that I was either a divorced woman, or a soap-box orator of the revolution.

9. Sylvia, in that first conversation, told me much about herself that she did not know she was telling. I became fairly certain, for instance, that she had not married Mr. Douglas van Tuiver for love. The young girl who has so married does not suffer from ennui in the first year, nor does she find her happiness depending upon her ability to solve the problem of charity in connection with her husband's wealth.

She would have ridden and talked longer, she said, but for a dinner engagement. She asked me to call on her, and I promised to come some morning, as soon as she set a day. When the car drew up before the door of her home, I thought of my first ride about the city in the "rubber-neck wagon," and how I had stared when the lecturer pointed out this mansion. We, the passengers, had thrilled as one soul, imagining the wonderful life which must go on behind those massive portals, the treasures outshining the wealth of Ormus and of Ind, which required those thick, bronze bars for their protection. And here was the mistress of all the splendour, inviting me to come and see it from within!

She wanted to send me home in the car, but I would not have that, on account of the push-cart men and the babies in my street; I got out and walked--my heart beating fast, my blood leaping with exultation. I reached home, and there on the bureau was the picture--but behold, how changed! It was become a miracle of the art of colour-photography; its hair was golden, its eyes a wonderful red-brown, its cheeks aglow with the radiance of youth! And yet more amazing, the picture spoke! It spoke with the most delicious of Southern drawls--referring to the "repo't" of my child-labour committee, shivering at the cold and bidding me pull the "fu-uzz" up round me. And when I told funny stories about the Italians and the Hebrews of my tenement-neighbourhood, it broke into silvery laughter, and cried: "Oh, de-ah me! How que-ah!" Little had I dreamed, when I left that picture in the morning, what a miracle was to be wrought upon it.

I knew, of course, what was the matter with me; the symptoms were unmistakable. After having made up my mind that I was an old woman, and that there was nothing more in life for me save labour--here the little archer had come, and with the sharpest of his golden arrows, had shot me through. I had all the thrills, the raptures and delicious agonies of first love; I lived no longer in myself, but in the thought of another person. Twenty times a day I looked at my picture, and cried aloud: "Oh, beautiful, beautiful!"

I do not know how much of her I have been able to give. I have told of our first talk--but words are so cold and dead! I stop and ask: What there is, in all nature, that has given me the same feeling? I remember how I watched the dragon-fly emerging from its chrysalis. It is soft and green and tender; it clings to a branch and dries its wings in the sun, and when the miracle is completed, there for a brief space it poises, shimmering with a thousand hues, quivering with its new-born ecstasy. And just so was Sylvia; a creature from some other world than ours, as yet unsoiled by the dust and heat of reality. It came to me with a positive shock, as a terrifying thing, that there should be in this world of strife and wickedness any young thing that took life with such intensity, that was so palpitating with eagerness, with hope, with sympathy. Such was the impression that one got of her, even when her words most denied it. She might be saying world-weary and cynical things, out of the maxims of Lady Dee; but there was still the eagerness, the sympathy, surging beneath and lifting her words.

The crown of her loveliness was her unconsciousness of self. Even though she might be talking of herself, frankly admitting her beauty, she was really thinking of other people, how she could get to them to help them. This I must emphasize, because, apart from jesting, I would not have it thought that I had fallen under the spell of a beautiful countenance, combined with a motor-car and a patrician name. There were things about Sylvia that were aristocratic, that could be nothing else; but she could be her same lovely self in a cottage--as I shall prove to you before I finish with the story of her life.

I was in love. At that time I was teaching myself German, and I sat one day puzzling out two lines of Goethe:

"Oden and Thor, these two thou knowest; Freya, the heavenly, knowest thou not."

And I remember how I cried aloud in sudden delight: *"I know her!"* For a long time that was one of my pet names--"Freya dis Himmlische!" I only heard of one other that I preferred--when in course of time she told me about Frank Shirley, and how she had loved him, and how their hopes had been wrecked. He had called her "Lady Sunshine"; he had been wont to call it over and over in his happiness, and as Sylvia repeated it to me--"Lady Sunshine! Lady Sunshine!" I could imagine that I caught an echo of the very tones of Frank Shirley's voice.

10. For several days I waited upon the postman, and when the summons came I dodged a committee-meeting, and ascended the marble stairs with trepidation, and underwent the doubting scrutiny of an English lackey, sufficiently grave in deport-ment and habiliments to have waited upon a bishop in his own land. I have a vague memory of an entrance-hall with panelled paintings and a double-staircase with a snow-white carpet, about which I had read in the newspapers that it was woven in one piece, and had cost an incredible sum. One did not have to profane it with his feet, as there was an elevator provided.

I was shown to Sylvia's morning-room, which had been "done" in pink and white and gold by some decorator who had known her colours. It was large enough to have held half-a-dozen of my own quarters, and the sun was allowed to flood it. Through a door at one side came Sylvia, holding out her hands to me.

She was really glad to see me! She began to apologize at once for the time she had taken to write. It was because she had so much to do. She had married into a world that took itself seriously: the "idle rich," who worked like slaves. "You know," she said, while we sat on a pink satin couch, and a footman brought us coffee: "you read that Mrs. So-and-so is a 'social queen,' and you think it's a newspaper phrase, but it isn't; she really feels that she's a queen, and other people feel it, and she goes through her ceremonies as solemnly as the Lord's anointed."

She went on to tell me some of her adventures. She had a keen sense of fun, and was evidently suffering for an outlet for it. She saw through the follies and pretences of people in a flash, but they were all such august and important people that, out of regard for her husband, she dared not let them suspect her clairvoyant power.

She referred to her experiences abroad. She had not liked Europe--being quite frankly a provincial person. To Castleman County a foreigner was a strange, dark person who mixed up his consonants, and was under suspicion of being a fiddler or an opera-singer. The people she had met under her husband's charge had been socially indubitable, but still, they were foreigners, and Sylvia could never really be sure what they meant.

There was, for instance, the young son of a German steel-king, a person of amazing savoir faire, who had made bold to write books and exhibit pictures, and had travelled so widely that he had even heard of Castleman County. He had taken Sylvia to show her the sights of Berlin, and had rolled her down the "Sieges Allée," making outrageous fun of his Kaiser's taste in art, and coming at last to a great marble column, with a female figure representing Victory upon the top. "You will observe," said the cultured young plutocrat, "that the Grecian lady stands a hundred meters in the air, and has no stairway. There is a popular saying about her which is delightful--that she is the only chaste woman in Berlin!"

I had been through the culture-seeking stage, and knew my Henry James; so I could read between the lines of Sylvia's experiences. I figured her as a person walking on volcanic ground, not knowing her peril, but vaguely disquieted by a smell of sulphur in the air. And once in a while a crack would open in the ground! There was the Duke of Something in Rome, for example, a melancholy young man, with whom she had coquetted, as she did, in her merry fashion, with every man she met. Being married, she had taken it for granted that she might be as winsome as she chose; but the young Italian had misunderstood the game, and had whispered words of serious import, which had so horrified Sylvia that she flew to her husband and told him the story--begging him incidentally not to horse-whip the fellow. In reply it had to be explained to her she had laid herself liable to the misadventure.

The ladies of the Italian aristocracy were severe and formal, and Sylvia had no right to expect an ardent young duke to understand her native wildness.

11. Something of that sort was always happening--something in each country to bewilder her afresh, and to make it necessary for her husband to remind her of the proprieties. In France, a cousin of van Tuiver's had married a marquis, and they had visited the chateau. The family was Catholic, of the very oldest and strictest, and the brother-in-law, a prelate of high degree, had invited the guests to be shown through his cathedral. "Imagine my bewilderment!" said Sylvia. "I thought I was going to meet a church dignitary, grave and reverent; but here was a wit, a man of the world. Such speeches you never heard! I was ravished by the grandeur of the building, and I said: 'If I had seen this, I would have come to you to be married.' 'Madame is an American,' he replied. 'Come the next time!' When I objected that I was not a Catholic, he said: 'Your beauty is its own religion!' When I protested that he would be doing me too great an honour, 'Madame,' said he, 'the *honneur* would be all to the church!' And because I was shocked at all this, I was considered to be a provincial person!"

Then they had come to London, a dismal, damp city where you "never saw the sun, and when you did see it it looked like a poached egg"; where you had to learn to eat fish with the help of a knife, and where you might speak of bitches, but must never on any account speak of your stomach. They went for a week-end to "Hazel-hurst," the home of the Dowager Duchess of Danbury, whose son van Tuiver, had entertained in America, and who, in the son's absence, claimed the right to repay the debt. The old lady sat at table with two fat poodle dogs in infants' chairs, one on each side of her, feeding out of golden trays. There was a visiting curate, a frightened little man at the other side of one poodle; in an effort to be at ease he offered the wheezing creature a bit of bread. "Don't feed my dogs!" snapped the old lady. "I don't allow anybody to feed my dogs!"

And then there was the Honourable Reginald Annersley, the youngest son of the family, home from Eton on vacation. The Honourable Reginald was twelve years of age, undersized and ill-nourished. ("They feed them badly," his mother had explained, "an' the teachin's no good either, but it's a school for gentlemen.") "Honestly," said Sylvia, "he was the queerest little mannikin--like the tiny waiter's assistants you see in hotels on the Continent. He wore his Eton suit, you understand-

-grown-up evening clothes minus the coat-tails, and a top hat. He sat at tea and chatted with the mincing graces of a cotillion-leader; you expected to find some of his hair gone when he took off his hat! He spoke of his brother, the duke, who had gone off shooting seals somewhere. 'The jolly rotter has nothing to do but spend his money; but we younger sons have to work like dogs when we grow up!' I asked what he'd do, and he said 'I suppose there's nothin' but the church. It's a beastly bore, but you do get a livin' out of it.'

"That was too much for me," said Sylvia. "I proceeded to tell the poor, blasé infant about my childhood; how my sister Celeste and I had caught half-tamed horses and galloped about the pasture on them, when we were so small that our little fat legs stuck out horizontally; how we had given ourselves convulsions in the green apple orchard, and had to be spanked every day before we had our hair combed. I told how we heard a war-story about a "train of gunpowder," and proceeded to lay such a train about the attic of Castleman Hall, and set fire to it. I might have spent the afternoon teaching the future churchman how to be a boy, if I hadn't suddenly caught a glimpse of my husband's face!"

12. I did not hear these stories all at once. I have put them together here because they make a little picture of her honeymoon, and also because they show how, without meaning it, she was giving me an account of her husband.

There had been even fewer adventures in the life of young Douglas van Tuiver than in the life of the Honourable Reginald Annersley. When one heard the details of the up-bringing of this "millionaire baby," one was able to forgive him for being self-centred. He had grown into a man who lived to fulfil his social duties, and he had taken to wife a girl who was reckless, high-spirited, with a streak of almost savage pride in her.

Sylvia's was the true aristocratic attitude towards the rest of the world. It could never have occurred to her to imagine that anywhere upon the whole earth there were people superior to the Castlemans of Castleman County. If you had been ignorant enough to suggest such an idea, you would have seen her eyes flash and her nostrils quiver; you would have been enveloped in a net of bewilderment and transfixed with a trident of mockery and scorn. That was what she had done in her husband-hunt. The trouble was that van Tuiver was not clever enough to realise this, and to trust her prowess against other beasts in the social jungle.

Strange to me were such inside glimpses into the life of these two favourites of the gods! I never grew weary of speculating about them, and the mystery of their alliance. How had Sylvia come to make this marriage? She was not happy with him; keen psychologist that she was, she must have foreseen that she would not be happy with him. Had she deliberately sacrificed herself, because of the good she imagined she could do to her family?

I was beginning to believe this. Irritated as she was by the solemn snobberies of van Tuiver's world, it was none the less true that she believed in money; she believed in it with a faith which appalled me as I came to realise it. Everybody had to have money; the social graces, the aristocratic virtues were impossible without it. The rich needed it--even the poor needed it! Could it be that the proud Castlemans of Castleman County had needed it also?

If that guess at her inmost soul was correct, then what a drama was her meeting with me! A person who despised money, who had proven it by grim deeds--and this a person of her own money-worshipping sex! What was the meaning of this phenomenon--this new religion that was challenging the priesthood of Mammon? So some Roman consul's daughter might have sat in her father's palace, and questioned in wonder a Christian slave woman, destined ere long to face the lions in the arena.

The exactness of this simile was not altered by the fact that in this case the slave woman was an agnostic, while the patrician girl had been brought up in the creed of Christ. Sylvia had long since begun to question the formulas of a church whose very pews were rented, and whose existence, she declared, had to be justified by charity to the poor. As we sat and talked, she knew this one thing quite definitely--that I had a religion, and she had none. That was the reason for the excitement which possessed her.

Nor was that fact ever out of my own mind for a moment. As she sat there in her sun-flooded morning-room, clad in an exquisite embroidered robe of pink Japanese silk, she was such a lovely thing that I was ready to cry out for joy of her; and yet there was something within me, grim and relentless, that sat on guard, warning me that she was of a different faith from mine, and that between those two faiths there could be no compromise. Some day she must find out what I thought of her husband's wealth, and the work it was doing in the world! Some day she must hear my real opinion of the religion of motor-cars and hand-woven carpets!

13. Nor was the day so very far off. She sat opposite me, leaning forward in her eagerness, declaring: "You must help to educate me. I shall never rest until I'm of some real use in the world."

"What have you thought of doing?" I inquired.

"I don't know yet. My husband has an aunt who's interested in a day-nursery for the children of working-women. I thought I might help this, but my husband says it does no good whatever--it only makes paupers of the poor. Do you think so?"

"I think more than that," I replied. "It sets women free to compete with men, and beat down men's wages."

"Oh, what a puzzle!" she exclaimed, and then: "Is there any way of helping the poor that wouldn't be open to the same objection?"

That brought us once more to the subject I had put aside at our last meeting. She had not forgotten it, and asked again for an explanation. What did I mean by the competitive wage system?

My purpose in this writing is to tell the story of Sylvia Castleman's life, to show, not merely what she was, but what she became. I have to make real to you a process of growth in her soul, and at this moment the important event is her discovery of the class-struggle and her reaction to it. You may say, perhaps, that you are not interested in the class-struggle, but you cannot alter the fact that you live in an age when millions of people are having the course of their lives changed by the discovery of it. Here, for instance, is a girl who has been taught to keep her promises, and has promised to love, honour and obey a man; she is to find the task more difficult, because she comes to understand the competitive wage-system while he does not understand it and does not wish to. If that seems to you strange material out of which to make a domestic drama, I can only tell you that you have missed some of the vital facts of your own time.

I gave her a little lesson in elementary economics. I showed her how, when a capitalist needed labour, he bought it in the open market, like any other commodity. He did not think about the human side of it, he paid the market-price, which came to be what the labourer had to have in order to live. No labourer could get more, because others would take less.

"If that be true," I continued, "one of the things that follows is the futility of charity. Whatever you do for the wage-worker on a general scale comes sooner or later out of his wages. If you take care of his children all day or part of the day, he can work for less; if he doesn't discover that someone else does, and underbids him and takes his place. If you feed his children at school, if you bury him free, if you insure his life, or even give him a dinner on Christmas Day, you simply enable his landlord to charge him more, or his employer to pay him less."

Sylvia sat for a while in thought, and then asked: "What can be done about such a fact?"

"The first thing to be done is to make sure that you understand it. Nine-tenths of the people who concern themselves with social questions don't, and so they waste their time in futilities. For instance, I read the other day an article by a benevolent old gentleman who believed that the social problem could be solved by teaching the poor to chew their food better, so that they would eat less. You may laugh at that, but it's not a bit more absurd than the idea of our men of affairs, that the thing to do is to increase the efficiency of the workers, and so produce more goods."

"You mean the working-man doesn't get more, even when he produces more?"

"Take the case of the glass factories. Men used to get eight dollars a day there, but someone invented a machine that did the work of a dozen men, and that machine is run by a boy for fifty cents a day."

A little pucker of thought came between her eyes. "Might there not be a law forbidding the employer to reduce wages?"

"A minimum wage law. But that would raise the cost of the product, and drive the trade to another state."

She suggested a national law, and when I pointed out that the trade would go to other countries, she fell back on the tariff. I felt like an embryologist--watching the individual repeating the history of the race!

"Protection and prosperity!" I said, with a smile. "Don't you see the increase in the cost of living? The working-man gets more money in his pay envelope, but he can't buy more with it because prices go up. And even supposing you could pass a minimum wage law, and stop competition in wages, you'd only change it to competition in efficiency--you'd throw the old and the feeble and the untrained into pauperism."

"You make the world seem a hard place to live in," protested Sylvia.

"I'm simply telling you the elementary facts of business. You can forbid the employer to pay less than a standard wage, but you can't compel him to employ people who aren't able to earn that wage. The business-man doesn't employ for fun, he does it for the profit there is in it."

"If that is true," said Sylvia, quickly, "then the way of employing people is cruel."

"But what other way could you have?"

She considered. "They could be employed so that no one would make a profit. Then surely they could be paid enough to live decently!"

"But whose interest would it be to employ them without profit?"

"The State should do it, if no one else will."

I had been playing a game with Sylvia, as no doubt you have perceived. "Surely," I said, "you wouldn't approve anything like that!"

"But why not?"

"Because, it would be Socialism."

She looked at me startled. "Is that Socialism?"

"Of course it is. It's the essence of Socialism."

"But then--what's the harm in it?"

I laughed. "I thought you said that Socialism was a menace, like divorce!"

I had my moment of triumph, but then I discovered how fond was the person who imagined that he could play with Sylvia. "I suspect you are something of a Socialist yourself," she remarked.

She told me a long time afterwards what had been her emotions during these early talks. It was the first time in her life that she had ever listened to ideas that were hostile to her order, and she did so with tremblings and hesitations, combating at every step an impulse to flee to the shelter of conventionality. She was more shocked by my last revelation than she let me suspect. It counted for little that I had succeeded in trapping her in proposing for herself the economic programme of Socialism, for what terrifies her class is not our economic programme, it is our threat of slave-rebellion. I had been brought up in a part of the world where democracy is a tradition, a word to conjure with, and I supposed that this would be the case with any American--that I would only have to prove that Socialism was democracy applied to industry. How could I have imagined the kind of "democracy" which had been taught to Sylvia by her Uncle Mandeville, the politician of the family, who believed that America was soon to have a king, to keep the "foreign riff-raff" in its place!

14. At this time I was living in a three-roomed apartment in one of the new "model tenements" on the East Side. I had a saying about the place, that it was "built for the proletariat and occupied by cranks." What an example for Sylvia of the futility of charity--the effort on the part of benevolent capitalists to civilise the poor by putting bath-tubs in their homes, and the discovery that the graceless creatures were using them for the storage of coals!

Having heard these strange stories, Sylvia was anxious to visit me, and I was, of course, glad to invite her. I purchased a fancy brand of tea, and some implements for the serving of it, and she came, and went into raptures over my three rooms and bath, no one of which would have made more than a closet in her own apartments. I suspected that this was her Southern ***noblesse oblige***, but I knew also that in my living room there were some rows of books, which would have meant more to Sylvia van Tuiver just then than the contents of several clothes-closets.

I was pleased to discover that my efforts had not been wasted. She had been thinking, and she had even found time, in the midst of her distractions, to read part of a book. In the course of our talks I had mentioned Veblen, and she had been reading snatches of his work on the Leisure Class, and I was surprised, and not a little amused, to observe her reaction to it.

When I talked about wages and hours of labour, I was dealing with things that were remote from her, and difficult to make real; but Veblen's theme, the idle rich, and the arts and graces whereby they demonstrate their power, was the stuff of which her life was made. The subtleties of social ostentation, the minute distinctions between the newly-rich and the anciently-rich, the solemn certainties of the latter and the quivering anxieties of the former--all those were things which Sylvia knew as a bird knows the way of the wind. To see the details of them analysed in learned, scientific fashion, explained with great mouthfuls of words which one had to look up in the dictionary--that was surely a new discovery in the book-world! "Conspicuous leisure!" "Vicarious consumption of goods!" "Oh, de-ah me, how que-ah!" exclaimed Sylvia.

And what a flood of anecdotes it let loose! A flood that bore us straight back to Castleman Hall, and to all the scenes of her young ladyhood! If only Lady Dee could have revised this book of Veblen's, how many points she could have given to him! No details had been too minute for the technique of Sylvia's great-aunt--the difference between the swish of the right kind of silk petticoats and the wrong kind; and yet her technique had been broad enough to take in a landscape. "Every girl should have a background," had been one of her maxims, and Sylvia had to have a special phaeton to drive, a special horse to ride, special roses which no one else was allowed to wear.

"Conspicuous expenditure of time," wrote Veblen. It was curious, said Sylvia, but nobody was free from this kind of vanity. There was dear old Uncle Basil, a more godly bishop never lived, and yet he had a foible for carving! In his opinion the one certain test of a gentleman was the ease with which he found the joints of all kinds of meat, and he was in arms against the modern tendency to turn such accomplishments over to butlers. He would hold forth on the subject, illustrating his theories with an elegant knife, and Sylvia remembered how her father and the Chilton boys had wired up the joints of a duck for the bishop to work on. In the struggle the bishop had preserved his dignity, but lost the duck, and the bishop's wife, being also high-born, and with a long line of traditions behind her, had calmly continued the conversation, while the butler removed the smoking duck from her lap!

Such was the way of things at Castleman Hall! The wild, care-free people--like half-grown children, romping their way through life! There was really nothing too crazy for them to do, if the whim struck them. Once a visiting cousin had ventured the remark that she saw no reason why people should not eat rats; a barn-rat was clean in its person, and far choicer in its food than a pig. Thereupon "Miss Margaret" had secretly ordered the yard-man to secure a barn-rat; she had had it broiled, and served in a dish of squirrels, and had sat by and watched the young lady enjoy it! And this, mind you, was Mrs. Castleman of Castleman Hall, mother of five children, and as stately a dame as ever led the grand march at the Governor's inaugural ball! "Major Castleman," she would say to her husband, "you may take me into my bedroom, and when you have locked the door securely, you may spit upon me, if you wish; but don't you dare even to *imagine* anything undignified about me in public!"

15. In course of time Sylvia and I became very good friends. Proud as she was, she was lonely, and in need of some one to open her eager mind to. Who was there safer to trust than this plain Western woman, who lived so far, both in reality and in ideas, from the great world of fashion?

Before we parted she considered it necessary to mention my relationship to this world. She had a most acute social conscience. She knew exactly what formalities she owed to everyone, just when she ought to call, and how long she ought to stay, and what she ought to ask the other person to do in return; she assumed that the other knew it all exactly as well, and would suffer if she failed in the slightest degree.

So now she had to throw herself upon my mercy. "You see," she explained, "my husband wouldn't understand. I may be able to change him gradually, but if I shock him all at once--"

"My dear Mrs. van Tuiver--" I smiled.

"You can't really imagine!" she persisted. "You see, he takes his social position so seriously! And when you are conspicuous--when everybody's talking about what you do--when everything that's the least bit unusual is magnified--"

"My dear girl!" I broke in again. "Stop a moment and let me talk!"

"But I hate to have to think--"

"Don't worry about my thoughts! They are most happy ones! You must understand that a Socialist cannot feel about such things as you do; we work out our economic interpretation of them, and after that they are simply so much data to us. I might meet one of your great friends, and she might snub me, but I would never think she had snubbed *me*--it would be my Western accent, and my forty-cent hat, and things like that which had put me in a class in her mind. My real self nobody can snub--certainly not until they've got at it."

"Ah!" said Sylvia, with shining eyes. "You have your own kind of aristocracy, I see!"

"What I want," I said, "is you. I'm an old hen whose chickens have grown up and left her, and I want something to mother. Your wonderful social world is just a bother to me, because it keeps me from gathering you into my arms as I'd like to. So what you do is to think of some role for me to play, so that I can come to see you; let me be advising you about your proposed day-nursery, or let me be a tutor of something, or a nice, respectable sewing-woman who darns the toes of your silk stockings!"

She laughed. "If you suppose that I'm allowed to wear my stockings until they have holes in them, you don't understand the perquisites of maids." She thought a moment, and then added: "You might come to trim hats for me."

By that I knew that we were really friends. If it does not seem to you a bold thing for Sylvia to have made a joke about my hat, it is only because you do not yet know her. I have referred to her money-consciousness and her social-consciousness; I would be idealizing her if I did not refer to another aspect of her which appalled me when I came to realise it--her clothes-consciousness. She knew every variety of fabric and every shade of colour and every style of design that ever had been delivered of the frenzied sartorial imagination. She had been trained in all the infinite minutiae which distinguished the right from the almost right; she would sweep a human being at one glance, and stick him in a pigeon hole of her mind for ever--because of his clothes. When later on she had come to be conscious of this clothes-consciousness, she told me that ninety-nine times out of a hundred she had found this method of appraisal adequate for the purposes of society life. What a curious comment upon our civilization--that all that people had to ask of one another, all they had to give to one another, should be expressible in terms of clothes!

16. I had set out to educate Mrs. Douglas van Tuiver in the things I thought she needed to know. A part of my programme was to find some people of modern sympathies whom she might meet without offence to her old prejudices. The first person I thought of was Mrs. Jessie Frothingham, who was the head of a fashionable girls' school, just around the corner from Miss Abercrombie's where Sylvia herself had received the finishing touch. Mrs. Frothingham's was as exclusive and expensive a school as the most proper person could demand, and great was Sylvia's consternation when I told her that its principal was a member of the Socialist party, and made no bones about speaking in public for us.

How in the world did she manage it? For one thing, I answered, she ran a good school--nobody had ever been heard to deny that. For another, she was an irresistibly serene and healthy person, who would look one of her millionaire "papas" in the eye and tell him what was what with so much decision; it would suddenly occur to the great man that if his daughter could be made into so capable a woman, he would not care what ticket she might vote.

Then too, it was testimony to the headway we are making that we are ceasing to be dangerous, and getting to be picturesque. In these days of strenuous social competition, when mammas are almost at their wits' end for some new device, when it costs incredible sums to make no impression at all--here was offered a new and inexpensive way of being unique. There could be no question that men were getting to like serious women; the most amazing subjects were coming up at dinner-parties, and you might hear the best people speak disrespectfully of their own money, which means that the new Revolution will have not merely its "Egalité Orleans," but also some of the ladies of his family!

I telephoned from Sylvia's house to Mrs. Frothingham, who answered: "Wouldn't you like Mrs. van Tuiver to hear a speech? I am to speak next week at the noon-day Wall Street meeting." I passed the question on, and Sylvia answered with an exclamation of delight: "Would a small boy like to attend a circus?"

It was arranged that Sylvia was to take us in her car. You may picture me with my grand friends--an old speckled hen in the company of two golden pheasants. I kept very quiet and let them get acquainted, knowing that my cause was safe in the hands of one so perfectly tailored as Mrs. Frothingham.

Sylvia expressed her delight at the idea of hearing a Socialist speech, and her amazement that the head of Mrs. Frothingham's should be so courageous, and meantime we threaded our way through the tangle of trucks and surface-cars on Broadway, and came to the corner of Wall Street. Here Mrs. Frothingham said she would get out and walk; it was quite likely that someone might recognise Mrs. Douglas van Tuiver, and she ought not to be seen arriving with the speaker. Sylvia, who would not willingly have committed a breach of etiquette towards a bomb-throwing anarchist, protested at this, but Mrs. Frothingham laughed good-naturedly, saying that it would be time enough for Mrs. van Tuiver to commit herself when she knew what she believed.

The speaking was to be from the steps of the Sub-treasury. We made a détour, and came up Broad Street, stopping a little way from the corner. These meetings had been held all through the summer and fall, so that people had learned to expect them; although it lacked some minutes of noon, there was already a crowd gathered. A group of men stood upon the broad steps, one with a red banner and several others with armfuls of pamphlets and books. With them was our friend, who looked at us and smiled, but gave no other sign of recognition.

Sylvia pushed back the collar of her sable coat, and sat erect in her shining blue velvet, her eyes and her golden hair shining beneath the small brim of a soft velvet hat. As she gazed eagerly at the busy throngs of men hurrying about this busy corner, she whispered to me: "I haven't been so excited since my début party!"

The crowd increased until it was difficult to get through Wall Street. The bell of Old Trinity was tolling the hour of noon, and the meeting was about to begin, when suddenly I heard an exclamation from Sylvia, and turning, saw a well-dressed man pushing his way from the office of Morgan and Company towards us. Sylvia clutched my hand where it lay on the seat of the car, and half gasped: "My husband!"

17. Of course I had been anxious to see Douglas van Tuiver. I had heard Claire Lepage's account of him, and Sylvia's, also I had seen pictures of him in the newspapers, and had studied them with some care, trying to imagine what sort of personage he might be. I knew that he was twenty-four, but the man who came towards us I would have taken to be forty. His face was sombre, with large features and strongly marked lines about the mouth; he was tall and thin, and moved with decision, betraying no emotion even in this moment of surprise. "What are you doing here?" were his first words.

For my part, I was badly "rattled"; I knew by the clutch of Sylvia's hand that she was too. But here I got a lesson in the nature of "social training." Some of the bright colour had faded from her face, but she spoke with the utmost coolness, the words coming naturally and simply: "We can't get through the crowd." And at the same time she looked about her, as much as to say: "You can see for yourself." (One of the maxims of Lady Dee had set forth that a lady never told a lie if she could avoid it.)

Sylvia's husband looked about, saying: "Why don't you call an officer?" He started to follow his own suggestion, and I thought then that my friend would miss her meeting. But she had more nerve than I imagined.

"No," she said. "Please don't."

"Why not?" Still there was no emotion in the cold, grey eyes.

"Because--I think there's something going on."

"What of that?"

"I'm not in a hurry, and I'd like to see."

He stood for a moment looking at the crowd. Mrs. Frothingham had come forward, evidently intending to speak. "What is this, Ferris?" he demanded of the chauffeur.

"I'm not sure, sir," said the man. "I think it's a Socialist meeting." (He was, of course, not missing the little comedy. I wondered what he thought!)

"A Socialist meeting?" said van Tuiver; then, to his wife: "You don't want to stay for that!"

Again Sylvia astonished me. "I'd like to very much," she answered simply.

He made no reply. I saw him stare at her, and then I saw his glance take me in. I sat in a corner as inconspicuous as I could make myself. I wondered whether I was a sempstress or a tutor, and whether either of these functionaries were introduced, and whether they shook hands or not.

Mrs. Frothingham had taken her stand at the base of Washington's statue. Had she by any chance identified the tall and immaculate gentleman who stood beside the automobile? Before she had said three sentences I made sure that she had done so, and I was appalled at her audacity.

"Fellow citizens," she began--"fellow-buccaneers of Wall Street." And when the mild laughter had subsided: "What I have to say is going to be addressed to one individual among you--the American millionaire. I assume there is one present--if no actual millionaire, then surely several who are destined to be, and not less than a thousand who aspire to be. So hear me, Mr. Millionaire," this with a smile, which gave you a sense of a reserve fund of energy and good humour. She had the crowd with her from the start--all but one. I stole a glance at the millionaire, and saw that he was not smiling.

"Won't you get in?" asked his wife, and he answered coldly: "No, I'll wait till you've had enough."

"Last summer I had a curious experience," said the speaker. "I was a guest at a tennis match, played upon the grounds of a State insane-asylum, the players being the doctors of the institution. Here, on a beautiful sunshiny afternoon, were ladies and gentlemen clad in festive white, enjoying a holiday, while in the background stood a frowning building with iron-barred gates and windows, from which one heard now and then the howlings of the maniacs. Some of the less fortunate of these victims of fate had been let loose, and while we played tennis, they chased the balls. All afternoon, while I sipped tea and chatted and watched the games, I said to myself: 'Here is the most perfect simile of our civilization that has ever come to me. Some people wear white and play tennis all day, while other people chase the balls, or howl in dungeons in the background!' And that is the problem I wish to put before my American millionaire--the problem of what I will call our lunatic- asylum stage of civilization. Mind you, this condition is all very well so long as we can say that the lunatics are incurable--that there is nothing we can do but shut our ears to their howling, and go ahead with our tennis. But suppose the idea were to dawn upon us that it is only because we played tennis all day that the lunatic- asylum is crowded, then might not the howls grow unendurable to us, and the game lose its charm?"

Stealing glances about me, I saw that several people were watching the forty-or-fifty-times-over millionaire; they had evidently recognised him, and were enjoying the joke. "Haven't you had enough of this?" he suddenly demanded of his wife, and she answered, guilelessly: "No, let's wait. I'm interested."

"Now, listen to me, Mr. American Millionaire," the speaker was continuing. "You are the one who plays tennis, and we, who chase the balls for you--we are the lunatics. And my purpose to-day is to prove to you that it is only because you play tennis all day that we have to chase balls all the day, and to tell you that some time soon we are going to cease to be lunatics, and that then you will have to chase your own balls! And don't, in your amusement over this illustration, lose sight of the serious nature of what I am talking about--the horrible economic lunacy which is known as poverty, and which is responsible for most of the evils we have in this world to-day--for crime and prostitution, suicide, insanity and war. My purpose is to show you, not by any guess of mine, or any appeals to your faith, but by cold business facts which can be understood in Wall Street, that this economic lunacy is one which can be cured; that we have the remedy in our hands, and lack nothing but the intelligence to apply it."

18. I do not want to bore you with a Socialist speech. I only want to give you an idea of the trap into which Mr. Douglas van Tuiver had been drawn. He stood

there, rigidly aloof while the speaker went on to explain the basic facts of wealth-production in modern society. She quoted from Kropotkin: "'Fields, Factories and Work- shops,' on sale at this meeting for a quarter!"--showing how by modern intensive farming--no matter of theory, but methods which were in commercial use in hundreds of places--it would be possible to feed the entire population of the globe from the soil of the British Isles alone. She showed by the bulletins of the United States Government how the machine process had increased the productive power of the individual labourer ten, twenty, a hundred fold. So vast was man's power of producing wealth today, and yet the labourer lived in dire want just as in the days of crude hand-industry!

So she came back to her millionaire, upon whom this evil rested. He was the master of the machine for whose profit the labourer had to produce. He could only employ the labourer to produce what could be sold at a profit; and so the stream of prosperity was choked at its source. "It is you, Mr. Millionaire, who are to blame for poverty; it is because so many millions of dollars must be paid to you in profits that so many millions of men must live in want. In other words, precisely as I declared at the outset, it is your playing tennis which is responsible for the lunatics chasing the balls!"

I wish that I might give some sense of the speaker's mastery of this situation, the extent to which she had communicated her good-humour to the crowd. You heard ripple after ripple of laughter, you saw everywhere about you eager faces, following every turn of the argument. No one could resist the contagion of interest--save only the American millionaire! He stood impassive, never once smiling, never once betraying a trace of feeling. Venturing to watch him more closely, however, I could see the stern lines deepening about his mouth, and his long, lean face growing more set.

The speaker had outlined the remedy--a change from the system of production for profit to one of production for use. She went on to explain how the change was coming; the lunatic classes were beginning to doubt the divine nature of the rules of the asylum, and they were preparing to mutiny, and take possession of the place. And here I saw that Sylvia's husband had reached his limit. He turned to her: "Haven't you had enough of this?"

"Why, no," she began. "If you don't mind--"

"I do mind very much," he said, abruptly. "I think you are committing a breach of taste to stay here, and I would be greatly obliged if you would leave."

And without really waiting for Sylvia's reply, he directed, "Back out of here, Ferris."

The chauffeur cranked up, and sounded his horn--which naturally had the effect of disturbing the meeting. People supposed we were going to try to get through the crowd ahead--and there was no place where anyone could move. But van Tuiver went to the rear of the car, saying, in a voice of quiet authority: "A little room here, please." And so, foot by foot, we backed away from the meeting, and when we had got clear of the throng, the master of the car stepped in, and we turned and made our way down Broad Street.

And now I was to get a lesson in the aristocratic ideal. Of course van Tuiver was angry; I believe he even suspected his wife of having known of the meeting. I supposed he would ask some questions; I supposed that at least he would express his opinion of the speech, his disgust that a woman of education should make such a spectacle of herself. Such husbands as I had been familiar with had never hesitated to vent their feelings under such circumstances. But from Douglas van Tuiver there came--not a word! He sat, perfectly straight, staring before him, like a sphinx; and Sylvia, after one or two swift glances at him, began to gossip cheerfully about her plans for the day-nursery for working-women!

So for a few blocks, until suddenly she leaned forward. "Stop here, Ferris." And then, turning to me, "Here is the American Trust Company."

"The American Trust Company?" I echoed, in my dumb stupidity.

"Yes--that is where the check is payable," said Sylvia, and gave me a pinch.

And so I comprehended, and gathered up my belongings and got out. She shook my hand warmly, and her husband raised his hat in a very formal salute, after which the car sped on up the street. I stood staring after it, in somewhat the state of mind of any humble rustic who may have been present when Elijah was borne into the heavens by the chariot of fire!

19. Sylvia had been something less than polite to me; and so I had not been home more than an hour before there came a messenger-boy with a note. By way of reassuring her, I promised to come to see her the next morning; and when I did, and saw her lovely face so full of concern, I forgot entirely her worldly greatness,

and did what I had longed to do from the beginning--put my arms about her and kissed her.

"My dear girl," I protested, "I don't want to be a burden in your life--I want to help you!'"

"But," she exclaimed, "what must you have thought--"

"I thought I had made a lucky escape!" I laughed.

She was proud--proud as an Indian; it was hard for her to make admissions about her husband. But then--we were like two errant school-girls, who had been caught m an escapade! "I don't know what I'm going to do about him," she said, with a wry smile. "He really won't listen--I can't make any impression on him."

"Did he guess that you'd come there on purpose?" I asked.

"I told him," she answered.

"You ***told*** him!"

"I'd meant to keep it secret--I wouldn't have minded telling him a fib about a little thing. But he made it so very serious!"

I could understand that it must have been serious after the telling. I waited for her to add what news she chose.

"It seems," she said, "that my husband has a cousin, a pupil of Mrs. Frothingham's. You can imagine!"

"I can imagine Mrs. Frothingham may lose a pupil."

"No; my husband says his Uncle Archibald always was a fool. But how can anyone be so narrow! He seemed to take Mrs. Frothingham as a personal affront."

This was the most definite bit of vexation against her husband that she had ever let me see. I decided to turn it into a jest. "Mrs. Frothingham will be glad to know she was understood," I said.

"But seriously, why can't men have open minds about politics and money?" She went on in a worried voice: "I knew he was like this when I met him at Harvard. He was living in his own house, aloof from the poorer men--the men who were most worth while, it seemed to me. And when I told him of the bad effect he was having on these men and on his own character as well, he said he would do whatever I asked--he even gave up his house and went to live in a dormitory. So I thought I had some influence on him. But now, here is the same thing again, only I find that one can't take a stand against one's husband. At least, he doesn't admit the right."

She hesitated. "It doesn't seem loyal to talk about it."

"My dear girl," I said with an impulse of candour, "there isn't much you can tell me about that problem. My own marriage went to pieces on that rock."

I saw a look of surprise upon her face. "I haven't told you my story yet," I said. "Some day I will--when you feel you know me well enough for us to exchange confidences."

There was more than a hint of invitation in this. After a silence, she said: "One's instinct is to hide one's troubles."

"Sylvia," I answered, "let me tell you about us. You must realise that you've been a wonderful person to me; you belong to a world I never had anything to do with, and never expected to get a glimpse of. It's the wickedness of our class-civilization that human beings can't be just human beings to each other--a king can hardly have a friend. Even after I've overcome the impulse I have to be awed by your luxury and your grandness; I'm conscious of the fact that everybody else is awed by them. If I so much as mention that I've met you, I see people start and stare at me--instantly I become a personage. It makes me angry, because I want to know *you*."

She was gazing at me, not saying a word. I went on: "I'd never have thought it possible for anyone to be in your position and be real and straight and human, but I realise that you have managed to work that miracle. So I want to love you and help you, in every way I know how. But you must understand, I can't ask for your confidence, as I could for any other woman's. There is too much vulgar curiosity about the rich and great, and I can't pretend to be unaware of that hatefulness; I can't help shrinking from it. So all I can say is--if you need me, if you ever need a real friend, why, here I am; you may be sure I understand, and won't tell your secrets to anyone else."

With a little mist of tears in her eyes, Sylvia put out her hand and touched mine. And so we went into a chamber alone together, and shut the cold and suspicious world outside.

20. We knew each other well enough now to discuss the topic which has been the favourite of women since we sat in the doorways of caves and pounded wild grain in stone mortars--the question of our lords, who had gone hunting, and who might be pleased to beat us on their return. I learned all that Sylvia had been taught on the subject of the male animal; I opened that amazing unwritten volume of

woman traditions, the maxims of Lady Dee Lysle.

Sylvia's maternal great-aunt had been a great lady out of a great age, and incidentally a grim and grizzled veteran of the sex-war. Her philosophy started from a recognition of the physical and economic inferiority of woman, as complete as any window-smashing suffragette could have formulated, but her remedy for it was a purely individualist one, the leisure-class woman's skill in trading upon her sex. Lady Dee did not use that word, of course--she would as soon have talked of her esophagus. Her formula was "charm," and she had taught Sylvia that the preservation of "charm" was the end of woman's existence, the thing by which she remained a lady, and without which she was more contemptible than the beasts.

She had taught this, not merely by example and casual anecdote, but by precepts as solemnly expounded as bible-texts. "Remember, my dear, a woman with a husband is like a lion-tamer with a whip!" And the old lady would explain what a hard and dangerous life was lived by lion-tamers, how their safety depended upon life-long distrustfulness of the creatures over whom they ruled. She would tell stories of the rending and maiming of luckless ones, who had forgotten for a brief moment the nature of the male animal! "Yes, my dear," she would say, "believe in love; but let the man believe first!" Her maxims never sinned by verbosity.

The end of all this was not merely food and shelter, a home and children, it was the supremacy of a sex, its ability to shape life to its whim. By means of this magic "charm"--a sort of perpetual individual sex-strike--a woman turned her handicaps into advantages and her chains into ornaments; she made herself a rare and wonderful creature, up to whom men gazed in awe. It was "romantic love," but preserved throughout life, instead of ceasing with courtship.

All the Castleman women understood these arts, and employed them. There was Aunt Nannie, when she cracked her whip the dear old bishop-lion would jump as if he had been shot! Did not the whole State know the story of how once he had been called upon at a banquet and had risen and remarked: "Ladies and gentlemen, I had intended to make a speech to you this evening, but I see that my wife is present, so I must beg you to excuse me." The audience roared, and Aunt Nannie was furious, but poor dear Bishop Chilton had spoken but the literal truth, that he could not spread the wings of his eloquence in the presence of his "better half."

And with Major Castleman, though it seemed different, it was really the same.

Sylvia's mother had let herself get stout--which seemed a dangerous mark of confidence in the male animal. But the major was fifteen years older than his wife, and she had a weak heart with which to intimidate him. Now and then the wilfulness of Castleman Lysle would become unendurable in the house, and his father would seize him and turn him over his knee. His screams would bring "Miss Margaret" flying to the rescue: "Major Castleman, how dare you spank one of *my* children?" And she would seize the boy and march off in terrible haughtiness, and lock herself and her child in her room, and for hours afterwards the poor major would wander about the house, suffering the lonelines of the guilty soul. You would hear him tapping gently at his lady's door. "Honey! Honey! Are you mad with me?" "Major Castleman," the stately answer would come, "will you oblige me by leaving one room in this house to which I may retire?"

21. I would give you a wrong idea of Sylvia if I did not make clear that along with this sophistication as to the play-aspects of sex, there went the most incredible ignorance as to its practical realities. In my arguments I had thought to appeal to her by referring to that feature of wage-slavery which more than even child-labour stirs the moral sense of women, but to my utter consternation I discovered that here was a woman nearly a year married who did not know what prostitution was. A suspicion had begun to dawn upon her, and she asked me, timidly: Could it be possible that that intimacy which was given in marriage could become a thing of barter in the market-place? When I told her the truth, I found her horror so great that it was impossible to go on talking economics. How could I say that women were driven to such things by poverty? Surely a woman who was not bad at heart would starve, before she would sell her body to a man!

Perhaps I should have been more patient with her, but I am bitter on these subjects. "My dear Mrs. van Tuiver," I said, "there is a lot of nonsense talked about this matter. There is very little sex-life for women without a money-price made clear in advance."

"I don't understand," she said.

"I don't know about your case," I replied, "but when I married, it was because I was unhappy and wanted a home of my own. And if the truth were told, that is why most women marry."

"But what has THAT to do with it?" she cried. She really did not see!

"What is the difference--except that such women stand out for a maintenance, while the prostitute takes cash?" I saw that I had shocked her, and I said: "You must be humble about these things, because you have never been poor, and you cannot judge those who have been. But surely you must have known worldly women who married rich men for their money. And surely you admit that that is prostitution?"

She fell suddenly silent, and I saw what I had done, and, no doubt, you will say I should have been ashamed of myself. But when one has seen as much of misery and injustice as I have, one cannot be so patient with the fine artificial delicacies and sentimentalities of the idle rich. I went ahead to tell her some stories, showing her what poverty actually meant to women.

Then, as she remained silent, I asked her how she had managed to remain so ignorant. Surely she must have met with the word "prostitution" in books; she must have heard allusions to the "demi-monde."

"Of course," she said, "I used to see conspicuous-looking women at the race-track in New Orleans; I've sat near them in restaurants, I've known by my mother's looks and her agitation that they must be bad women. But you see, I didn't know what it meant--I had nothing but a vague feeling of something dreadful."

I smiled. "Then Lady Dee did not tell you everything about the possibilities of her system of 'charm.'"

"No," said Sylvia. "Evidently she didn't!" She sat staring at me, trying to get up the courage to go on with this plain speaking.

And at last the courage came. "I think it is wrong," she exclaimed. "Girls ought not to be kept so ignorant! They ought to know what such things mean. Why, I didn't even know what marriage meant!"

"Can that be true?" I asked.

"All my life I had thought of marriage, in a way; I had been trained to think of it with every eligible man I met--but to me it meant a home, a place of my own to entertain people in. I pictured myself going driving with my husband, giving dinner-parties to his friends. I knew I'd have to let him kiss me, but beyond that--I had a vague idea of something, but I didn't think. I had been deliberately trained not to let myself think--to run away from every image that came to me. And I went on dreaming of what I'd wear, and how I'd greet my husband when he came home in the evening."

"Didn't you think about children?"

"Yes--but I thought of the CHILDREN. I thought what they'd look like, and how they'd talk, and how I'd love them. I don't know if many young girls shut their minds up like that."

She was speaking with agitation, and I was gazing into her eyes, reading more than she knew I was reading. I was nearer to solving the problem that had been baffling me. And I wanted to take her hands in mine, and say: "You would never have married him if you'd understood!"

22. Sylvia thought she ought to have been taught, but when she came to think of it she was unable to suggest who could have done the teaching. "Your mother?" I asked, and she had to laugh, in spite of the seriousness of her mood. "Poor dear mamma! When they sent me up here to boarding school, she took me off and tried to tell me not to listen to vulgar talk from the girls. She managed to make it clear that I mustn't listen to something, and I managed not to listen. I'm sure that even now she would rather have her tongue cut out than talk to me about such things."

"I talked to my children," I assured her.

"And you didn't feel embarrassed?"

"I did in the beginning--I had the same shrinkings to overcome. But I had a tragedy behind me to push me on."

I told her the story of my nephew, a shy and sensitive lad, who used to come to me for consolation, and became as dear to me as my own children. When he was seventeen he grew moody and despondent; he ran away from home for six months and more, and then returned and was forgiven--but that seemed to make no difference. One night he came to see me, and I tried hard to get him to tell me what was wrong. He wouldn't, but went away, and several hours later I found a letter he had shoved under the table-cloth. I read it, and rushed out and hitched up a horse and drove like mad to my brother-in-law's, but I got there too late, the poor boy had taken a shot-gun to his room, and put the muzzle into his mouth, and set off the trigger with his foot. In the letter he told me what was the matter--he had got into trouble with a woman of the town, and had caught syphilis. He had gone away and tried to get cured, but had fallen into the hands of a quack, who had taken all his money and left his health worse than ever, so in despair and shame the poor boy had shot his head off.

I paused, uncertain if Sylvia would understand the story. "Do you know what syphilis is?" I asked.

"I suppose--I have heard of what we call a 'bad disease'" she said.

"It's a very bad disease. But if the words convey to you that it's a disease that bad people get, I should tell you that most men take the chance of getting it; yet they are cruel enough to despise those upon whom the ill-luck falls. My poor nephew had been utterly ignorant--I found out that from his father, too late. An instinct had awakened in him of which he knew absolutely nothing; his companions had taught him what it meant, and he had followed their lead. And then had come the horror and the shame--and some vile, ignorant wretch to trade upon it, and cast the boy off when he was penniless. So he had come home again, with his gnawing secret; I pictured him wandering about, trying to make up his mind to confide in me, wavering between that and the horrible deed he did."

I stopped, because even to this day I cannot tell the story without tears. I cannot keep a picture of the boy in my room, because of the self-reproaches that haunt me. "You can understand," I said to Sylvia, "I never could forget such a lesson. I swore a vow over the poor lad's body, that I would never let a boy or girl that I could reach go out in ignorance into the world. I read up on the subject, and for a while I was a sort of fanatic--I made people talk, young people and old people. I broke down the taboos wherever I went, and while I shocked a good many, I knew that I helped a good many more."

All that was, of course, inconceivable to Sylvia. How curious was the contrast of her one experience in the matter of venereal disease. She told me how she had been instrumental in making a match between her friend, Harriet Atkinson and a young scion of an ancient and haughty family of Charleston, and how after the marriage her friend's health had begun to give way, until now she was an utter wreck, living alone in a dilapidated antebellum mansion, seeing no one but negro servants, and praying for death to relieve her of her misery.

"Of course, I don't really know," said Sylvia. "Perhaps it was this--this disease that you speak of. None of my people would tell me--I doubt if they really know themselves. It was just before my own wedding, so you can understand it had a painful effect upon me. It happened that I read something in a magazine, and I thought that--that possibly my fiancée--that someone ought to ask him, you understand--"

She stopped, and the blood was crimson in her cheeks, with the memory of her old excitement, and some fresh excitement added to it. There are diseases of the mind as well as of the body, and one of them is called prudery.

"I can understand," I said. "It was certainly your right to be reassured on such a point."

"Well, I tried to talk to my Aunt Varina about it; then I wrote to Uncle Basil, and asked him to write to Douglas. At first he refused--he only consented to do it when I threatened to go to my father."

"What came of it in the end?"

"Why, my uncle wrote, and Douglas answered very kindly that he understood, and that it was all right--I had nothing to fear. I never expected to mention the incident to anyone again."

"Lots of people have mentioned such things to me," I responded, to reassure her. Then after a pause: "Tell me, how was it, if you didn't know the meaning of marriage, how could you connect the disease with it?"

She answered, gazing with the wide-open, innocent eyes: "I had no idea how people gave it to each other. I thought maybe they got it by kissing."

I thought to myself again: The horror of this superstition of prudery! Can one think of anything more destructive to life than the placing of a taboo upon such matters? Here is the whole of the future at stake--the health, the sanity, the very existence of the race. And what fiend has been able to contrive it that we feel like criminals when we mention the subject?

23. Our intimacy progressed, and the time came when Sylvia told me about her marriage. She had accepted Douglas van Tuiver because she had lost Frank Shirley, and her heart was broken. She could never imagine herself loving any other man; and not knowing exactly what marriage meant, it had been easier for her to think of her family, and to follow their guidance. They had told her that love would come; Douglas had implored her to give him a chance to teach her to love him. She had considered what she could do with his money--both for her home-people and for those she spoke of vaguely as "the poor." But now she was making the discovery that she could not do very much for these "poor."

"It isn't that my husband is mean," she said. "On the contrary, the slightest hint will bring me any worldly thing I want. I have homes in half a dozen parts of America--I have ***carte blanche*** to open accounts in two hemispheres. If any of my people need money I can get it; but if I want it for myself, he asks me what I'm doing with it--and so I run into the stone-wall of his ideas."

At first the colliding with this wall had merely pained and bewildered her. But now the combination of Veblen and myself had helped her to realize what it meant. Douglas van Tuiver spent his money upon a definite system: whatever went to the maintaining of his social position, whatever added to the glory, prestige and power of the van Tuiver name--that money was well-spent; while money spent to any other end was money wasted--and this included all ideas and "causes." And when the master of the house knew that his money was being wasted, it troubled him.

"It wasn't until after I married him that I realized how idle his life is," she remarked. "At home all the men have something to do, running their plantations, or getting elected to some office. But Douglas never does anything that I can possibly think is useful."

His fortune was invested in New York City real-estate, she went on to explain. There was an office, with a small army of clerks and agents to attend to it--a machine which had been built up and handed on to him by his ancestors. It sufficed if he dropped in for an hour or two once a week when he was in the city, and signed a batch of documents now and then when he was away. His life was spent in the company of people whom the social system had similarly deprived of duties; and they had, by generations of experiment, built up for themselves a new set of duties, a life which was wholly without relationship to reality. Into this unreal existence Sylvia had married, and it was like a current sweeping her in its course. So long as she went with it, all was well; but let her try to catch hold of something and stop, and it would tear her loose and almost strangle her.

As time went on, she gave me strange glimpses into this world. Her husband did not seem really to enjoy its life. As Sylvia put it, "He takes it for granted that he has to do all the proper things that the proper people do. He hates to be conspicuous, he says. I point out to him that the proper things are nearly always conspicuous, but he replies that to fail to do them would be even more conspicuous."

It took me a long time to get really acquainted with Sylvia, because of the extent to which this world was clamouring for her. I used to drop in when she 'phoned me she had half an hour. I would find her dressing for something, and she would send her maid away, and we would talk until she would be late for some function; and that might be a serious matter, because somebody would feel slighted. She was always "on pins and needles" over such questions of precedent; it seemed as if everybody in her world must be watching everybody else. There was a whole elaborate science of how to treat the people you met, so that they would not feel slighted--or so that they would feel slighted, according to circumstances.

To the enjoyment of such a life it was essential that the person should believe in it. Douglas van Tuiver did believe in it; it was his religion, the only one he had. (Churchman as he was, his church was a part of the social routine.) He was proud of Sylvia, and apparently satisfied when he could take her at his side; and Sylvia went, because she was his wife, and that was what wives were for. She had tried her best to be happy; she had told herself that she *was* happy yet all the time realizing that a woman who is really happy does not have to tell herself.

Earlier in life she had quaffed and enjoyed the wine of applause. I recollect vividly her telling me of the lure her beauty had been to her--the most terrible temptation that could come to a woman. "I walk into a brilliant room, and I feel the thrill of admiration that goes through the crowd. I have a sudden sense of my own physical perfection--a glow all over me! I draw a deep breath--I feel a surge of exaltation. I say, 'I am victorious--I can command! I have this supreme crown of womanly grace--I am all-powerful with it--the world is mine!'"

As she spoke the rapture was in her voice, and I looked at her--and yes, she was beautiful! The supreme crown was hers!

"I see other beautiful women," she went on--and swift anger came into her voice. "I see what they are doing with this power! Gratifying their vanity--turning men into slaves of their whim! Squandering money upon empty pleasures--and with the dreadful plague of poverty spreading in the world! I used to go to my father, 'Oh, papa, why must there be so many poor people? Why should we have servants--why should they have to wait on me, and I do nothing for them?' He would try to explain to me that it was the way of Nature. Mamma would tell me it was the will of the Lord--'The poor ye have always with you'--'Servants, obey your masters'--and so on. But in spite of the Bible texts, I felt guilty. And now I come to Douglas with the same plea--and it only makes him angry! He has been to college and has a lot of scientific phrases--he tells me it's 'the struggle for existence,' 'the elimination of the unfit'--and so on. I say to him, 'First we make people unfit, and then we have to eliminate them.' He cannot see why I do not accept what learned people tell me--why I persist in questioning and suffering."

She paused, and then added, "It's as if he were afraid I might find out something he doesn't want me to! He's made me give him a promise that I won't see Mrs. Frothingham again!" And she laughed. "I haven't told him about you!"

I answered, needless to say, that I hoped she would keep the secret!

24. All this time I was busy with my child-labour work. We had an important bill before the legislature that session, and I was doing what I could to work up sentiment for it. I talked at every gathering where I could get a hearing; I wrote letters to newspapers; I sent literature to lists of names. I racked my mind for new schemes, and naturally, at such times, I could not help thinking of Sylvia. How much she could do, if only she would!

I spared no one, least of all myself, and so it was not easy to spare her. The fact that I had met her was the gossip of the office, and everybody was waiting for something to happen. "How about Mrs. van Tuiver?" my "chief" would ask, at intervals. "If she would *only* go on our press committee" my stenographer would sigh.

The time came when our bill was in committee, a place of peril for bills. I went to Albany to see what could be done. I met half a hundred legislators, of whom perhaps half-a-dozen had some human interest in my subject; the rest, well, it was discouraging. Where was the force that would stir them, make them forget their own particular little grafts, and serve the public welfare in defiance to hostile interests?

Where was it? I came back to New York to look for it, and after a blue luncheon with the members of our committee, I came away with my mind made up--I would sacrifice my Sylvia to this desperate emergency.

I knew just what I had to do. So far she had heard speeches about social wrongs, or read books about them; she had never been face to face with the reality of them. Now I persuaded her to take a morning off, and see some of the sights of the underworld of toil. We foreswore the royal car, and likewise the royal furs and velvets; she garbed herself in plain appearing dark blue and went down town in the Subway like common mortals, visiting paper-box factories and flower factories, tenement homes where whole families sat pasting toys and gimcracks for fourteen or sixteen hours a day, and still could not buy enough food to make full-sized men and women of them.

She was Dante, and I was Virgil, our inferno was an endless procession of tortured faces--faces of women, haggard and mournful, faces of little children, starved and stunted, dulled and dumb. Several times we stopped to talk with these people--one little Jewess girl I knew whose three tiny sisters had been roasted alive in a sweatshop fire. This child had jumped from a fourth-story window, and been miraculously caught by a fireman. She said that some man had started the fire, and been caught, but the police had let him get away. So I had to explain to Sylvia that curious bye-product (sic) of the profit system known as the "Arson Trust." Authorities estimated that incendiarism was responsible for the destruction of a quarter of a billion dollars worth of property in America every year. So, of course, the business of starting fires was a paying one, and the "fire-bug," like the "cadet" and the dive-keeper, was a part of the "system." So it was quite a possible thing that the man who had burned up this little girl's three sisters might have been allowed to escape.

I happened to say this in the little girl's hearing, and I saw her pitiful strained eyes fixed upon Sylvia. Perhaps this lovely, soft-voiced lady was a fairy god-mother, come to free her sisters from an evil spell and to punish the wicked criminal! I saw Sylvia turn her head away, and search for her handkerchief; as we groped our way down the dark stairs, she caught my hand, whispering: "Oh, my God! my God!"

It had even more effect than I had intended; not only did she say that she would do something--anything that would be of use--but she told me as we rode back home that her mind was made up to stop the squandering of her husband's money. He had been planning a costume ball for a couple of months later, an event which would keep the van Tuiver name in condition, and would mean that he and other people would spend many hundreds of thousands of dollars. As we rode home in the roaring Subway, Sylvia sat beside me, erect and tense, saying that if the ball were given, it would be without the presence of the hostess.

I struck while the iron was hot, and got her permission to put her name upon our committee list. She said, moreover, that she would get some free time, and be more than a mere name to us. What were the duties of a member of our committee?

"First," I said, "to know the facts about child-labour, as you have seen them to-day, and second, to help other people to know."

"And how is that to be done?"

"Well, for instance, there is that hearing before the legislative committee. You remember I suggested that you appear."

"Yes," she said in a low voice. I could almost hear the words that were in her mind: "What would *he* say?"

25. Sylvia's name went upon our letter-heads and other literature, and almost at once things began to happen. In a day or two there came a reporter, saying he had noticed her name. Was it true that she had become interested in our work? Would I please give him some particulars, as the public would naturally want to know.

I admitted that Mrs. van Tuiver had joined the committee; she approved of our work and desired to further it. That was all. He asked: Would she give an interview? And I answered that I was sure she would not. Then would I tell something about how she had come to be interested in the work? It was a chance to assist our propaganda, added the reporter, diplomatically.

I retired to another room, and got Sylvia upon the 'phone, "The time has come for you to take the plunge," I said.

"Oh, but I don't want to be in the papers!" she cried "Surely, you wouldn't advise it!"

"I don't see how you can avoid having something appear. Your name is given out, and if the man can't get anything else, he'll take our literature, and write up your doings out of his imagination."

"And they'll print my picture with it!" she exclaimed. I could not help laughing. "It's quite possible."

"Oh, what will my husband do? He'll say 'I told you so!'"

It is a hard thing to have one's husband say that, as I knew by bitter experience. But I did not think that reason enough for giving up.

"Let me have time to think it over," said Sylvia. "Get him to wait till to-morrow, and meantime I can see you."

So it was arranged. I think I told Sylvia the truth when I said that I had never before heard of a committee member who was unwilling to have his purposes discussed in the newspapers. To influence newspapers was one of the main purposes of committees, and I did not see how she could expect either editors or readers to take any other view.

"Let me tell the man about your trip down town," I suggested, "then I can go on to discuss the bill and how it bears on the evils you saw. Such a statement can't possibly do you harm."

She consented, but with the understanding that she was not to be quoted directly. "And don't let them make me picturesque!" she exclaimed. "That's what my husband seems most to dread."

I wondered if he didn't think she was picturesque, when she sat in a splendid, shining coach, and took part in a public parade through Central Park. But I did not say this. I went off, and swore my reporter to abstain from the "human touch," and he promised and kept his word. There appeared next morning a dignified "write-up" of Mrs. Douglas van Tuiver's interest in child-labour reform. Quoting me, it described some of the places she had visited, and some of the sights which had shocked her; it went on to tell about our committee and its work, the status of our bill in the legislature, the need of activity on the part of our friends if the measure was to be forced through at this session. It was a splendid "boost" for our work, and everyone in the office was in raptures over it. The social revolution was at hand! thought my young stenographer.

But the trouble with this business of publicity is that, however carefully you control your interviewer, you cannot control the others who use his material. The "afternoon men" came round for more details, and they made it clear that it was personal details they wanted. And when I side-stepped their questions, they went off and made up answers to suit themselves, and printed Sylvia's pictures, together with photographs of child-workers taken from our pamphlets.

I called Sylvia up while she was dressing for dinner, to explain that I was not responsible for any of this picturesqueness. "Oh, perhaps I am to blame myself!" she exclaimed. "I think I interviewed a reporter."

"How do you mean?"

"A woman sent up her card--she told the footman she was a friend of mine. And I thought--I couldn't be sure if I'd met her--so I went and saw her. She said she'd met me at Mrs. Harold Cliveden's, and she began to talk to me about child-labour, and this and that plan she had, and what did I think of them, and suddenly it flashed over me: 'Maybe this is a reporter playing a trick on me!'"

I hurried out before breakfast next morning and got all the papers, to see what this enterprising lady had done. There was nothing, so I reflected that probably she had been a "Sunday" lady.

But then, when I reached my office, the 'phone rang, and I heard the voice of Sylvia: "Mary, something perfectly dreadful has happened!"

"What?" I cried.

"I can't tell you over the 'phone, but a certain person is furiously angry. Can I see you if I come down right away?"

26. Such terrors as these were unguessed by me in the days of my obscurity. Uneasy lies the head that wears a crown, uneasy also, lies the wife of that head, and the best friend of the wife. I dismissed my stenographer, and spent ten or fifteen restless minutes until Sylvia appeared.

Her story was quickly told. A couple of hours ago the acting-manager of Mr. van Tuiver's office had telephoned to ask if he might call upon a matter of importance. He had come. Naturally, he had the most extreme reluctance to say anything which might seem to criticise the activities of Mr. van Tuiver's wife, but there was something in the account in the newspapers which should be brought to her husband's attention. The articles gave the names and locations of a number of firms in whose factories it was alleged that Mrs. van Tuiver had found unsatisfactory conditions, and it happened that two of these firms were located in premises which belonged to the van Tuiver estates!

A story coming very close to melodrama, I perceived. I sat dismayed at what I had done. "Of course, dear girl," I said, at last, "you understand that I had no idea who owned these buildings."

"Oh, don't say that!" exclaimed Sylvia. "I am the one who should have known!"

Then for a long time I sat still and let her suffer. "Tenement sweat-shops! Little children in factories!" I heard her whisper.

At last I put my hand on hers. "I tried to put it off for a while," I said. "But I knew it would have to come."

"Think of me!" she exclaimed, "going about scolding other people for the way they make their money! When I thought of my own, I had visions of palatial hotels and office-buildings--everything splendid and clean!"

"Well, my dear, you've learned now, and you will be able to do something--"

She turned upon me suddenly, and for the first time I saw in her face the passions of tragedy. "Do you believe I will be able to do anything? No! Don't have any such idea!"

I was struck dumb. She got up and began to pace the room. "Oh, don't make any mistake, I've paid for my great marriage in the last hour or two. To think that he cares about nothing save the possibility of being found out and made ridiculous! All his friends have been 'muckraked,' as he calls it, and he has sat aloft and smiled over their plight; he was the landed gentleman, the true aristrocrat, whom the worries of traders and money-changers didn't concern. Now perhaps he's caught, and his name is to be dragged in the mire, and it's my flightiness, my lack of common-sense that has done it!"

"I shouldn't let that trouble me," I said. "You could not know--"

"Oh, it's not that! It's that I hadn't a single courageous word to say to him--not a hint that he ought to refuse to wring blood-money from sweat-shops! I came away without having done it, because I couldn't face his anger, because it would have meant a quarrel!"

"My dear," I said gently, "it is possible to survive a quarrel."

"No, you don't understand! We should never make it up again, I know--I saw it in his words, in his face. He will never change to please me, no, not even a simple thing like the business-methods of the van Tuiver estates."

I could not help smiling. "My dear Sylvia! A simple thing!"

She came and sat beside me. "That's what I want to talk about. It is time I was growing up. It it time that I knew about these things. Tell me about them."

"What, my dear?"

"About the methods of the van Tuiver estates, that can't be changed to please me. I made out one thing, we had recently paid a fine for some infraction of the law in one of those buildings, and my husband said it was because we had refused to pay more money to a tenement-house inspector. I asked him: 'Why should we pay any money at all to a tenement-house inspector? Isn't it bribery?' He answered: 'It's a custom--the same as you give a tip to a hotel waiter.' Is that true?"

I could not help smiling. "Your husband ought to know, my dear," I said.

I saw her compress her lips. "What is the tip for?"

"I suppose it is to keep out of trouble with him."

"But why can't we keep out of trouble by obeying the law?"

"My dear, sometimes the law is inconvenient, and sometimes it is complicated and obscure. It might be that you are violating it without knowing the fact. It might be uncertain whether you are violating it or not, so that to settle the question would mean a lot of expense and publicity. It might even be that the law is impossible to obey--that it was not intended to be obeyed."

"What do you mean by that?"

"I mean, maybe it was passed to put you at the mercy of the politicians."

"But," she protested, "that would be blackmail."

"The phrase," I replied, "is 'strike-legislation.'"

"But at least, that wouldn't be our fault!"

"No, not unless you had begun it. It generally happens that the landlord discovers it's a good thing to have politicians who will work with him. Maybe he wants his assessments lowered; maybe he wants to know where new car lines are to go, so that he can buy intelligently; maybe he wants the city to improve his neighbourhood; maybe he wants influence at court when he has some heavy damage suit."

"So we bribe everyone!"

"Not necessarily. You may simply wait until campaign-time, and then make your contribution to the machine. That is the basis of the 'System.'."

"The 'System '?"

"A semi-criminal police-force, and everything that pays tribute to it; the saloon and the dive, the gambling hell the white-slave market, and the Arson trust."

I saw a wild look in her eyes. "Tell me, do you *know* that all these things are true? Or are you only guessing about them?"

"My dear Sylvia," I answered, "you said it was time you grew up. For the present I will tell you this: Several months before I met you, I made a speech in which I named some of the organised forces of evil in the city. One was Tammany Hall, and another was the Traction Trust, and another was the Trinity Church Corporation, and yet another was the van Tuiver estates."

27. The following Sunday there appeared a "magazine story" of an interview with the infinitely beautiful young wife of the infinitely rich Mr. Douglas van Tuiver, in which the views of the wife on the subject of child-labour were liberally

interlarded with descriptions of her reception-room and her morning-gown. But mere picturesqueness by that time had been pretty well discounted in our minds. So long as the article did not say anything about the ownership of child-labour tenements!

I did not see Sylvia for several weeks after that. I took it for granted that she would want some time to get herself together and make up her mind about the future. I did not feel anxious; the seed had sprouted, and I felt sure it would continue to grow.

Then one day she called me up, asking if I could come to see her. I suggested that afternoon, and she said she was having tea with some people at the Palace Hotel, and could I come there just after tea-time? I remember the place and the hour, because of the curious adventure into which I got myself. One hears the saying, when unexpected encounters take place, "How small the world is!" But I thought the world was growing really too small when I went into a hotel tea-room to wait for Sylvia, and found myself face to face with Claire Lepage!

The place appointed had been the "orange-room"; I stood in the door-way, sweeping the place with my eyes, and I saw Mrs. van Tuiver at the same moment that she saw me. She was sitting at a table with several other people and she nodded, and I took a seat to wait. From my position I could watch her, in animated conversation; and she could send me a smile now and then. So I was decidedly startled when I heard a voice, "Why, how do you do?" and looked up and saw Claire holding out her hand to me.

"Well, for heaven's sake!" I exclaimed.

"You don't come to see me any more," she said.

"Why, no--no, I've been busy of late." So much I managed to ejaculate, in spite of my confusion.

"You seem surprised to see me," she remarked--observant as usual, and sensitive to other people's attitude to her.

"Why, naturally," I said. And then, recollecting that it was not in the least natural--since she spent a good deal of her time in such places--I added, "I was looking for someone else."

"May I do in the meantime?" she inquired, taking a seat beside me. "What are you so busy about?"

"My child-labour work," I answered. Then, in an instant, I was sorry for the words, thinking she must have read about Sylvia's activities. I did not want her to know that I had met Sylvia, for it would mean a flood of questions, which I did not want to answer--nor yet to refuse to answer.

But my fear was needless. "I've been out of town," she said.

"Whereabouts?" I asked, making conversation.

"A little trip to Bermuda."

My mind was busy with the problem of getting rid of her. It would be intolerable to have Sylvia come up to us; it was intolerable to know that they were in sight of each other.

Even as the thought came to me, however, I saw Claire start. "Look!" she exclaimed.

"What is it?"

"That woman there--in the green velvet! The fourth table."

"I see her."

"Do you know who she is?"

"Who?" (I remembered Lady Dee's maxim about lying!)

"Sylvia Castleman!" whispered Claire. (She always referred to her thus--seeming to say, "I'm as much van Tuiver as she is!")

"Are you sure?" I asked--in order to say something.

"I've seen her a score of times. I seem to be always running into her. That's Freddie Atkins she's talking to."

"Indeed!" said I.

"I know most of the men I see her with. But I have to walk by as if I'd never seen them. A queer world we live in, isn't it?"

I could assent cordially to that proposition. "Listen," I broke in, quickly. "Have you got anything to do? If not, come down to the Royalty and have tea with me."

"Why not have it here?"

"I've been waiting for someone from there, and I have to leave a message. Then I'll be free."

She rose, to my vast relief, and we walked out. I could feel Sylvia's eyes following me; but I dared not try to send her a message--I would have to make up some explanation afterwards. "Who was your well-dressed friend?" I could imagine her asking; but my mind was more concerned with the vision of what would happen if, in full sight of her companion, Mr. Freddie Atkins, she were to rise and walk over to Claire and myself!

28. Seated in the palm-room of the other hotel, I sipped a cup of tea which I felt I had earned, while Claire had a little glass of the fancy-coloured liquids which the ladies in these places affect. The room was an aviary, with tropical plants and splashing fountains--and birds of many gorgeous hues; I gazed from one to another of the splendid creatures, wondering how many of them were paying for their plumage in the same way as my present companion. It would have taken a more practiced eye than mine to say which, for if I had been asked, I would have taken Claire for a diplomat's wife. She had not less than a thousand dollars' worth of raiment upon her, and its style made clear to all the world the fact that it had not been saved over from a previous season of prosperity. She was a fine creature, who could carry any amount of sail; with her bold, black eyes she looked thoroughly competent, and it was hard to believe in the fundamental softness of her character.

I sat, looking about me, annoyed at having missed Sylvia, and only half listening to Claire. But suddenly she brought me to attention. "Well," she said, "I've met him."

"Met whom?"

"Douglas."

I stared at her. "Douglas van Tuiver?"

She nodded; and I suppressed a cry.

"I told you he'd come back," she added, with a laugh.

"You mean he came to see you?"

I could not hide my concern. But there was no need to, for it flattered Claire's vanity. "No--not yet, but he will. I met him at Jack Taylor's--at a supper-party."

"Did he know you were to be there?"

"No. But he didn't leave when he saw me."

There was a pause. I could not trust myself to say anything. But Claire had no intention of leaving me curious. "I don't think he's happy with her," she remarked.

"What makes you say that?"

"Oh, several things. I know him, you know. He wouldn't say he was."

"Perhaps he didn't want to discuss it with you."

"Oh, no--not that. He isn't reserved with me."

"I should think it was dangerous to discuss one's wife under such circumstances," I laughed.

Claire laughed also. "You should have heard what Jack had to say about his wife! She's down at Palm Beach."

"She'd better come home," I ventured.

"He was telling what a dance she leads him; she raises Cain if a woman looks at him--and she damns every woman he meets before the woman has a chance to look. Jack said marriage was hell--just hell. Reggie Channing thought it was like a pair of old slippers that you got used to." Jack laughed and answered, "You're at the stage where you think you can solve the marriage problem by deceiving your wife!"

I made no comment. Claire sat for a while, busy with her thoughts; then she repeated, "He wouldn't say he was happy! And he misses me, too. When he was going, I held his hand, and said: 'Well, Douglas, how goes it?'"

"And then?" I asked; but she would not say any more.

I waited a while, and then began, "Claire, let him alone. Give them a chance to be happy."

"Why should I?" she demanded, in a voice of hostility.

"She never harmed you," I said. I knew I was being foolish, but I would do what I could.

"She took him away from me, didn't she?" And Claire's eyes were suddenly alight with the hatred of her outcast class. "Why did she get him? Why is she Mrs. van Tuiver, and I nobody? Because her father was rich, because she had power and position, while I had to scratch for myself in the world. Is that true, or isn't it?"

I could not deny that it might be part of the truth. "But they're married now," I said, "and he loves her."

"He loves me, too. And I love him still, in spite of the way he's treated me. He's the only man I ever really loved. Do you think I'm going off and hide in a hole, while she spends his money and plays the princess up and down the Avenue? Not much!"

I fell silent. Should I set out upon another effort at "moulding water"? Should

I give Claire one more scolding--tell her, perhaps, how her very features were becoming hard and ugly, as a result of the feelings she was harbouring? Should I recall the pretences of generosity and dignity she had made when we first met? I might have attempted this--but something held me back. After all, the one person who could decide this issue was Douglas van Tuiver.

I rose. "Well, I have to be going. But I'll drop round now and then, and see what success you have."

She became suddenly important. "Maybe I won't tell!"

To which I answered, indifferently, "All right, it's your secret." But I went off without much worry over that part of it. Claire must have some one to whom to recount her troubles--or her triumphs, as the case might be.

29. I had my talk with Sylvia a day or two later, and made my excuse--a friend from the West who had been going out of town in a few hours later.

The seed had been growing, I found. Ever since we had last met, her life had consisted of arguments over the costume-ball on which her husband had set his heart, and at which she had refused to play the hostess.

"Of course, he's right about one thing," she remarked. "We can't stay in New York unless we give some big affair. Everyone expects it, and there is no explanation except one he could not offer."

"I've made a big breach in your life, Sylvia," I said.

"It wasn't all you. This unhappiness has been in me--it's been like a boil, and you've been the poultice." (She had four younger brothers and sisters, so these domestic similes came naturally.)

"Boils," I remarked, "are disfiguring, when they come to a head."

There was a pause. "How is your child-labour bill?" she asked, abruptly.

"Why, it's all right."

"Didn't I see a letter in the paper saying it had been referred to a sub-committee, some trick to suppress it for this session?"

I could not answer. I had been hoping she had not seen that letter.

"If I were to come forward now," she said, "I could possibly block that move, couldn't I?"

Still I said nothing.

"If I were to take a bold stand--I mean if I were to speak at a public meeting, and denounce the move."

"I suppose you could," I had to admit.

For a long time she sat with her head bowed. "The children will have to wait," she said, at last, half to herself.

"My dear," I answered (What else was there to answer?) "the children have waited a long time."

"I hate to turn back--to have you say I'm a coward--"

"I won't say that, Sylvia."

"You will be too kind, no doubt, but that will be the truth."

I tried to reassure her. But the acids I had used--intended for tougher skins than hers--had burned into the very bone, and now it was not possible to stop their action. "I must make you understand," she said, "how serious a thing it seems to me for a wife to stand out against her husband. I've been brought up to feel that it was the most terrible thing a woman could do."

She stopped, and when she went on again her face was set like one enduring pain. "So this is the decision to which I have come. If I do anything of a public nature now, I drive my husband from me; on the other hand, if I take a little time, I may be able to save the situation. I need to educate myself, and I'm hoping I may be able to educate him at the same time. If I can get him to read something--if it's only a few paragraphs everyday--I may gradually change his point of view, so that he will tolerate what I believe. At any rate, I ought to try; I am sure that is the wise and kind and fair thing to do."

"What will you do about the ball?" I asked.

"I am going to take him away, out of this rush and distraction, this dressing and undressing, hurrying about meeting people and chattering about nothing."

"He is willing?"

"Yes; in fact, he suggested it himself. He thinks my mind is turned, with all the things I've been reading, and with Mrs. Frothingham, and Mrs. Allison, and the rest. He hopes that if I go away, I may quiet down and come to my senses. We have a good excuse. I have to think of my health just now---"

She stopped, and looked away from my eyes. I saw the colour spreading in a slow wave over her cheeks; it was like those tints of early dawn that are so ravishing to the souls of poets. "In four or five months from now---" And she stopped again.

I put my big hand gently over her small one. "I have three children of my own," I said.

"So," she went on, "it won't seem so unreasonable. Some people know, and the rest will guess, and there won't be any talk--I mean, such as there would be if it was rumoured that Mrs. Douglas van Tuiver had got interested in Socialism, and refused to spend her husband's money."

"I understand," I replied. "It's quite the most sensible thing, and I'm glad you've found a way out. I shall miss you, of course, but we can write each other long letters. Where are you going?"

"I'm not absolutely sure. Douglas suggests a cruise in the West Indies, but I think I should rather be settled in one place. He has a lovely house in the mountains of North Carolina, and wants me to go there; but it's a show-place, with rich homes all round, and I know I'd soon be in a social whirl. I thought of the camp in the Adirondacks. It would be glorious to see the real woods in winter; but I lose my nerve when I think of the cold--I was brought up in a warm place."

"A 'camp' sounds rather primitive for one in your condition," I suggested.

"That's because you haven't been there. In reality it's a big house, with twenty-five rooms, and steam-heat and electric lights, and half a dozen men to take care of it when it's empty--as it has been for several years."

I smiled--for I could read her thought. "Are you going to be unhappy because you can't occupy all your husband's homes?"

"There's one other I prefer," she continued, unwilling to be made to smile. "They call it a 'fishing lodge,' and it's down in the Florida Keys. They're putting a railroad through there, but meantime you can only get to it by a launch. From the pictures, it's the most heavenly spot imaginable. Fancy running about those wonderful green waters in a motor-boat!"

"It sounds quite alluring," I replied. "But isn't it remote for you?"

"We're not so very far from Key West; and my husband means to have a physician with us in any case. The advantage of being in a small place is that we couldn't entertain if we wanted to. I can have my Aunt Varina come to stay with me, a dear, sweet soul who loves me devotedly; and then if I find I have to have some new ideas, perhaps you can come---"

"I don't think your husband would favour that," I said.

She put her hand out to me in a quick gesture. "I don't mean to give up our friendship! I want you to understand, I intend to go on studying and growing. I am doing what he asked me--it's right that I should think of his wishes, and of the health of my child. But the child will be growing up, and sooner or later my husband must grant me the right to think, to have a life of my own. You must stand by me and help me, whatever happens."

I gave her my hand on that, and so we parted--for some time, as it proved. I went up to Albany once more, in a last futile effort to save our precious bill; and while I was there I got a note from her, saying that she was leaving for the Florida Keys.

BOOK II
SYLVIA AS MOTHER

For three months after this I had nothing but letters from Sylvia. She proved to be an excellent letter-writer, full of verve and colour. I would not say that she poured out her soul to me, but she gave me glimpses of her states of mind, and the progress of her domestic drama.

First, she described the place to which she had come; a ravishing spot, where any woman ought to be happy. It was a little island, fringed with a border of cocoa-nut-palms, which rustled and whispered day and night in the breeze. It was covered with tropical foliage, and there was a long, rambling bungalow, with screened "galleries," and a beach of hard white sand in front. The water was blue, dazzling with sunshine, and dotted with distant green islands; all of it, air, water, and islands, were warm. "I don't realize till I get here," she said, "I am never really happy in the North. I wrap myself against the assaults of a cruel enemy. But here I am at home; I cast off my furs, I stretch out my arms, I bloom. I believe I shall quite cease to think for a while--I shall forget all storms and troubles, and bask on the sand like a lizard.

"And the water! Mary, you cannot imagine such water; why should it be blue on top, and green when you look down into it? I have a little skiff of my own in which I drift, and I have been happy for hours, studying the bottom; you see every colour of the rainbow, and all as clear as in an aquarium. I have been fishing, too, and have caught a tarpon. That is supposed to be a great adventure, and it really is quite thrilling to feel the monstrous creature struggling with you--though, of course, my arms soon gave out, and I had to turn him over to my husband. This is one of the famous fishing-grounds of the world, and I am glad of that, because it will keep the men happy while I enjoy the sunshine.

"I have discovered a fascinating diversion," she wrote, in a second letter. "I make them take me in the launch to one of the loneliest of the keys; they go off to fish, and I have the whole day to myself, and am as happy as a child on a picnic! I roam the beach, I take off my shoes and stockings--there are no newspaper reporters snapping pictures. I dare not go far in, for there are huge black creatures with dangerous stinging tails; they rush away in a cloud of sand when I approach, but the thought of stepping upon one by accident is terrifying. However, I let the little wavelets wash round my toes, and I try to grab little fish, and I pick up lovely shells; and then I go on, and I see a huge turtle waddling to the water, and I dash up, and would stop him if I dared, and then I find his eggs--such an adventure!

"I am the prey of strange appetites and cravings. I have a delicious luncheon with me, but suddenly the one thing in the world I want to eat is turtle-eggs. I have no matches with me, and I do not know how to build a fire like the Indians, so I have to hide the eggs back in the sand until to-morrow. I hope the turtle does not move them--and that I have not lost my craving in the meantime!

"Then I go exploring inland. These islands were once the haunts of pirates, so I may imagine all sorts of romantic things. What I find are lemon-trees. I do not know if they are wild, or if the key was once cultivated; the lemons are huge in size, and nearly all skin, but the flavour is delicious. Turtle-eggs with wild lemon-juice! And then I go on and come to a mangrove-swamp--dark and forbidding, a grisly place; you imagine the trees are in torment, with limbs and roots tangled like writhing serpents. I tiptoe in a little way, and then get frightened, and run back to the beach.

"I see on the sand a mysterious little yellow creature, running like the wind; I make a dash, and get between him and his hole; and so he stands, crouching on guard, staring at me, and I at him. He is some sort of crab, but he stands on two legs like a caricature of a man; he has two big weapons upraised for battle, and staring black eyes stuck out on long tubes. He is an uncanny thing to look at; but then suddenly the idea comes, How do I seem to him? I realize that he is alive; a tiny mite of hunger for life, of fear and resolution. I think, How lonely he must be! And I want to tell him that I love him, and would not hurt him for the world; but I have no way to make him understand me, and all I can do is to go away and leave him. I go, thinking what a strange place the world is, with so many living things, each shut away apart by himself, unable to understand the others or make the others understand him. This is what is called philosophy, is it not? Tell me some books where these things are explained....

"I am reading all you sent me. When I grew tired of exploring the key, I lay down in the shade of a palm-tree, and read--guess what? 'Number Five John Street'! So all this loveliness vanished, and I was back in the world's nightmare. An extraordinary book! I decided that it would be good for my husband, so I read him a few paragraphs; but I found that it only irritated him. He wants me to rest, he says--he can't see why I've come away to the Florida Keys to read about the slums of London.

"My hope of gradually influencing his mind has led to a rather appalling discovery--that he has the same intention as regards me! He too has brought a selection of books, and reads to me a few pages every day, and explains what they mean. He calls *this* resting! I am no match for him, of course--I never realized more keenly the worthlessness of my education. But I see in a general way where his arguments tend--that life is something that has grown, and is not in the power of men to change; but even if he could convince me of this, I should not find it a source of joy. I have a feeling always that if you were here, you would know something to answer.

"The truth is that I am so pained by the conflict between us that I cannot argue at all. I find myself wondering what our marriage would have been like if we had discovered that we had the same ideas and interests. There are days and nights at a time when I tell myself that I ought to believe what my husband believes, that I ought never have allowed myself to think of anything else. But that really won't do as a life-programme; I tried it years ago with my dear mother and father. Did I ever tell you that my mother is firmly convinced in her heart that I am to suffer eternally in a real hell of fire because I do not believe certain things about the Bible? She still has visions of it--though not so bad since she turned me over to a husband!

"Now it is my husband who is worried about my ideas. He is reading a book by Burke, a well-known old writer. The book deals with English history, which I don't know much about, but I see that it resents modern changes, and the whole spirit of change. And Mary, why can't I feel that way? I really ought to love those old and stately things, I ought to be reverent to the past; I was brought up that way. Sometimes I tremble when I realize how very flippant and cynical I am. I seem to see the wrong side of everything, so that I couldn't believe in it if I wanted to!"

2. Her letters were full of the wonders of Nature about her. There was a snow-white egret who made his home upon her island; she watched his fishing operations, and meant to find his nest, so as to watch his young. The men made a trip into the Everglades, and brought back wonder-tales of flocks of flamingoes making scarlet clouds in the sky, huge colonies of birds' nests crowded like a city. They had brought home a young one, which screamed all day to be stuffed with fish.

A cousin of Sylvia's, Harley Chilton, had come to visit her. He had taken van Tuiver on hunting-trips during the latter's courtship days, and now was a good fishing-companion. He was not allowed to discover the state of affairs between Sylvia and her husband, but he saw his cousin reading serious books, and his contribution to the problem was to tell her that she would get wrinkles in her face, and that even her feet would grow big, like those of the ladies in New England.

Also, there was the young physician who kept watch over Sylvia's health; a dapper little man with pink and white complexion, and a brown moustache from which he could not keep his fingers. He had a bungalow to himself, but sometimes he went along on the launch-trips, and Sylvia thought she observed wrinkles of amusement round his eyes whenever she differed from her husband on the subject of Burke. She suspected this young man of not telling all his ideas to his multi-millionaire patients, and she was entertained by the prospect of probing him.

Then came Mrs. Varina Tuis; who since the tragic cutting of her own domestic knot, had given her life to the service of the happier members of the Castleman line. She was now to be companion and counsellor to Sylvia; and on the very day of her arrival she discovered the chasm that was yawning in her niece's life.

"It's wonderful," wrote Sylvia, "the intuition of the Castleman women. We were in the launch, passing one of the viaducts of the new railroad, and Aunt Varina exclaimed, 'What a wonderful piece of work!' 'Yes,' put in my husband, 'but don't let Sylvia hear you say it.' 'Why not?' she asked; and he replied, 'She'll tell you how many hours a day the poor Dagoes have to work.' That was all; but I saw Aunt Varina give a quick glance at me, and I saw that she was not fooled by my efforts to make conversation. It was rather horrid of Douglas, for he knows that I love these old people, and do not want them to know about my trouble. But it is characteristic of him--when he is annoyed he seldom tries to spare others.

"As soon as we were alone, Aunt Varina began, 'Sylvia, my dear, what does it mean? What have you done to worry your husband?'

"You would be entertained if I could remember the conversation. I tried to dodge the trouble by answering off-hand, 'Douglas had eaten too many turtle-eggs for luncheon '--this being a man-like thing, that any dear old lady would understand. But she was too shrewd. I had to explain to her that I was learning to think, and this sent her into a perfect panic.

"'You actually mean, my child, that you are thinking about subjects to which your husband objects, and you refuse to stop when he asks you to? Surely you must know that he has some good reason for objecting.'

"'I suppose so,' I said, 'but he has not made that reason clear to me; and certainly I have a right--'

"She would not hear any more than that. 'Right, Sylvia? Right? Are you claiming the right to drive your husband from you?'

"'But surely I can't regulate all my thinking by the fear of driving my husband from me!'

"'Sylvia, you take my breath away. Where did you get such ideas?'

"'But answer me, Aunt Varina--can I?'

"'What thinking is as important to a woman as thinking how to please a good, kind husband? What would become of her family if she no longer tried to do this?'

"So you see, we opened up a large subject. I know you consider me a backward person, and you may be interested to learn that there are some to whom I seem a terrifying rebel. Picture poor Aunt Varina, her old face full of concern, repeating over and over, 'My child, my child, I hope I have come in time! Don't scorn the advice of a woman who has paid bitterly for her mistakes. You have a good husband, a man who loves you devotedly; you are one of the most fortunate of women--now do not throw your happiness away!'

"'Aunt Varina,' I said (I forget if I ever told you that her husband gambled and drank, and finally committed suicide) 'Aunt Varina, do you really believe that every man is so anxious to get away from his wife that it must take her whole stock of energy, her skill in diplomacy, to keep him?'

"'Sylvia,' she answered, "you put things so strangely, you use such horribly crude language, I don't know how to talk to you!' (That must be your fault, Mary. I never heard such a charge before.) 'I can only tell you this--that the wife who permits herself to think about other things than her duty to her husband and her children is taking a frightful risk. She is playing with fire, Sylvia--she will realize too late what it means to set aside the wisdom of her sex, the experience of other women for ages and ages!'

"So there you are, Mary! I am studying another unwritten book, the Maxims of Aunt Varina!

"She has found the remedy for my troubles, the cure for my disease of thought--I am to sew! I tell her that I have more clothes than I can wear in a dozen seasons, and she answers, in an awesome voice, 'There is the little stranger!' When I point out that the little stranger will be expected to have a 'layette' costing many thousands of dollars, she replies, 'They will surely permit him to wear some of the things his mother's hands have made.' So, behold me, seated on the gallery, learning fancy stitches--and with Kautsky on the Social Revolution hidden away in the bottom of my sewing-bag!"

3. The weeks passed. The legislature at Albany adjourned, without regard to our wishes; and so, like the patient spider whose web is destroyed, we set to work upon a new one. So much money must be raised, so many articles must be written, so many speeches delivered, so many people seized upon and harried and wrought to a state of mind where they were dangerous to the future career of legislators. Such is the process of social reform under the private property régime; a process which the pure and simple reformers imagine we shall tolerate for ever--God save us!

Sylvia asked me for the news, and I told it to her--how we had failed, and what we had to do next. So pretty soon there came by registered mail a little box, in which I found a diamond ring. "I cannot ask him for money just now," she explained, "but here is something that has been mine from girlhood. It cost about four hundred dollars--this for your guidance in selling it. Not a day passes that I do not see many times that much wasted; so take it for the cause." Queen Isabella and her jewels!

In this letter she told me of a talk she had had with her husband on the "woman-problem." She had thought at first that it was going to prove a helpful talk--he had been in a fairer mood than she was usually able to induce. "He evaded some of my questions," she explained, "but I don't think it was deliberate; it is simply the evasive attitude of mind which the whole world takes. He says he does not think that women are inferior to men, only that they are different; the mistake is for them to try to become *like* men. It is the old proposition of 'charm,' you see. I put that to him, and he admitted that he did like to be 'charmed.'

"I said, 'You wouldn't, if you knew as much about the process as I do.'

"'Why not?' he asked.

"'Because, it's not an honest process. It's not a straight way for one sex to deal with the other.'

"He asked what I meant by that; but then, remembering the cautions of my great-aunt, I laughed. 'If you are going to compel me to use the process, you can hardly expect me to tell you the secret of it.'

"'Then there's no use trying to talk,' he said.

"'Ah, but there is!' I exclaimed. 'You admit that I have 'charm'--dozens of other men admitted it. And so it ought to count for something if I declare that I know it's not an honest thing--that it depends upon trickery, and appeals to the worst qualities in a man. For instance, his vanity. "Flatter him," Lady Dee used to say. "He'll swallow it." And he will--I never knew a man to refuse a compliment in my life. His love of domination. "If you want anything, make him think that *he* wants it!" His egotism. She had a bitter saying--I can hear the very tones of her voice: "When in doubt, talk about HIM." That is what is called "charm"!'

"'I don't seem to feel it,' he said.

"' No, because now you are behind the scenes. But when you were in front, you felt it, you can't deny. And you would feel it again, any time I chose to use it. But I want to know if there is not some honest way a woman can interest a man. The question really comes to this--Can a man love a woman for what she really is?'

"'I should say,' he said, 'that it depends upon the woman.'

"I admitted this was a plausible answer. 'But you loved me, when I made myself a mystery to you. But now that I am honest with you, you have made it clear that you don't like it, that you won't have it. And that is the problem that women have to face. It is a fact that the women of our family have always ruled the men; but they've done it by indirection--nobody ever thought seriously of "women's rights" in Castleman County. But you see, women *have* rights; and somehow or other they will fool the men, or else the men must give up the idea that they are the superior sex, and have the right, or the ability, to rule women.'

"Then I saw how little he had followed me. 'There has to be a head to the family,' he said.

"I answered, 'There have been cases in history of a king and queen ruling together, and getting along very well. Why not the same thing in a family?'

"'That's all right, so far as the things of the family are concerned. But such affairs as business and politics are in the sphere of men; and women cannot meddle in them without losing their best qualities as women.'

"And so there we were. I won't repeat his arguments, for doubtless you have read enough anti-suffrage literature. The thing I noticed was that if I was very tactful and patient, I could apparently carry him along with me; but when the matter came up again, I would discover that he was back where he had been before. A woman must accept the guidance of a man; she must take the man's word for the things that he understands. 'But suppose the man is *wrong?*' I said; and there we stopped--there we shall stop always, I begin to fear. I agree with him that woman should obey man--so long as man is right!"

4. Her letters did not all deal with this problem. In spite of the sewing, she found time to read a number of books, and we argued about these. Then, too, she had been probing her young doctor, and had made interesting discoveries about him. For one thing, he was full of awe and admiration for her; and her awakening mind found material for speculation in this.

"Here is this young man; he thinks he is a scientist, he rather prides himself upon being cold-blooded; yet a cunning woman could twist him round her finger. He had an unhappy love-affair when he was young, so he confided to me; and now, in his need and loneliness, a beautiful woman is transformed into something supernatural in his imagination--she is like a shimmering soap-bubble, that he blows with his own breath. I know that I could never get him to see the real truth about me; I might tell him that I have let myself be tied up in a golden net--but he would only marvel at my spirituality. Oh, the women I have seen trading upon the credulity of men! And when I think how I did this myself! If men were wise, they would give us the vote, and a share in the world's work--anything that would bring us out into the light of day, and break the spell of mystery that hangs round us!

"By the way," she wrote in another letter, "there will be trouble if you come down here. I was telling Dr. Perrin about you, and your ideas about fasting, and mental healing, and the rest of your fads. He got very much excited. It seems that he takes his diploma seriously, and he's not willing to be taught by amateur experiments. He wanted me to take some pills, and I refused, and I think now he blames you for it. He has found a bond of sympathy with my husband, who proves his respect for authority by taking whatever he is told to take. Dr. Perrin got his medical training here in the South, and I imagine he's ten or twenty years behind the rest of the medical world. Douglas picked him out because he'd met him socially. It makes no difference to me--because I don't mean to have any doctoring done to me!"

Then, on top of these things, would come a cry from her soul. "Mary, what will you do if some day you get a letter from me confessing that I am not happy? I dare not say a word to my own people. I am supposed to be at the apex of human triumph, and I have to play that role to keep from hurting them. I know that if my dear old father got an inkling of the truth, it would kill him. My one real solid consolation is that I have helped him, that I have lifted a money-burden from his life; I have done that, I tell myself, over and over; but then I wonder, have I done anything but put the reckoning off? I have given all his other children a new excuse for extravagance, an impulse towards worldliness which they did not need.

"There is my sister Celeste, for example. I don't think I have told you about her. She made her début *last fall, and was coming up to New York to stay with me this winter. She had it all arranged in her mind to make a rich marriage; I was to give her the* entrée *--and now I have been selfish, and thought of my own desires, and gone away. Can I say to her, Be warned by me, I have made a great match, and it has not brought me happiness? She would not understand, she would say I was foolish. She would say, 'If I had your luck,* I would be happy.' And the worst of it is, it would be true.

"You see the position I am in with the rest of the children. I cannot say, 'You are spending too much of papa's money, it is wrong for you to sign cheques and trust to his carelessness.' I have had my share of the money, I have lined my own nest. All I can do is to buy dresses and hats for Celeste; and know that she will use these to fill her girl-friends with envy, and make scores of other families live beyond their means."

5. Sylvia's pregnancy was moving to its appointed end. She wrote me beautifully about it, much more frankly and simply than she could have brought herself to talk. She recalled to me my own raptures, and also, my own heartbreak. "Mary! Mary! I felt the child to-day! Such a sensation, I could not have credited it if anyone had told me. I almost fainted. There is something in me that wants to turn back, that is afraid to go on with such experiences. I do not wish to be seized in spite of myself, and made to feel things beyond my control. I wander off down the beach, and hide myself, and cry and cry. I think I could almost pray again."

And then again, "I am in ecstasy, because I am to bear a child, a child of my own! Oh, wonderful, wonderful! But suddenly my ecstasy is shot through with terror, because the father of this child is a man I do not love. There is no use trying to deceive myself--nor you! I must have one human soul with whom I can talk about it as it really is. I do not love him, I never did love him, I never shall love him!

"Oh, how could they have all been so mistaken? Here is Aunt Varina--one of those who helped to persuade me into this marriage. She told me that love would come; it seemed to be her idea--my mother had it too--that you had only to submit yourself to a man, to follow and obey him, and love would take possession of your heart. I tried credulously, and it did not happen as they promised. And now, I am to bear him a child; and that will bind us together for ever!

"Oh, the despair of it--I do not love the father of my child! I say, The child will be partly his, perhaps more his than mine. It will be like him--it will have this quality and that, the very qualities, perhaps, that are a source of distress to me in the father. So I shall have these things before me day and night, all the rest of my life; I shall have to see them growing and hardening; it will be a perpetual crucifixion of my mother-love. I seek to comfort myself by saying, The child can be trained differently, so that he will not have these qualities. But then I think, No, you cannot train him as you wish. Your husband will have rights to the child, rights superior to your own. Then I foresee the most dreadful strife between us.

"A shrewd girl-friend once told me that I ought to be better or worse; I ought not to see people's faults as I do, or else I ought to love people less. And I can see that I ought to have been too good to make this marriage, or else not too good to make the best of it. I know that I might be happy as Mrs. Douglas van Tuiver, if I could think of the worldly advantages, and the fact that my child will inherit them. But instead, I see them as a trap, in which not only ourselves but the child is caught, and from which I cannot save us. Oh, what a mistake a woman makes when she marries a man with the idea that she is going to change him! He will not change, he will not have the need of change suggested to him. He wants *peace* in his home--which means that he wants to be what he is.

"Sometimes I can study the situation quite coolly, and as if it didn't concern me at all. He has required me to subject my mind to his. But he will not be content with a general capitulation; he must have a surrender from each individual soldier, from every rebel hidden in the hills. He tracks them out (my poor, straggling, feeble ideas) and either they take the oath of allegiance, or they are buried where they lie. The process is like the spoiling of a child, I find; the more you give him, the more he wants. And if any little thing is refused, then you see him set out upon a regular campaign to break you down and get it."

A month or more later she wrote: "Poor Douglas is getting restless. He has caught every kind of fish there is to catch, and hunted every kind of animal and bird, in and out of season. Harley has gone home, and so have our other guests; it would be embarrassing to me to have company now. So Douglas has no one but the doctor and myself and my poor aunt. He has spoken several times of our going away; but I do not want to go, and I think I ought to consider my own health at this critical time. It is hot here, but I simply thrive in it--I never felt in better health. So I asked him to go up to New York, or visit somewhere for a while, and let me stay here until my baby is born. Does that seem so very unreasonable? It does not to me, but poor Aunt Varina is in agony about it--I am letting my husband drift away from me!

"I speculate about my lot as a woman; I see the bitterness and the sorrow of my sex through the ages. I have become physically misshapen, so that I am no longer attractive to him. I am no longer active and free, I can no longer go about with him; on the contrary, I am a burden, and he is a man who never tolerated a burden before. What this means is that I have lost the magic hold of sex.

"As a woman it was my business to exert all my energies to maintain it. And I know how I could restore it now; there is young Dr. Perrin! *He* does not find me a burden, *he* would tolerate any deficiencies! And I can see my husband on the alert in an instant, if I become too much absorbed in discussing your health-theories with my handsome young guardian!

"This is one of the recognized methods of keeping your husband; I learned from Lady Dee all there is to know about it. But I would find the method impossible now, even if my happiness were dependent upon retaining my husband's love. I should think of the rights of my friend, the little doctor. That is one point to note for the 'new' woman, is it not? You may mention it in your next suffrage-speech!

"There are other methods, of course. I have a mind, and I might turn its powers to entertaining him, instead of trying to solve the problems of the universe. But to do this, I should have to believe that it was the one thing in the world for me to do; and I have permitted a doubt of that to gain entrance to my brain! My poor aunt's exhortations inspire me to efforts to regain the faith of my mothers, but I simply cannot--I cannot! She sits by me with the terror of all the women of all the ages in her eyes. I am losing a man!

"I don't know if you have ever set out to hold a man--deliberately, I mean. Probably you haven't. That bitter maxim of Lady Dee's is the literal truth of it--'When in doubt, talk about HIM!' If you will tactfully and shrewdly keep a man talking about himself, his tastes, his ideas, his work and the importance of it, there is never the least possibility of your boring him. You must not just tamely agree with him, of course; if you hint a difference now and then, and make him convince you, he will find that stimulating; or if you can manage not to be quite convinced, but sweetly open to conviction, he will surely call again. 'Keep him busy every minute,' Lady Dee used to say. 'Run away with him now and then--like a spirited horse!' And she would add, 'But don't let him drop the reins!'

"You can have no idea how many women there are in the world deliberately playing such parts. Some of them admit it; others just do the thing that is easiest, and would die of horror if they were told what it is. It is the whole of the life of a successful society woman, young or old. Pleasing a man! Waiting upon his moods, piquing him, flattering him, feeding his vanity--'charming' him! That is what Aunt Varina wants me to do now; if I am not too crude in my description of the process, she has no hesitation in admitting the truth. It is what she tried to do, it is what almost every woman has done who has held a family together and made a home. I was reading ***Jane Eyre*** the other day. ***There*** is your woman's ideal of an imperious and impetuous lover! Listen to him, when his mood is on him!--

"I am disposed to be gregarious and communicative to-night; and that is why I sent for you; the fire and the chandelier were not sufficient company for me; nor would Pilot have been, for none of these can talk. To-night I am resolved to be at ease; to dismiss what importunes, and recall what pleases. It would please me now to draw you out--to learn more of you--therefore speak!"

6. It was now May, and Sylvia's time was little more than a month off. She had been urging me to come and visit her, but I had refused, knowing that my presence must necessarily be disturbing to both her husband and her aunt. But now she wrote that her husband was going back to New York. "He was staying out of a sense of duty to me," she said. "But his discontent was so apparent that I had to point out to him that he was doing harm to me as well as to himself.

"I doubt if you will want to come here now. The last of the winter visitors have left. It is really hot, so hot that you cannot get cool by going into the water. Yet I am revelling in it; I wear almost nothing, and that white; and even the suspicious Dr. Perrin cannot but admit that I am thriving; his references to pills are purely formal.

"Lately I have not permitted myself to think much about the situation between my husband and myself. I cannot blame him, and I cannot blame myself, and I am trying to keep my peace of mind till my baby is born. I have found myself following half-instinctively the procedure you told me about; I talk to my own subconscious mind, and to the baby--I command them to be well. I whisper to them things that are not so very far from praying; but I don't think my poor dear mamma would recognize it in its new scientific dress!

"But sometimes I can't help thinking of the child and its future, and then all of a sudden my heart is ready to break with pity for the child's father! I have the consciousness that I do not love him, and that he has always known it--and that makes me remorseful. But I told him the truth before we married--he promised to be patient with me till I had learned to love him! Now I want to burst into tears and cry aloud, 'Oh, why did you do it? Why did I let myself be persuaded into this marriage?'

"I tried to have a talk with him last night, after he had decided to go away. I was full of pity, and a desire to help. I said I wanted him to know that no matter how much we might disagree about some things, I meant to learn to live happily with him. We must find some sort of compromise, for the sake of the child, if not for ourselves; we must not let the child suffer. He answered coldly that there would be no need for the child to suffer, the child would have the best the world could afford. I suggested that there might arise some question as to just what the best was; but to that he said nothing. He went on to rebuke my discontent; had he not given me everything a woman could want? he asked. He was too polite to mention money; but he said that I had leisure and entire freedom from care. I was persisting in assuming cares, while he was doing all in his power to prevent it.

"And that was as far as we got. I gave up the discussion, for we should only have gone the old round over again.

"Douglas has taken up a saying that my cousin brought with him: 'What you don't know won't hurt you!' I think that before he left, Harley had begun to suspect that all was not well between my husband and myself, and he felt it necessary to give me a little friendly counsel. He was tactful, and politely vague, but I understood him--my worldly-wise young cousin. I think that saying of his sums up the philosophy that he would teach to all women--'What you don't know won't hurt you!'"

7. A week or so later Sylvia wrote me that her husband was in New York. And I waited another week, for good measure, and then one morning dropped in for a call upon Claire Lepage.

Why did I do it? you ask. I had no definite purpose--only a general opposition to the philosophy of Cousin Harley.

I was ushered into Claire's boudoir, which was still littered with last evening's apparel. She sat in a dressing-gown with resplendent red roses on it, and brushed the hair out of her eyes, and apologized for not being ready for callers.

"I've just had a talking to from Larry," she explained.

"Larry?" said I, inquiringly; for Claire had always informed me elaborately that van Tuiver had been her one departure from propriety, and always would be.

Apparently she had now reached a stage in her career where pretences were too much trouble. "I've come to the conclusion that I don't know how to manage men," she said. "I never can get along with one for any time."

I remarked that I had had the same experience; though of course I had only tried it once. "Tell me," I said, "who's Larry?"

"There's his picture." She reached into a drawer of her dresser.

I saw a handsome blonde gentleman, who looked old enough to know better. "He doesn't seem especially forbidding," I said.

"That's just the trouble--you can never tell about men!"

I noted a date on the picture. "He seems to be an old friend. You never told me about him."

"He doesn't like being told about. He has a troublesome wife."

I winced inwardly, but all I said was, "I see."

"He's a stock-broker; and he got 'squeezed,' so he says, and it's made him cross--and careful with his money, too. That's trying, in a stock-broker, you must admit." She laughed. "And still he's just as particular--wants to have his own way in every-thing, wants to say whom I shall know and where I shall go. I said, 'I have all the inconveniences of matrimony, and none of the advantages.'"

I made some remark upon the subject of the emancipation of woman; and Claire, who was now leaning back in her chair, combing out her long black tresses, smiled at me out of half-closed eyelids. "Guess whom he's objecting to!" she said. And when I pronounced it impossible, she looked portentous. "There are bigger fish in the sea than Larry Edgewater!"

"And you've hooked one?" I asked, innocently.

"Well, I don't mean to give up all my friends."

I went on casually to talk about my plans for the summer; and a few minutes later, after a lull--"By the way," remarked Claire, "Douglas van Tuiver is in town."

"How do you know?"

"I've seen him."

"Indeed! Where?"

"I got Jack Taylor to invite me again. You see, when Douglas fell in love with his peerless southern beauty, Jack predicted he'd get over it even more quickly. Now he's interested in proving he was right."

I waited a moment, and then asked, carelessly, "Is he having any success?"

"I said, 'Douglas, why don't you come to see me?' He was in a playful mood. 'What do you want? A new automobile?' I answered, 'I haven't any automobile, new or old, and you know it. What I want is you. I always loved you--surely I proved that to you.' 'What you proved to me was that you were a sort of wild-cat. I'm afraid of you. And anyway, I'm tired of women. I'll never trust another one.'"

"About the same conclusion as you've come to regarding men," I remarked.

"'Douglas,' I said, 'come and see me, and we'll talk over old times. You may trust me, I swear I'll not tell a living soul.' 'You've been consoling yourself with someone else,' he said. But I knew he was only guessing. He was seeking for something that would worry me, and he said, 'You're drinking too much. People that drink can't be trusted.' 'You know,' I replied, 'I didn't drink too much when I was with you. I'm not drinking as much as you are, right now.' He answered, 'I've been off on a desert island for God knows how many months, and I'm celebrating my escape.' 'Well,' I answered, 'let me help celebrate!'"

"What did he say to that?"

Claire resumed the combing of her silken hair, and smiled a slow smile at me. "'You may trust me, Douglas,' I said. 'I swear I'll not tell a living soul!'"

"Of course," I remarked, appreciatively, "that means he said he'd come!"

"*I* haven't told you!" was the reply.

8. I knew that I had only to wait for Claire to tell me the rest of the story. But her mind went off on another tack. "Sylvia's going to have a baby," she remarked, suddenly.

"That ought to please her husband," I said.

"You can see him beginning to swell with paternal pride!--so Jack said. He sent for a bottle of some famous kind of champagne that he has, to celebrate the new 'millionaire baby.' (They used to call Douglas that, once upon a time.) Before they got through, they had made it triplets. Jack says Douglas is the one man in New York who can afford them."

"Your friend Jack seems to be what they call a wag," I commented.

"It isn't everybody that Douglas will let carry on with him like that. He takes himself seriously, as a rule. And he expects to take the new baby seriously."

"It generally binds a man tighter to his wife, don't you think?"

I watched her closely, and saw her smile at my naiveté. "No," she said, "I don't. It leaves them restless. It's a bore all round."

I did not dispute her authority; she ought to know her husbands, I thought.

She was facing the mirror, putting up her hair; and in the midst of the operation she laughed. "All that evening, while we were having a jolly time at Jack Taylor's, Larry was here waiting."

"Then no wonder you had a row!" I said.

"He hadn't told me he was coming. And was I to sit here all night alone? It's always the same--I never knew a man who really in his heart was willing for you to have any friends, or any sort of good time without him."

"Perhaps," I replied, "he's afraid you mightn't be true to him." I meant this for a jest, of the sort that Claire and her friends would appreciate. Little did I foresee where it was to lead us!

I remember how once on the farm my husband had a lot of dynamite, blasting out stumps; and my emotions when I discovered the children innocently playing with a stick of it. Something like these children I seem now to myself, looking back on this visit to Claire, and our talk.

"You know," she observed, without smiling, "Larry's got a bee in his hat. I've seen men who were jealous, and kept watch over women, but never one that was obsessed like him."

"What's it about?"

"He's been reading a book about diseases, and he tells me tales about what may happen to me, and what may happen to him. When you've listened a while, you can see microbes crawling all over the walls of the room."

"Well----" I began.

"I was sick of his lecturing, so I said, 'Larry, you'll have to do like me--have everything there is, and get over it, and then you won't need to worry.'"

I sat still, staring at her; I think I must have stopped breathing. At the end of an eternity, I said, "You've not really had any of these diseases, Claire?"

"Who hasn't?" she countered.

Again there was a pause. "You know," I observed, "some of them are dangerous----"

"Oh, of course," she answered, lightly. "There's one that makes your nose fall in and your hair fall out--but you haven't seen anything like that happening to me!"

"But there's another," I hinted--"one that's much more common." And when she did not take the hint, I continued, "Also it's more serious than people generally realize."

She shrugged her shoulders. "What of it? Men bring you these things, and it's part of the game. So what's the use of bothering?"

9. There was a long silence; I had to have time to decide what course to take. There was so much that I wanted to get from her, and so much that I wanted to hide from her!

"I don't want to bore you, Claire," I began, finally, "but really this is a matter of importance to you. You see, I've been reading up on the subject as well as Larry. The doctors have been making new discoveries. They used to think this was just a local infection, like a cold, but now they find it's a blood disease, and has the gravest consequences. For one thing, it causes most of the surgical operations that have to be performed on women."

"Maybe so," she said, still indifferent. "I've had two operations. But it's ancient history now."

"You mayn't have reached the end yet," I persisted. "People suppose they are cured of gonorrhea, when really it's only suppressed, and is liable to break out again at any time."

"Yes, I knew. That's some of the information Larry had been making love to me with."

"It may get into the joints and cause rheumatism; it may cause neuralgia; it's been known to affect the heart. Also it causes two-thirds of all the blindness in infants----"

And suddenly Claire laughed. "That's Sylvia Castleman's lookout it seems to me!"

"Oh! OH!" I whispered, losing my self-control.

"What's the matter?" she asked, and I noticed that her voice had become sharp.

"Do you really mean what you've just implied?"

"That Mrs. Douglas van Tuiver may have to pay something for what she has done to me? Well, what of it?" And suddenly Claire flew into a passion, as she always did when our talk came to her rival. "Why shouldn't she take chances the same as the rest of us? Why should I have it and she get off?"

I fought for my composure. After a pause, I said: "It's not a thing we want anybody to have, Claire. We don't want anybody to take such a chance. The girl ought to have been told."

"Told? Do you imagine she would have given up her great catch?"

"She might have, how can you be sure? Anyhow, she should have had the chance."

There was a long silence. I was so shaken that it was hard for me to find words. "As a matter of fact," said Claire, grimly, "I thought of warning her myself. There'd have been some excitement at least! You remember--when they came out of church. You helped to stop me! "

"It would have been too late then," I heard myself saying.

"Well," she exclaimed, with fresh excitement, "it's Miss Sylvia's turn now! We'll see if she's such a grand lady that she can't get my diseases!"

I could no longer contain myself. "Claire," I cried, "you are talking like a devil!"

She picked up a powder-puff, and began to use it diligently. "I know," she said--and I saw her burning eyes in the glass--"you can't fool me. You've tried to be kind, but you despise me in your heart. You think I'm as bad as any woman of the street. Very well then, I speak for my class, and I tell you, this is where we prove our humanity. They throw us out, but you see we get back in!"

"My dear woman," I said, "you don't understand. You'd not feel as you do, If you knew that the person to pay the penalty might be an innocent little child."

" *Their* child! Yes, it's too bad if there has to be anything the matter with the little prince! But I might as well tell you the truth--I've had that in mind all along. I didn't know just what would happen, or how--I don't believe anybody does, the doctors who pretend to are just faking you. But I knew Douglas was rotten, and maybe his children would be rotten, and they'd all of them suffer. That was one of the things that kept me from interfering and smashing him up."

I was speechless now, and Claire, watching me, laughed. "You look as if you'd had no idea of it. Don't you know that I told you at the time?"

"You told me at the time!"

"I suppose, you didn't understand. I'm apt to talk French when I'm excited. We have a saying: 'The wedding present which the mistress leaves in the basket of the bride.' That was pretty near telling, wasn't it?"

"Yes," I said, in a low voice.

And the other, after watching me for a moment more, went on: "You think I'm revengeful, don't you? Well, I used to reproach myself with this, and I tried to fight it down; but the time comes when you want people to pay for what they take from you. Let me tell you something that I never told to anyone, that I never expected to tell. You see me drinking and going to the devil; you hear me talking the care-free talk of my world, but in the beginning I was really in love with Douglas van Tuiver, and I wanted his child. I wanted it so that it was an ache to me. And yet, what chance did I have? I'd have been the joke of his set for ever if I'd breathed it; I'd have been laughed out of the town. I even tried at one time to trap him--to get his child in spite of him, but I found that the surgeons had cut me up, and I could never have a child. So I have to make the best of it--I have to agree with my friends that it's a good thing, it saves me trouble! But *she* comes along, and she has what I wanted, and all the world thinks it wonderful and sublime. She's a beautiful young mother! What's she ever done in her life that she has everything, and I go without? You may spend your time shedding tears over her and what may happen to her but for my part, I say this--let her take her chances! Let her take her chances with the other women in the world--the women she's too good and too pure to know any-thing about!"

10. I came out of Claire's house, sick with horror. Not since the time when I had read my poor nephew's letter had I been so shaken. Why had I not thought long ago of questioning Claire about these matters. How could I have left Sylvia all this time exposed to peril?

The greatest danger was to her child at the time of birth. I figured up, accord-ing to the last letter I had received; there was about ten days yet, and so I felt some relief. I thought first of sending a telegram, but reflected that it would be difficult, not merely to tell her what to do in a telegram, but to explain to her afterwards why I had chosen this extraordinary method. I recollected that in her last letter she had mentioned the name of the surgeon who was coming from New York to attend her during her confinement. Obviously the thing for me to do was to see this surgeon.

"Well, madame?" he said, when I was seated in his inner office.

He was a tall, elderly man, immaculately groomed, and formal and precise in his manner. "Dr. Overton," I began, "my friend, Mrs. Douglas van Tuiver writes me that you are going to Florida shortly."

"That is correct," he said.

"I have come to see you about a delicate matter. I presume I need hardly say that I am relying upon the seal of professional secrecy."

I saw his gaze become suddenly fixed. "Certainly, madame," he said.

"I am taking this course because Mrs. van Tuiver is a very dear friend of mine, and I am concerned about her welfare. It has recently come to my knowledge that she has become exposed to infection by a venereal disease."

He would hardly have started more if I had struck him. "HEY?" he cried, forgetting his manners.

"It would not help you any," I said, "if I were to go into details about this unfortunate matter. Suffice it to say that my information is positive and precise--that it could hardly be more so."

There was a long silence. He sat with eyes rivetted upon me. "What is this disease?" he demanded, at last.

I named it, and then again there was a pause. "How long has this--this possibility of infection existed?"

"Ever since her marriage, nearly eighteen months ago."

That told him a good part of the story. I felt his look boring me through. Was I a mad woman? Or some new kind of blackmailer? Or, was I, possibly, a Claire? I was grateful for my forty-cent bonnet and my forty-seven years.

"Naturally," he said at length, "this information startles me."

"When you have thought it over," I responded, "you will realise that no possible motive could bring me here but concern for the welfare of my friend."

He took a few moments to consider. "That may be true, madame, but let me add that when you say you KNOW this----"

He stopped. "I MEAN that I know it," I said, and stopped in turn.

"Has Mrs. van Tuiver herself any idea of this situation?"

"None whatever. On the contrary, she was assured before her marriage that no such possibility existed."

Again I felt him looking through me, but I left him to make what he could of my information. "Doctor," I continued, "I presume there is no need to point out to a man in your position the seriousness of this matter, both to the mother and to the child."

"Certainly there is not."

"I assume that you are familiar with the precautions that have to be taken with regard to the eyes of the child?"

"Certainly, madame." This with just a touch of HAUTEUR, and then, suddenly: "Are you by any chance a nurse?"

"No," I replied, "but many years ago I was forced by tragedy in my own family to realise the seriousness of the venereal peril. So when I learned this fact about my friend, my first thought was that you should be informed of it. I trust that you will appreciate my position."

"Certainly, madame, certainly," he made haste to say. "You are quite right, and you may rest assured that everything will be done that our best knowledge directs. I only regret that the information did not come to me sooner."

"It only came to me about an hour ago," I said, as I rose to leave. "The blame, therefore, must rest upon another person."

I needed to say no more. He bowed me politely out, and I walked down the street, and realised that I was restless and wretched. I wandered at random for a while. trying to think what else I could do, for my own peace of mind, if not for Sylvia's welfare. I found myself inventing one worry after another. Dr. Overton had not said just when he was going, and suppose she were to need someone at once? Or suppose something were to happen to him--if he were to be killed upon the long train-journey? I was like a mother who has had a terrible dream about her child--she must rush and fling her arms about the child. I realised that I wanted to see Sylvia!

She had begged me to come; and I was worn out and had been urged by the office to take a rest. Suddenly I bolted into a store, and telephoned the railroad station about trains to Southern Florida. I hailed a taxi-cab, rode to my home post-haste, and flung a few of my belongings into a bag and the waiting cab sped with me to the ferry. In little more than two hours after Claire had told me the dreadful tidings, I was speeding on my way to Sylvia.

11. From a train-window I had once beheld a cross-section of America from West to East; now I beheld another from North to South. In the afternoon were the farms and country-homes of New Jersey; and then in the morning endless wastes of wilderness, and straggling fields of young corn and tobacco; turpentine forests,

with half-stripped negroes working, and a procession of "depots," with lanky men chewing tobacco, and negroes basking in the blazing sun. Then another night, and there was the pageant of Florida: palmettos, and other trees of which one had seen pictures in the geography books; stretches of vine-tangled swamps, where one looked for alligators; orange-groves in blossom, and gardens full of flowers beyond imagining. Every hour, of course, it got hotter; I was not, like Sylvia, used to it, and whenever the train stopped I sat by the open window, mopping the perspiration from my face.

We were due at Miami in the afternoon; but there was a freight-train off the track ahead of us, and so for three hours I sat chafing with impatience, worrying the conductor with futile questions. I had to make connections at Miami with a train which ran to the last point on the mainland, where the construction-work over the keys was going forward. And if I missed that last train, I would have to wait in Miami till morning. I had better wait there, anyhow, the conductor argued; but I insisted that my friends, to whom I had telegraphed two days before, would meet me with a launch and take me to their place that night.

We got in half an hour late for the other train; but this was the South, I discovered, and they had waited for us. I shifted my bag and myself across the platform, and we moved on. But then another problem arose; we were running into a storm. It came with great suddenness; one minute all was still, with a golden sunset, and the next it was so dark that I could barely see the palm-trees, bent over, swaying madly--like people with arms stretched out, crying in distress. I could hear the roaring of the wind above that of the train, and I asked the conductor in consternation if this could be a hurricane. It was not the season for hurricanes, he replied; but it was "some storm, all right," and I would not find any boat to take me to the keys until it was over.

It was absurd of me to be nervous, I kept telling myself; but there was something in me that cried out to be there, to be there! I got out of the train, facing what I refrain from calling a hurricane out of deference to local authority. It was all I could do to keep from being blown across the station-platform, and I was drenched with the spray and bewildered by the roaring of the waves that beat against the pier beyond. Inside the station, I questioned the agent. The launch of the van Tuivers had not been in that day; if it had been on the way, it must have sought shelter somewhere. My telegram to Mrs. van Tuiver had been received two days before, and delivered by a boatman whom they employed for that purpose. Presumably, therefore, I would be met. I asked how long this gale was apt to last; the answer was from one to three days.

Then I asked about shelter for the night. This was a "jumping-off" place, said the agent, with barracks and shanties for a construction-gang; there were saloons, and what was called a hotel, but it wouldn't do for a lady. I pleaded that I was not fastidious--being anxious to nullify the effect which the name van Tuiver had produced. But the agent would have it that the place was unfit for even a Western farmer's wife; and as I was not anxious to take the chance of being blown overboard in the darkness, I spent the night on one of the benches in the station. I lay, listening to the incredible clamour of wind and waves, feeling the building quiver, and wondering if each gust might not blow it away.

I was out at dawn, the force of the wind having abated somewhat by that time. I saw before me a waste of angry foam-strewn water, with no sign of any craft upon it. Late in the morning came the big steamer which ran to Key West, in connection with the railroad; it made a difficult landing, and I interviewed the captain, with the idea of bribing him to take me to my destination. But he had his schedule, which neither storms nor the name of van Tuiver could alter. Besides, he pointed out, he could not land me at their place, as his vessel drew too much water to get anywhere near; and if he landed me elsewhere, I should be no better off, "If your friends are expecting you, they'll come here," he said, "and their launch can travel when nothing else can."

To pass the time I went to inspect the viaduct of the railway-to-be. The first stretch was completed, a long series of concrete arches, running out, apparently, into the open sea. It was one of the engineering wonders of the world, but I fear I did not appreciate it. Towards mid-afternoon I made out a speck of a boat over the water, and my friend, the station-agent, remarked, "There's your launch."

I expressed my amazement that they should have ventured out in such weather. I had had in mind the kind of tiny open craft that one hears making day and night hideous at summer-resorts; but when the "Merman" drew near, I realized afresh what it was to be the guest of a multi-millionaire. She was about fifty feet long, a vision of polished brass and shining, new-varnished cedar. She rammed her shoulder into the waves and flung them contemptuously to one side; her cabin was tight, dry as the saloon of a liner.

Three men emerged on deck to assist in the difficult process of making a landing. One of them sprang to the dock, and confronting me, inquired if I was Mrs. Abbott. He explained that they had set out to meet me the previous afternoon, but had had to take refuge behind one of the keys.

"How is Mrs. van Tuiver?" I asked, quickly.

"She is well."

"I don't suppose--the baby----" I hinted.

"No, ma'am, not yet," said the man; and after that I felt interested in what he had to say about the storm and its effects. We could return at once, it seemed, if I did not mind being pitched about.

"How long does it take?" I asked.

"Three hours, in weather like this. It's about fifty miles."

"But then it will be dark," I objected.

"That won't matter, ma'am--we have plenty of light of our own. We shan't have trouble, unless the wind rises, and there's a chain of keys all the way, where we can get shelter if it does. The worst you have to fear is spending a night on board."

I reflected that I could not well be more uncomfortable than I had been the previous night, so I voted for a start. There was mail and some supplies to be put on board; then I made a spring for the deck, as it surged up towards me on a rising wave, and in a moment more the cabin-door had shut behind me, and I was safe and snug, in the midst of leather and mahogany and electric-lighted magnificence. Through the heavy double windows I saw the dock swing round behind us, and saw the torrents of green spray sweep over us and past. I grasped at the seat to keep myself from being thrown forward, and then grasped behind, to keep from going in that direction. I had a series of sensations as of an elevator stopping suddenly-- and then I draw the curtains of the "Merman's" cabin, and invite the reader to pass by. This is Sylvia's story, and not mine, and it is of no interest what happened to me during that trip. I will only remind the reader that I had lived my life in the far West, and there were some things I could not have foreseen.

12. "We are there, ma'am," I heard one of the boatmen say, and I realised vaguely that the pitching had ceased. He helped me to sit up, and I saw the search-

light of the craft sweeping the shore of an island. "It passes off 'most as quick as it comes, ma'am," added my supporter, and for this I murmured feeble thanks.

We came to a little bay, where the power was shut off, and we glided towards the shore. There was a boat-house, a sort of miniature dry-dock, with a gate which closed behind us. I had visions of Sylvia waiting to meet me, but apparently our arrival had not been noted, and for this I was grateful. There were seats in the boat-house, and I sank into one, and asked the man to wait a few minutes while I recovered myself. When I got up and went to the house, what I found made me quickly forget that I had such a thing as a body.

There was a bright moon, I remember, and I could see the long, low bungalow, with windows gleaming through the palm-trees. A woman's figure emerged from the house and came down the white shell-path to meet me. My heart leaped. My beloved!

But then I saw it was the English maid, whom I had come to know in New York; I saw, too, that her face was alight with excitement. "Oh, my lady!" she cried. "The baby's come!"

It was like a blow in the face. "***What?***" I gasped.

"Came early this morning. A girl."

"But--I thought it wasn't till next week!"

"I know, but it's here. In that terrible storm, when we thought the house was going to be washed away! Oh, my lady, it's the loveliest baby!"

I had presence of mind enough to try to hide my dismay. The semi-darkness was a fortunate thing for me. "How is the mother?" I asked.

"Splendid. She's asleep now."

"And the child?"

"Oh! Such a dear you never saw!"

"And it's all right?"

"It's just the living image of its mother! You shall see!"

We moved towards the house, slowly, while I got my thoughts together. "Dr. Perrin is here?" I asked.

"Yes. He's gone to his place to sleep."

"And the nurse?"

"She's with the child. Come this way."

We went softly up the steps of the veranda. All the rooms opened upon it, and we entered one of them, and by the dim-shaded light I saw a white-clad woman bending over a crib. "Miss Lyman, this is Mrs. Abbott," said the maid.

The nurse straightened up. "Oh! so you got here! And just at the right time!"

"God grant it may be so!" I thought to myself. "So this is the child!" I said, and bent over the crib. The nurse turned up the light for me.

It is the form in which the miracle of life becomes most apparent to us, and dull indeed must be he who can encounter it without being stirred to the depths. To see, not merely new life come into the world, but life which has been made by ourselves, or by those we love--life that is a mirror and copy of something dear to us! To see this tiny mite of warm and living flesh, and to see that it was Sylvia! To trace each beloved lineament, so much alike, and yet so different--half a portrait and half a caricature, half sublime and half ludicrous! The comical little imitation of her nose, with each dear little curve, with even a remainder of the tiny groove underneath the tip, and the tiny corresponding dimple underneath the chin! The soft silken fuzz which was some day to be Sylvia's golden glory! The delicate, sensitive lips, which were some day to quiver with feeling! I gazed at them and saw them moving, I saw the breast moving--and a wave of emotion swept over me, and the tears half-blinded me as I knelt.

But I could not forget the reason for my coming. It meant little that the child was alive and seemingly well; I was not dealing with a disease which, like syphilis, starves and deforms in the very womb. The little one was asleep, but I moved the light so as to examine its eyelids. Then I turned to the nurse and asked: "Miss Lyman, doesn't it seem to you the eyelids are a trifle inflamed?"

"Why, I hadn't noticed it," she answered.

"Were the eyes washed?" I inquired.

"I washed the baby, of course--"

"I mean the eyes especially. The doctor didn't drop anything into them?"

"I don't think he considered it necessary."

"It's an important precaution," I replied; "there are always possibilities of infection."

"Possibly," said the other. "But you know, we did not expect this. Dr. Overton was to be here in three or four days."

"Dr. Perrin is asleep?" I asked.

"Yes. He was up all last night."

"I think I will have to ask you to waken him," I said.

"Is it as serious as that?" she inquired, anxiously, having sensed some of the emotion I was trying to conceal.

"It might be very serious," I said. "I really ought to have a talk with the doctor."

13. The nurse went out, and I drew up a chair and sat by the crib, watching the infant go back to sleep. I was glad to be alone, to have a chance to get myself together. But suddenly I heard a rustle of skirts in the doorway behind me, and turned and saw a white-clad figure; an elderly gentlewoman, slender and fragile, grey-haired and rather pale, wearing a soft dressing-gown. Aunt Varina!

I rose. "This must be Mrs. Abbott," she said. Oh, these soft, caressing Southern voices, that cling to each syllable as a lover to a hand at parting.

She was a very prim and stately little lady, and I think she did not intend to shake hands; but I felt pretty certain that under her coating of formality, she was eager for a chance to rhapsodize. "Oh, what a lovely child!" I cried; and instantly she melted.

"You have seen our babe!" she exclaimed; and I could not help smiling. A few months ago, "the little stranger," and now "our babe"!

She bent over the cradle, with her dear old sentimental, romantic soul in her eyes. For a minute or two she quite forgot me; then, looking up, she murmured, "It is as wonderful to me as if it were my own!"

"All of us who love Sylvia feel that," I responded.

She rose, and suddenly remembering hospitality, asked me as to my present needs. Then she said, "I must go and see to sending some telegrams."

"Telegrams?" I inquired.

"Yes. Think what this news will mean to dear Douglas! And to Major Castleman!"

"You haven't informed them?"

"We couldn't send any smaller boat on account of the storm. We must telegraph Dr. Overton also, you understand."

"To tell him not to come?" I ventured. "But don't you think, Mrs. Tuis, that he may wish to come anyhow?"

"Why should he wish that?"

"I'm not sure, but--I think he might." How I longed for a little of Sylvia's skill in social lying! "Every newly-born infant ought to be examined by a specialist, you know; there may be a particular régime, a diet for the mother--one cannot say."

"Dr. Perrin didn't consider it necessary."

"I am going to have a talk with Dr. Perrin at once," I said.

I saw a troubled look in her eyes. "You don't mean you think there's anything the matter?"

"No--no," I lied. "But I'm sure you ought to wait before you have the launch go. Please do."

"If you insist," she said. I read bewilderment in her manner, and just a touch of resentment. Was it not presumptuous of me, a stranger, and one--well, possibly not altogether a lady? She groped for words; and the ones that came were: "Dear Douglas must not be kept waiting."

I was too polite to offer the suggestion that "dear Douglas" might be finding ways to amuse himself. The next moment I heard steps approaching on the veranda, and turned to meet the nurse with the doctor.

14. "How do you do, Mrs. Abbott?" said Dr. Perrin. He was in his dressing-gown, and had a newly-awakened look. I started to apologize, but he replied, "It's pleasant to see a new face in our solitude. Two new faces!"

That was behaving well, I thought, for a man who had been routed out of sleep. I tried to meet his mood. "Dr. Perrin, Mrs. van Tuiver tells me that you object to amateur physicians. But perhaps you won't mind regarding me as a midwife. I have three children of my own, and I've had to help bring others into the world."

"All right," he smiled. "We'll consider you qualified. What is the matter?"

"I wanted to ask you about the child's eyes. It is a wise precaution to drop some nitrate of silver into them, to provide against possible infection."

I waited for my answer. "There have been no signs of any sort of infection in this case," he said, at last.

"Perhaps not. But it is not necessary to wait, in such a matter. You have not taken the precaution?"

"No, madam."

"You have some of the drug, of course?"

Again there was a pause. "No, madam, I fear that I have not."

I winced, involuntarily. I could not hide my distress. "Dr. Perrin," I exclaimed, "you came to attend a confinement case, and you omitted to provide something so essential!"

There was nothing left of the little man's affability now. "In the first place," he said, "I must remind you that I did not come to attend a confinement case. I came to look after Mrs. van Tuiver's condition up *to* the time of confinement."

"But you knew there would always be the possibility of an accident!"

"Yes, to be sure."

"And you didn't have any nitrate of silver!"

"Madam," he said, stiffly, "there is no use for this drug except in one contingency."

"I know," I cried, "but it is an important precaution. It is the practice to use it in all maternity hospitals."

"Madam, I have visited hospitals, and I think I know something of what the practice is."

So there we were, at a deadlock. There was silence for a space.

"Would you mind sending for the drug?" I asked, at last.

"I presume," he said, with *hauteur,* "it will do no harm to have it on hand."

I was aware of an elderly lady watching us, with consternation written upon every sentimental feature. "Dr. Perrin," I said, "if Mrs. Tuis will pardon me, I think I ought to speak with you alone." The nurse hastily withdrew; and I saw the elderly lady draw herself up with terrible dignity--and then suddenly quail, and turn and follow the nurse.

I told the little man what I knew. After he had had time to get over his consternation, he said that fortunately there did not seem to be any sign of trouble.

"There does seem so to me," I replied. "It may be only my imagination, but I think the eyelids are inflamed."

I held the baby for him, while he made an examination. He admitted that there seemed to be ground for uneasiness. His professional dignity was now gone, and he was only too glad to be human.

"Dr. Perrin," I said, "there is only one thing we can do--to get some nitrate of silver at the earliest possible moment. Fortunately, the launch is here."

"I will have it start at once," he said. "It will have to go to Key West."

"And how long will that take?"

"It depends upon the sea. In good weather it takes us eight hours to go and re-turn." I could not repress a shudder. The child might be blind in eight hours!

But there was no time to be wasted in foreboding. "About Dr. Overton," I said. "Don't you think he had better come?" But I ventured to add the hint that Mr. van Tuiver would hardly wish expense to be considered in such an emergency; and in the end, I persuaded the doctor not merely to telegraph for the great surgeon, but to ask a hospital in Atlanta to send the nearest eye-specialist by the first train.

We called back Mrs. Tuis, and I apologized abjectly for my presumption, and Dr. Perrin announced that he thought he ought to see Dr. Overton, and another doctor as well. I saw fear leap into Aunt Varina's eyes. "Oh, what is it?" she cried. "What is the matter with our babe?"

I helped the doctor to answer polite nothings to all her questions. "Oh, the poor, dear lady!" I thought to myself. The poor, dear lady! What a tearing away of veils and sentimental bandages was written in her book of fate for that night!

15. I find myself lingering over these preliminaries, dreading the plunge into the rest of my story. We spent our time hovering over the child's crib, and in two or three hours the little eyelids had become so inflamed that there could no longer be any doubt what was happening. We applied alternate hot and cold cloths; we washed the eyes in a solution of boric acid, and later, in our desperation, with blue-stone. But we were dealing with the virulent gonococcus, and we neither expected nor obtained much result from these measures. In a couple of hours more the eyes were beginning to exude pus, and the poor infant was wailing in torment.

"Oh, what can it be? Tell me what is the matter?" cried Mrs. Tuis. She sought to catch the child in her arms, and when I quickly prevented her, she turned upon me in anger. "What do you mean?"

"The child must be quiet," I said.

"But I wish to comfort it!" And when I still insisted, she burst out wildly: "What *right* have you?"

"Mrs. Tuis," I said, gently, "it is possible the infant may have a very serious in-fection. If so, you would be apt to catch it."

She answered with a hysterical cry: "My precious innocent! Do you think that I would be afraid of anything it could have?"

"You may not be afraid, but we are. We should have to take care of you, and one case is more than enough."

Suddenly she clutched me by the arm. "Tell me what this awful thing is! I demand to know!"

"Mrs. Tuis," said the doctor, interfering, "we are not yet sure what the trouble is, we only wish to take precautions. It is really imperative that you should not handle this child or even go near it. There is nothing you can possibly do."

She was willing to take orders from him; he spoke the same dialect as herself, and with the same quaint stateliness. A charming little Southern gentleman--I could realise how Douglas van Tuiver had "picked him out for his social qualities." In the old-fashioned Southern medical college where he had got his training, I suppose they had taught him the old-fashioned idea of gonorrhea. Now he was acquiring our extravagant modern notions in the grim school of experience!

It was necessary to put the nurse on her guard as to the risks we were running. We should have had concave glasses to protect our eyes, and we spent part of our time washing our hands in bichloride solution.

"Mrs. Abbott, what is it?" whispered the woman.

"It has a long name," I replied--" ***opthalmia neonatorum.***"

"And what has caused it?"

"The original cause," I responded, "is a man." I was not sure if that was according to the ethics of the situation, but the words came.

Before long the infected eye-sockets were two red and yellow masses of inflammation, and the infant was screaming like one of the damned. We had to bind up its eyes; I was tempted to ask the doctor to give it an opiate for fear lest it should scream itself into convulsions. Then as poor Mrs. Tuis was pacing the floor, wringing her hands and sobbing hysterically, Dr. Perrin took me to one side and said: "I think she will have to be told."

The poor, poor lady!

"She might as well understand now as later," he continued. "She will have to help keep the situation from the mother."

"Yes," I said, faintly; and then, "Who shall tell her?"

"I think," suggested the doctor, "she might prefer to be told by a woman."

So I shut my lips together and took the distracted lady gently by the arm and led her to the door. We stole like two criminals down the veranda, and along the path to the beach, and near the boathouse we stopped, and I began.

"Mrs. Tuis, you may remember a circumstance which your niece mentioned to me--that just before her marriage she urged you to have certain inquiries made as to Mr. van Tuiver's health, his fitness for marriage?"

Never shall I forget her face at that moment. "Sylvia told you that!"

"The inquiries were made," I went on, "but not carefully enough, it seems. Now you behold the consequence of this negligence."

I saw her blank stare. I added: "The one to pay for it is the child."

"You--you mean--" she stammered, her voice hardly a whisper. "Oh--it is impossible!" Then, with a flare of indignation: "Do you realise what you are implying--that Mr. van Tuiver--"

"There is no question of implying," I said, quietly. "It is the facts we have to face now, and you will have to help us to face them."

She cowered and swayed before me, hiding her face in her hands. I heard her sobbing and murmuring incoherent cries to her god. I took the poor lady's hand, and bore with her as long as I could, until, being at the end of my patience with prudery and purity and chivalry, and all the rest of the highfalutin romanticism of the South, I said: "Mrs Tuis, it is necessary that you should get yourself together. You have a serious duty before you--that you owe both to Sylvia and her child."

"What is it?" she whispered. The word "duty" had motive power for her.

"At all hazards, Sylvia must be kept in ignorance of the calamity for the present. If she were to learn of it it would quite possibly throw her into a fever, and cost her life or the child's. You must not make any sound that she can hear, and you must not go near her until you have completely mastered your emotions."

"Very well," she murmured. She was really a brave little body, but I, not knowing her, and thinking only of the peril, was cruel in hammering things into her consciousness. Finally, I left her, seated upon the steps of the deserted boat-house, rocking back and forth and sobbing softly to herself--one of the most pitiful figures it has ever been my fortune to encounter in my pilgrimage through a world of sentimentality and incompetence.

16. I went back to the house, and because we feared the sounds of the infant's crying might carry, we hung blankets before the doors and windows of the room, and sat in the hot enclosure, shuddering, silent, grey with fear. After an hour or two, Mrs. Tuis rejoined us, stealing in and seating herself at one side of the room, staring from one to another of us with wide eyes of fright.

By the time the first signs of dawn appeared, the infant had cried itself into a state of exhaustion. The faint light that got into the room revealed the three of us, listening to the pitiful whimpering. I was faint with weakness, but I had to make an effort and face the worst ordeal of all. There came a tapping at the door--the maid, to say that Sylvia was awake and had heard of my arrival and wished to see me. I might have put off our meeting for a while, on the plea of exhaustion, but I preferred to have it over with, and braced myself and went slowly to her room.

In the doorway I paused for an instant to gaze at her. She was exquisite, lying there with the flush of sleep still upon her, and the ecstasy of her great achievement in her face. I fled to her, and we caught each other in our arms. "Oh, Mary, Mary! I'm so glad you've come!" And then: "Oh, Mary, isn't it the loveliest baby!"

"Perfectly glorious!" I exclaimed.

"Oh, I'm so happy--so happy as I never dreamed! I've no words to tell you about it."

"You don't need any words--I've been through it," I said.

"Oh, but she's so *beautiful!* Tell me, honestly, isn't that really so?"

"My dear," I said, "she is like you."

"Mary," she went on, half whispering, "I think it solves all my problems--all that I wrote you about. I don't believe I shall ever be unhappy again. I can't believe that such a thing has really happened--that I've been given such a treasure. And she's my own! I can watch her little body grow and help to make it strong and beautiful! I can help mould her little mind--see it opening up, one chamber of wonder after another! I can teach her all the things I have had to grope so to get!"

"Yes," I said, trying to speak with conviction. I added, hastily: "I'm glad you don't find motherhood disappointing."

"Oh, it's a miracle!" she exclaimed. "A woman who could be dissatisfied with anything afterwards would be an ingrate!" She paused, then added: "Mary, now she's here in flesh, I feel she'll be a bond between Douglas and me. He must see her rights, her claim upon life, as he couldn't see mine."

I assented gravely. So that was the thing she was thinking most about--a bond between her husband and herself! A moment later the nurse appeared in the doorway, and Sylvia set up a cry: "My baby! Where's my baby? I want to see my baby!"

"Sylvia, dear," I said, "there's something about the baby that has to be explained."

Instantly she was alert. "What is the matter?"

I laughed. "Nothing, dear, that amounts to anything. But the little one's eyes are inflamed--that is to say, the lids. It's something that happens to newly-born infants."

"Well, then?" she said.

"Nothing, only the doctor's had to put some salve on them, and they don't look very pretty."

"I don't mind that, if it's all right."

"But we've had to put a bandage over them, and it looks forbidding. Also the child is apt to cry."

"I must see her at once!" she exclaimed.

"Just now she's asleep, so don't make us disturb her."

"But how long will this last?"

"Not very long. Meantime you must be sensible and not mind. It's something I made the doctor do, and you mustn't blame me, or I'll be sorry I came to you."

"You dear thing," she said, and put her hand in mine. And then, suddenly: "Why did you take it into your head to come, all of a sudden?"

"Don't ask me," I smiled. "I have no excuse. I just got homesick and had to see you."

"It's perfectly wonderful that you should be here now," she declared. "But you look badly. Are you tired?"

"Yes, dear," I said. (Such a difficult person to deceive!) "To tell the truth, I'm pretty nearly done up. You see, I was caught in the storm, and I was desperately sea-sick."

"Why, you poor dear! Why didn't you go to sleep?"

"I didn't want to sleep. I was too much excited by everything. I came to see one Sylvia and I found two!"

"Isn't it absurd," she cried, "how she looks like me? Oh, I want to see her again. How long will it be before I can have her?"

"My dear," I said, "you mustn't worry--"

"Oh, don't mind me, I'm just playing. I'm so happy, I want to squeeze her in my arms all the time. Just think, Mary, they won't let me nurse her, yet--a whole day now! Can that be right?"

"Nature will take care of that," I said.

"Yes, but how can you be sure what Nature means? Maybe it's what the child is crying about, and it's the crying that makes its eyes red."

I felt a sudden spasm grip my heart. "No, dear, no," I said, hastily. "You must let Dr. Perrin attend to these things, for I've just had to interfere with his arrangements, and he'll be getting cross pretty soon."

"Oh," she cried with laughter in her eyes, "you've had a scene with him? I knew you would! He's so quaint and old-fashioned!"

"Yes," I said, "and he talks exactly like your aunt."

"Oh! You've met her too! I'm missing all the fun!"

I had a sudden inspiration--one that I was proud of. "My dear girl," I said, "maybe *you* call it fun!" And I looked really agitated.

"Why, what's the matter?" she cried.

"What could you expect?" I asked. "I fear, my dear Sylvia, I've shocked your aunt beyond all hope."

"What have you done?"

"I've talked about things I'd no business to--I've bossed the learned doctor-- and I'm sure Aunt Varina has guessed I'm not a lady."

"Oh, tell me about it!" cried Sylvia, full of delight.

But I could not keep up the game any longer. "Not now, dear," I said. "It's a long story, and I really am exhausted. I must go and get some rest."

I rose, and she caught my hand, whispering: "I shall be happy, Mary! I shall be really happy now!" And then I turned and fled, and when I was out of sight of the doorway, I literally ran. At the other end of the veranda I sank down upon the steps, and wept softly to myself.

17. The launch arrived, bringing the nitrate of silver. A solution was dropped into the baby's eyes, and then we could do nothing but wait. I might have lain down

and really tried to rest; but the maid came again, with the announcement that Sylvia was asking for her aunt. Excuses would have tended to excite her suspicions; so poor Mrs. Tuis had to take her turn at facing the ordeal, and I had to drill and coach her for it. I had a vision of the poor lady going in to her niece, and suddenly collapsing. Then there would begin a cross-examination, and Sylvia would worm out the truth, and we might have a case of puerperal fever on our hands.

This I explained afresh to Mrs. Tuis, having taken her into her own room and closed the door for that purpose. She clutched me with her shaking hands and whispered, "Oh, Mrs. Abbott, you will **never** let Sylvia find out what caused this trouble?"

I drew on my reserve supply of patience, and answered, "What I shall let her find out in the end, I don't know. We shall be guided by circumstances, and this is no time to discuss the matter. The point is now to make sure that you can go in and stay with her, and not let her get an idea there's anything wrong."

"Oh, but you know how Sylvia reads people!" she cried, in sudden dismay.

"I've fixed it for you," I said. "I've provided something you can be agitated about."

"What is that?"

"It's **me.**" Then, seeing her look of bewilderment, "You must tell her that I've affronted you, Mrs. Tuis; I've outraged your sense of propriety. You're indignant with me and you don't see how you can remain in the house with me--"

"Why, Mrs. Abbott!" she exclaimed, in horror.

"You know it's truth to some extent," I said.

The good lady drew herself up. "Mrs. Abbott, don't tell me that I have been so rude--"

"Dear Mrs. Tuis," I laughed, "don't stop to apologize just now. You have not been lacking in courtesy, but I know how I must seem to you. I am a Socialist. I have a raw, Western accent, and my hands are big--I've lived on a farm all my life, and done my own work, and even plowed sometimes. I have no idea of the charms and graces of life that are everything to you. What is more than that, I am forward, and thrust my opinions upon other people--"

She simply could not hear me. She was a-tremble with a new excitement. Worse even than **opthalmia neonatorum** was plain speaking to a guest! "Mrs. Abbott, you humiliate me!"

Then I spoke harshly, seeing that I would actually have to shock her. "I assure you, Mrs. Tuis, that if you don't feel that way about me, it's simply because you don't know the truth. It is not possible that you would consider me a proper person to visit Sylvia. I don't believe in your religion; I don't believe in anything that you would call religion, and I argue about it at the least provocation. I deliver violent harangues on street-corners, and have been arrested during a strike. I believe in woman's suffrage, I even argue in approval of window-smashing. I believe that women ought to earn their own living, and be independent and free from any man's control. I am a divorced woman--I left my husband because I wasn't happy with him, what's more, I believe that any woman has a right to do the same--I'm liable to teach such ideas to Sylvia, and to urge her to follow them."

The poor lady's eyes were wide and large. "So you see," I exclaimed, "you really couldn't approve of me! Tell her all this; she knows it already, but she will be horrified, because I have let you and the doctor find it out!"

Whereupon Mrs. Tuis started to ascend the pedestal of her dignity. "Mrs. Abbott, this may be your idea of a jest----"

"Now come," I cried, "let me help you fix your hair, and put on just a wee bit of powder--not enough to be noticed, you understand----"

I took her to the wash-stand, and poured out some cold water for her, and saw her bathe her eyes and face, and dry them, and braid her thin grey hair. While with a powder puff I was trying deftly to conceal the ravages of the night's crying, the dear lady turned to me, and whispered in a trembling voice, "Mrs. Abbott, you really don't mean that dreadful thing you said just now?"

"Which dreadful thing, Mrs. Tuis?"

"That you would tell Sylvia it could possibly be right for her to leave her husband?"

18. In the course of the day we received word that Dr. Gibson, the specialist for whom we had telegraphed, was on his way. The boat which brought his message took back a letter from Dr. Perrin to Douglas van Tuiver, acquainting him with the calamity which had befallen. We had talked it over and agreed that there was nothing to be gained by telegraphing the information. We did not wish any hint of the child's illness to leak into the newspapers.

I did not envy the great man the hour when he read that letter; although I knew that the doctor had not failed to assure him that the victim of his misdeeds should be kept in ignorance. Already the little man had begun to drop hints to me on this subject. Unfortunate accidents happened, which were not always to be blamed upon the husband, nor was it a thing to contemplate lightly, the breaking up of a family. I gave a non-committal answer, and changed the subject by asking the doctor not to mention my presence in the household. If by any chance van Tuiver were to carry his sorrows to Claire, I did not want my name brought up.

We managed to prevent Sylvia's seeing the child that day and night, and the next morning came the specialist. He held out no hope of saving any remnant of the sight, but the child might be so fortunate as to escape disfigurement--it did not appear that the eyeballs were destroyed, as happens generally in these cases. This bit of consolation I still have: that little Elaine, who sits by me as I write, has left in her pupils a faint trace of the soft red-brown--just enough to remind us of what we have lost, and keep fresh in our minds the memory of these sorrows. If I wish to see what her eyes might have been, I look above my head to the portrait of Sylvia's noble ancestress, a copy made by a "tramp artist" in Castleman County, and left with me by Sylvia.

There was the question of the care of the mother--the efforts to stay the ravages of the germ in the tissues broken and weakened by the strain of child-birth. We had to invent excuses for the presence of the new doctor--and yet others for the presence of Dr. Overton, who came a day later. And then the problem of the nourishing of the child. It would be a calamity to have to put it upon the bottle, but on the other hand, there were many precautions necessary to keep the infection from spreading.

I remember vividly the first time that the infant was fed: all of us gathered round, with matter-of-course professional air, as if these elaborate hygienic ceremonies were the universal custom when newly-born infants first taste their mothers' milk. Standing in the background, I saw Sylvia start with dismay, as she noted how pale and thin the poor little one had become. It was hunger that caused the whimpering, so the nurse declared, busying herself in the meantime to keep the tiny hands from the mother's face. The latter sank back and closed her eyes--nothing, it seemed, could prevail over the ecstasy of that first marvellous sensation, but afterwards she asked that I might stay with her, and as soon as the others were gone, she unmasked the batteries of her suspicion upon me. "Mary! What in the world has happened to my baby?"

So began a new stage in the campaign of lying. "It's nothing, nothing. Just some infection. It happens frequently."

"But what is the cause of it?"

"We can't tell. It may be a dozen things. There are so many possible sources of infection about a birth. It's not a very sanitary thing, you know."

"Mary! Look me in the face!"

"Yes, dear?"

"You're not deceiving me?"

"How do you mean?"

"I mean--it's not really something serious? All these doctors--this mystery-- this vagueness!"

"It was your husband, my dear Sylvia, who sent the doctors--it was his stupid man's way of being attentive." (This at Aunt Varina's suggestion--the very subtle lady!).

"Mary, I'm worried. My baby looks so badly, and I feel something is wrong."

"My dear Sylvia," I chided, "if you worry about it you will simply be harming the child. Your milk may go wrong."

"Oh, that's just it! That's why you would not tell me the truth!"

We persuade ourselves that there are certain circumstances under which lying is necessary, but always when we come to the lies we find them an insult to the soul. Each day I perceived that I was getting in deeper--and each day I watched Aunt Varina and the doctor busied to push me deeper yet.

There had come a telegram from Douglas van Tuiver to Dr. Perrin, revealing the matter which stood first in that gentleman's mind. "I expect no failure in your supply of the necessary tact." By this vagueness we perceived that he too was trusting no secrets to telegraph operators. Yet for us it was explicit and illuminative. It recalled the tone of quiet authority I had noted in his dealings with his chauffeur, and it sent me off by myself for a while to shake my fist at all husbands.

19. Mrs. Tuis, of course, had no need of any warning from the head of the house. The voice of her ancestors guided her in all such emergencies. The dear lady

had got to know me quite well, at the more or less continuous dramatic rehearsals we conducted; and now and then her trembling hands would seek to fasten me in the chains of decency. "Mrs. Abbott, think what a scandal there would be if Mrs. Douglas van Tuiver were to break with her husband!"

"Yes, my dear Mrs. Tuis-but on the other hand, think what might happen if she were kept in ignorance in this matter. She might bear another child."

I got a new realization of the chasms that lay between us. "Who are we," she whispered, "to interfere in these sacred matters? It is of souls, Mrs. Abbot, and not bodies, that the Kingdom of Heaven is made."

I took a minute or so to get my breath, and then I said, "What generally happens in these cases is that God afflicts the woman with permanent barrenness."

The old lady bowed her head, and I saw the tears falling into her lap. "My poor Sylvia!" she moaned, only half aloud.

There was a silence; I too almost wept. And finally, Aunt Varina looked up at me, her faded eyes full of pleading. "It is hard for me to understand such ideas as yours. You must tell me-can you really believe that it would help Sylvia to know this-this dreadful secret?"

"It would help her in many ways," I said. "She will be more careful of her health-she will follow the doctor's orders---"

How quickly came the reply! "I will stay with her, and see that she does that! I will be with her day and night."

"But are you going to keep the secret from those who attend her? Her maid--the child's nurses--everyone who might by any chance use the same towel, or a wash-basin, or a drinking-glass?"

"Surely you exaggerate the danger! If that were true, more people would meet with these accidents!"

"The doctors," I said, "estimate that about ten per cent. of cases of this disease are innocently acquired."

"Oh, these modern doctors!" she cried. "I never heard of such ideas!"

I could not help smiling. "My dear Mrs. Tuis, what do you imagine you know about the prevalence of gonorrhea? Consider just one fact--that I heard a college professor state publicly that in his opinion eighty-five per cent. of the men students at his university were infected with some venereal disease. And that is the pick of our young manhood--the sons of our aristocracy!"

"Oh, that can't be!" she exclaimed. "People would know of it!"

"Who are 'people'? The boys in your family know of it--if you could get them to tell you. My two sons studied at a State university, and they would bring me home what they heard--the gossip, the slang, the horrible obscenity. Fourteen fellows in one dormitory using the same bathroom--and on the wall you saw a row of fourteen syringes! And they told that on themselves, it was the joke of the campus. They call the disease a 'dose'; and a man's not supposed to be worthy the respect of his fellows until he's had his 'dose'--the sensible thing is to get several, till he can't get any more. They think it's 'no worse than a bad cold'; that's the idea they get from the 'clap-doctors,' and the women of the street who educate our sons in sex matters."

"Oh, spare me, spare me!" cried Mrs. Tuis. "I beg you not to force these horrible details upon me!"

"That is what is going on among our boys," I said. "The Castleman boys, the Chilton boys! It's going on in every fraternity house, every 'prep school' dormitory in America. And the parents refuse to know, just as you do!"

"But what could I possibly do, Mrs. Abbott?"

"I don't know, Mrs. Tuis. What *I* am going to do is to teach the young girls."

She whispered, aghast, "You would rob the young girls of their innocence. Why, with their souls full of these ideas their faces would soon be as hard--oh, you horrify me!"

"My daughter's face is not hard," I said. "And I taught her. Stop and think, Mrs. Tuis--ten thousand blind children every year! A hundred thousand women under the surgeon's knife! Millions of women going to pieces with slowly creeping diseases of which they never hear the names! I say, let us cry this from the housetops, until every woman knows--and until every man knows that she knows, and that unless he can prove that he is clean he will lose her! That is the remedy, Mrs. Tuis!"

Poor dear lady! I got up and went away, leaving her there, with clenched hands and trembling lips. I suppose I seemed to her like the mad women who were just then rising up to horrify the respectability of England--a phenomenon of Nature too portentous to be comprehended, or even to be contemplated, by a gentlewoman of the South!

20. There came in due course a couple of letters from Douglas van Tuiver. The one to Aunt Varina, which was shown to me, was vague and cautious--as if the writer were uncertain how much this worthy lady knew. He merely mentioned that Sylvia was to be spared every particle of "painful knowledge." He would wait in great anxiety, but he would not come, because any change in his plans might set her to questioning.

The letter to Dr. Perrin was not shown to me; but I judged that it must have contained more strenuous injunctions. Or had Aunt Varina by any chance got up the courage to warn the young doctor against me? His hints, at any rate, became more pointed. He desired me to realize how awkward it would be for him, if Sylvia were to learn the truth; it would be impossible to convince Mr. van Tuiver that this knowledge had not come from the physician in charge.

"But, Dr. Perrin," I objected, "it was I who brought the information to you! And Mr. van Tuiver knows that I am a radical woman; he would not expect me to be ignorant of such matters."

"Mrs. Abbott," was the response, "it is a grave matter to destroy the possibility of happiness of a young married couple."

However I might dispute his theories, in practice I was doing what he asked. But each day I was finding the task more difficult; each day it became more apparent that Sylvia was ceasing to believe me. I realized at last, with a sickening kind of fright, that she knew I was hiding something from her. Because she knew me, and knew that I would not do such a thing lightly, she was terrified. She would lie there, gazing at me, with a dumb fear in her eyes--and I would go on asseverating blindly, like an unsuccessful actor before a jeering audience.

A dozen times she made an effort to break through the barricade of falsehood; and a dozen times I drove her back, all but crying to her, "No, No! Don't ask me!" Until at last, late one night, she caught my hand and clung to it in a grip I could not break. "Mary! Mary! You must tell me the *truth!*"

"Dear girl--" I began.

"Listen!" she cried. "I know you are deceiving me! I know why--because I'll make myself ill. But it won't do any longer; it's preying on me, Mary--I've taken to imagining things. So you must tell me the truth!"

I sat, avoiding her eyes, beaten; and in the pause I could feel her hands shaking.

"Mary, what is it? Is my baby going to die?"

"No, dear, indeed no!" I cried.

"Then what?"

"Sylvia," I began, as quietly as I could, "the truth is not as bad as you imagine--"

"Tell me what it is!"

"But it is bad, Sylvia. And you must be brave. You must be, for your baby's sake."

"Make haste!" she cried.

"The baby," I said, "may be blind."

"Blind!" There we sat, gazing into each other's eyes, like two statues of women. But the grasp of her hand tightened, until even my big fist was hurt. "Blind!" she whispered again.

"Sylvia," I rushed on, "it isn't so bad as it might be! Think--if you had lost her altogether!"

" *Blind!*"

"You will have her always; and you can do things for her--take care of her. They do wonders for the blind nowadays--and you have the means; to do everything. Really, you know, blind children are not unhappy--some of them are happier than other children, I think. They haven't so much to miss. Think--"

"Wait, wait," she whispered; and again there was silence, and I clung to her cold hands.

"Sylvia," I said, at last, "you have a newly-born infant to nurse, and its very life depends upon your health now. You cannot let yourself grieve."

"No," she responded. "No. But, Mary, what caused this?"

So there was the end of my spell of truth-telling. "I don't know, dear. Nobody knows. There might be a thousand things--"

"Was it born blind?"

"No."

"Then was it the doctor's fault?"

"No, it was nobody's fault. Think of the thousands and tens of thousands of babies that become blind! It's a dreadful accident that happens." So I went on--possessed with a dread that had been with me for days, that had kept me awake for hours in the night: Had I, in any of my talks with Sylvia about venereal disease, mentioned blindness in infants as one of the consequences? I could not rememher; but now was the time I would find out!

She lay there, immovable, like a woman who had died in grief; until at last I flung my arms about her and whispered, "Sylvia! Sylvia! Please cry!"

"I can't cry!" she whispered, and her voice sounded hard.

So, after a space, I said, "Then, dear, I think I will have to make you laugh."

"Laugh, Mary?"

"Yes-I will tell you about the quarrel between Aunt Varina and myself. You know what times we've been having-how I shocked the poor lady?"

She was looking at me, but her eyes were not seeing me. "Yes, Mary," she said, in the same dead tone.

"Well, that was a game we made for you. It was very funny!"

"Funny?"

"Yes! Because I really did shock her-though we started out just to give you something else to think about!"

And then suddenly I saw the healing tears begin to come. She could not weep for her own grief-but she could weep because of what she knew we two had had to suffer for her!

21. I went out and told the others what I had done; and Mrs. Tuis rushed in to her niece and they wept in each other's arms, and Mrs. Tuis explained all the mysteries of life by her formula, "the will of the Lord."

Later on came Dr. Perrin, and it was touching to see how Sylvia treated him. She had, it appeared, conceived the idea that the calamity must be due to some blunder on his part, and then she had reflected that he was young, and that chance had thrown upon him a responsibility for which he had not bargained. He must be reproaching himself bitterly, so she had to persuade him that it was really not so bad as we were making it-that a blind child was a great joy to a mother's soul-in some ways even a greater joy than a perfectly sound child, because it appealed so to her protective instinct! I had called Sylvia a shameless payer of compliments, and now I went away by myself and wept.

Yet it was true in a way. When the infant was brought in to be nursed again, how she clung to it, a very picture of the sheltering and protecting instinct of motherhood! She knew the worst now--her mind was free, and she could partake of what happiness was allowed her. The child was hers to love and care for, and she would find ways to atone to it for the harshness of fate.

So little by little we got our existence upon a working basis. We lived a peaceful, routine life, to the music of cocoanut-palms rustling in the warm breezes which blew incessantly off the Mexican Gulf. Aunt Varina had, for the time, her undisputed way with the family; her niece reclined upon the veranda in true Southern lady fashion, and was read aloud to from books of indisputable respectability. I remember Aunt Varina selected the "Idylls of the King," and they two were in a mood to shed tears over these solemn, sorrowful tales. So it came that the little one got her name, after a pale and unhappy heroine.

I remember the long discussions of this point, the family-lore which Aunt Varina brought forth. It did not seem to her quite the thing to call a blind child after a member of one's family. Something strange, romantic, wistful--yes, Elaine was the name! Mrs. Tuis, it transpired, had already baptised the infant, in the midst of the agonies and alarms of its illness. She had called it "Sylvia," and now she was tremulously uncertain whether this counted--whether perhaps the higher powers might object to having to alter their records. But in the end a clergyman came out from Key West and heard Aunt Varina's confession, and gravely concluded that the error might be corrected by a formal ceremony. How strange it all seemed to me--being carried back two or three hundred years in the world's history! But I gave no sign of what was going on in my rebellious mind.

22. Dr. Overton on his return to New York, sent a special nurse to take charge of Sylvia's case. There was also an infant's nurse, and both had been taken into the doctor's confidence. So now there was an elaborate conspiracy--no less than five women and two men, all occupied in keeping a secret from Sylvia. It was a thing so contrary to my convictions that I was never free from the burden of it for a moment. Was it my duty to tell her?

Dr. Perrin no longer referred to the matter--I realised that both he and Dr. Gibson considered the matter settled. Was it conceivable that anyone of sound mind could set out, deliberately and in cold blood, to betray such a secret? But I had maintained all my life the right of woman to know the truth, and was I to back down now, at the first test of my convictions?

When the news reached Douglas van Tuiver that his wife had been informed of the infant's blindness, there came a telegram saying that he was coming. There was much excitement, of course, and Aunt Varina came to me, in an attempt to secure a definite pledge of silence. When I refused it, Dr. Perrin came again, and we fought the matter over for the better part of a day and night.

He was a polite little gentleman, and he did not tell me that my views were those of a fanatic, but he said that no woman could see things in their true proportion, because of her necessary ignorance concerning the nature of men, and the temptations to which they were exposed. I replied that I believed I understood these matters thoroughly, and I went on, quite simply and honestly, to make clear to him that this was so. In the end my pathetically chivalrous little Southern gentleman admitted everything I asked. Yes, it was true that these evils were ghastly, and that they were increasing, and that women were the worst sufferers from men. There might even be something in my idea that the older women of the community should devote themselves to this service, making themselves race-mothers, and helping, not merely in their homes, but in the schools and churches, to protect and save the future generations. But all that was in the future, he argued, while here was a case which had gone so far that "letting in the light" could only blast the life of two people, making it impossible for a young mother ever again to tolerate the father of her child. I argued that Sylvia was not of the hysterical type, but I could not make him agree that it was possible to predict what the attitude of any woman would be. His ideas were based on one peculiar experience he had had--a woman patient who had said to him: "Doctor, I know what is the matter with me, but for God's sake don't let my husband find out that I know, because then I should feel that my self-respect required me to leave him!"

23. The Master-of-the-House was coming! You could feel the quiver of excitement in the air of the place. The boatmen were polishing the brasses of the launch; the yard-man was raking up the dry strips of palm from beneath the cocoanut trees; Aunt Varina was ordering new supplies, and entering into conspiracies with the cook. The nurses asked me timidly, what was He like, and even Dr. Gibson, a testy old gentleman who had clashed violently with me on the subject of woman's suffrage, and had avoided me ever since as a suspicious character, now came and confided his troubles. He had sent home for a trunk, and the graceless express compa-

nies had sent it astray. Now he was wondering if it was necessary for him to journey to Key West and have a suit of dinner clothes made over night. I told him that I had not sent for any party-dresses, and that I expected to meet Mr. Douglas van Tuiver at his dinner-table in plain white linen. His surprise was so great that I suspected the old gentleman of having wondered whether I meant to retire to a "second-table" when the Master-of-the-House arrived.

I went away by myself, seething with wrath. Who was this great one whom we honoured? Was he an inspired poet, a maker of laws, a discoverer of truth? He was the owner of an indefinite number of millions of dollars--that was all, and yet I was expected, because of my awe of him, to abandon the cherished convictions of my lifetime. The situation was one that challenged my fighting blood. This was the hour to prove whether I really meant the things I talked.

On the morning of the day that van Tuiver was expected, I went early to Aunt Varina's room. She was going in the launch, and was in a state of flustration, occupied in putting on her best false hair. "Mrs. Tuis," I said, "I want you to let me go to meet Mr. van Tuiver instead of you."

I will not stop to report the good lady's outcries. I did not care, I said, whether it was proper, nor did I care whether, as she finally hinted, it might not be agreeable to Mr. van Tuiver. I was sorry to have to thrust myself upon him, but I was determined to go, and would let nothing prevent me. And all at once she yielded, rather surprising me by the suddenness of it. I suppose she concluded that van Tuiver was the man to handle me, and the quicker he got at it the better.

It is a trying thing to deal with the rich and great. If you treat them as the rest of the world does, you are a tuft-hunter; if you treat them as the rest of the world pretends to, you are a hypocrite; whereas, if you deal with them truly, it is hard not to seem, even to yourself, a bumptious person. I remember trying to tell myself on the launch-trip that I was not in the least excited; and then, standing on the platform of the railroad station, saying: "How can you expect not to be excited, when even the railroad is excited?"

"Will Mr. van Tuiver's train be on time?" I asked, of the agent.

"'Specials' are not often delayed," he replied, "at least, not Mr. van Tuiver's."

The engine and its two cars drew up, and the traveller stepped out upon the platform, followed by his secretary and his valet. I went forward to meet him. "Good morning, Mr. van Tuiver."

I saw at once that he did not remember me. "Mrs. Abbott," I prompted. "I came to meet you."

"Ah," he said. He had never got clear whether I was a sewing-woman, or a tutor, or what, and whenever he erred in such matters, it was on the side of caution.

"Your wife is doing well," I said, "and the child as well as could be expected."

"Thank you," he said. "Did no one else come?"

"Mrs. Tuis was not able," I said, diplomatically, and we moved towards the launch.

24. He did not offer to help me into the vessel, but I, crude Western woman, did not miss the attention. We seated ourselves in the upholstered leather seats in the stern, and when the "luggage" had been stowed aboard, the little vessel swung away from the pier. Then I said: "If you will pardon me, Mr. van Tuiver, I should like to talk with you privately."

He looked at me for a moment, and then answered, abruptly: "Yes, madam." The secretary rose and went forward.

The whirr of the machinery and the strong breeze made by the boat's motion, made it certain that no one could hear us, and so I began my attack: "Mr. van Tuiver, I am a friend of your wife's. I came here to help her in this crisis, and I came today to meet you because it was necessary for someone to talk to you frankly about the situation. You will understand, I presume, that Mrs. Tuis is not-- not very well informed about the matters in question."

His gaze was fixed intently upon me, but he said not a word. After waiting, I continued: "Perhaps you will wonder why your wife's physicians could not have handled the matter. The reason is, there is a woman's side to such questions and often it is difficult for men to understand it. If Sylvia knew the truth, she could speak for herself; so long as she does not know it, I shall have to take the liberty of speaking for her."

Again there was a pause. He did nothing more than watch me, yet I could feel his affronted maleness rising up for battle. I waited on purpose to compel him to speak.

"May I ask," he inquired, at last, "what you mean by the 'truth' that you refer to?"

"I mean," I said, "the cause of the infant's affliction."

His composure was a thing to wonder at. He did not show by the flicker of an eyelash any sign of uneasiness.

"Let me explain one thing," I continued. "I owe it to Dr. Perrin to make clear that he had nothing whatever to do with my coming into possession of the secret. In fact, as he will no doubt tell you, I knew it before he did; it is possible that you owe it to me that the infant is not disfigured as well as blind."

I paused again. "If that be true," he said, with unshaken formality, "I am obliged to you." What a man!

I continued: "My one desire and purpose is to protect my friend. So far, the secret has been kept from her. I consented to this, because her very life was at stake, it seemed to us all. But now she is well enough to know, and the question is SHALL she know. I need hardly tell you that Dr. Perrin thinks she should not, and that he has been using his influence to persuade me to agree with him; so also has Mrs. Tuis----"

Then I saw the first trace of uncertainty in his eyes. "There was a critical time," I explained, "when Mrs. Tuis had to be told. You may be sure, however, that no hint of the truth will be given by her. I am the only person who is troubled with the problem of Sylvia's rights."

I waited. "May I suggest, Mrs.--Mrs. Abbott--that the protection of Mrs. van Tuiver's rights can be safely left to her physicians and her husband?"

"One would wish so, Mr. van Tuiver, but the medical books are full of evidence that women's rights frequently need other protection."

I perceived that he was nearing the end of his patience now. "You make it difficult for me to talk to you," he said. "I am not accustomed to having my affairs taken out of my hands by strangers."

"Mr. van Tuiver," I replied, "in this most critical matter it is necessary to speak without evasion. Before her marriage Sylvia made an attempt to safeguard herself in this very matter, and she was not dealt with fairly."

At last I had made a hole in the mask! His face was crimson as he replied: "Madam, your knowledge of my private affairs is most astonishing. May I inquire how you learned these things?"

I did not reply at once, and he repeated the question. I perceived that this was to him the most important matter--his wife's lack of reserve!

"The problem that concerns us here," I said, "is whether you are willing to repair the error you made. Will you go frankly to your wife and admit your responsibility----"

He broke in, angrily: "Madam, the assumption you are making is one I see no reason for permitting."

"Mr. van Tuiver," said I, "I hoped that you would not take that line of argument. I perceive that I have been *naive.*"

"Really, madam!" he replied, with cruel intent, "you have not impressed me so!"

I continued unshaken: "In this conversation it will be necessary to assume that you are responsible for the presence of the disease."

"In that case," he replied, haughtily, "I can have no further part in the conversation, and I will ask you to drop it at once."

I might have taken him at his word and waited, confident that in the end he would have to come and ask for terms. But that would have seemed childish to me, with the grave matters we had to settle. After a minute or two, I said, quietly: "Mr. van Tuiver, you wish me to believe that previous to your marriage you had always lived a chaste life?"

He was equal to the effort it cost to control himself. He sat examining me with his cold grey eyes. I suppose I must have been as new and monstrous a phenomenon to him as he was to me.

At last, seeing that he would not reply, I said, coldly: "It will help us to get forward if you will give up the idea that it is possible for you to put me off, or to escape this situation."

"Madam," he cried, suddenly, "come to the point! What is it that you want? Money?"

I had thought I was prepared for everything; but this was an aspect of his world which I could hardly have been expected to allow for. I stared at him and then turned from the sight of him. "And to think that Sylvia is married to such a man!" I whispered, half to myself.

"Mrs. Abbott," he exclaimed, "how can anyone understand what you are driving at?"

But I turned away without answering, and for a long time sat gazing over the water. What was the use of pleading with such a man? What was the use of pouring out one's soul to him? I would tell Sylvia the truth at once, and leave him to her!

25. I heard him again, at last; he was talking to my back, his tone a trifle less aloof. "Mrs. Abbott, do you realize that I know nothing whatever about you--your character, your purpose, the nature of your hold upon my wife? So what means have I of judging? You threaten me with something that seems to me entirely insane--and what can I make of it? If you wish me to understand you, tell me in plain words what you want."

I reflected that I was in the world, and must take it as I found it. "I have told you what I want," I said; "but I will tell you again, if it is necessary. I hoped to persuade you that it was your duty to go to your wife and tell her the truth."

He took a few moments to make sure of his self-possession. "And would you explain what good you imagine that could do?"

"Your wife," I said, "must be put in position to protect herself in future. There is no means of making sure in such a matter, except to tell her the truth. You love her--and you are a man who has never been accustomed to do without what he wants."

"Great God, woman!" he cried. "Don't you suppose one blind child is enough?"

It was the first human word that he had spoken, and I was grateful for it. "I have already covered that point," I said, in a low voice. "The medical books are full of painful evidence that several blind children are often not enough. There can be no escaping the necessity--Sylvia must *know.* The only question is, who shall tell her? You must realize that in urging you to be the person, I am thinking of your good as well as hers. I will, of course, not mention that I have had anything to do with persuading you, and so it will seem to her that you have some realization of the wrong you have done her, some desire to atone for it, and to be honourable and fair in your future dealings with her. When she has once been made to realize that you are no more guilty than other men of your class--hat you have done no worse than all of them----"

"You imagine she could be made to believe that?" he broke in, impatiently.

"I will undertake to see that she believes it," I replied.

"You seem to have great confidence in your ability to manage my wife!"

"If you continue to resent my existence," I answered, gravely, "you will make it impossible for me to help you."

"Pardon me," he said--but he did not say it cordially.

I went on: "There is much that can be said in your behalf. I realize it is quite possible that you were not wholly to blame when you wrote to Bishop Chilton that you were fit to marry; I know that you may have believed it--that you might even have found physicians to tell you so. There is wide-spread ignorance on the subject of this disease. Men have the idea that the chronic forms of it cannot be communicated to women, and it is difficult to make them realize what modern investigations have proven. You can explain that to Sylvia, and I will back you up in it. You were in love with her, you wanted her. Go to her now, and admit to her honestly that you have wronged her. Beg her to forgive you, and to let you help make the best of the cruel situation that has arisen."

So I went on, pouring out my soul. And when I had finished, he said, "Mrs. Abbott, I have listened patiently to your most remarkable proposition. My answer is that I must ask you to withdraw from this intimate matter, which concerns only my wife and myself."

He was back where we started! Trying to sweep aside these grim and terrible realities with the wave of a conventional hand! Was this the way he met Sylvia's arguments? I felt moved to tell him what I thought of him.

"You are a proud man, Mr. van Tuiver--an obstinate man, I fear. It is hard for you to humble yourself to your wife--to admit a crime and beg forgiveness. Tell me--is that why you hesitate? Is it because you fear you will have to take second place in your family from now on--that you will no longer be able to dominate Sylvia? Are you afraid of putting into her hands a weapon of self-defence?"

He made no response.

"Very well," I said, at last. "Let me tell you, then--I will not help any man to hold such a position in a woman's life. Women have to bear half the burdens of marriage, they pay half, or more than half, the penalties; and so it is necessary that they have a voice in its affairs. Until they know the truth, they can never have a voice."

Of course my little lecture on Feminism might as well have been delivered to a sphinx. "How stupid you are!" I cried. "Don't you know that some day Sylvia must find out the truth for herself?"

This was before the days when newspapers and magazines began to discuss such matters frankly; but still there were hints to be picked up. I had a newspaper-item in my bag--the board of health in a certain city had issued a circular giving instructions for the prevention of blindness in newly-born infants, and discussing the causes thereof; and the United States post office authorities had barred the circular from the mails. I said, "Suppose that item had come under Sylvia's eyes; might it not have put her on the track. It was in her newspaper the day before yesterday; and it was only by accident that I got hold of it first. Do you suppose that can go on forever?"

"Now that I am here," he replied, "I will be glad to relieve you of such responsibilities."

Which naturally made me cross. I drew from my quiver an arrow that I thought would penetrate his skin. "Mr. van Tuiver," I said, "a man in your position must always be an object of gossip and scandal. Suppose some enemy were to send your wife an anonymous letter? Or suppose there were some woman who thought that you had wronged her?"

I stopped. He gave me one keen look--and then again the impenetrable mask! "My wife will have to do as other women in her position do--pay no attention to scandal-mongers of any sort."

I paused, and then went on: "I believe in marriage. I consider it a sacred thing; I would do anything in my power to protect and preserve a marriage. But I hold that it must be an equal partnership. I would fight to make it that; and wherever I found that it could not be that, I would say it was not marriage, but slavery, and I would fight just as hard to break it. Can you not understand that attitude upon a woman's part?"

He gave no sign that he could understand. But still I would not give up my battle. "Mr. van Tuiver," I pleaded, "I am a much older person than you. I have seen a great deal of life--I have seen suffering even worse than yours. And I am trying most earnestly to help you. Can you not bring yourself to talk to me frankly? Perhaps you have never talked with a woman about such matters--I mean, with a good woman. But I assure you that other men have found it possible, and never regretted the confidence they placed in me."

I went on to tell him about my own sons, and what I had done for them; I told him of a score of other boys in their class who had come to me, making me a sort of mother-confessor. I do not think that I was entirely deceived by my own eloquence--there was, I am sure, a minute or two when he actually wavered. But then the habits of a precocious life-time reasserted themselves, and he set his lips and told himself that he was Douglas van Tuiver. Such things might happen in raw Western colleges, but they were not according to the Harvard manner, nor the tradition of life in Fifth Avenue clubs.

He could not be a boy! He had never had any boyhood, any childhood--he had been a state personage ever since he had known that he was anything. I found myself thinking suddenly of the thin-lipped old family lawyer, who had had much to do with shaping his character, and whom Sylvia described to me, sitting at her dinner-table and bewailing the folly of people who "admitted things." That was what made trouble for family lawyers--not what people did, but what they admitted. How easy it was to ignore impertinent questions! And how few people had the wit to do it!-it seemed as if the shade of the thin-lipped old family lawyer were standing by Douglas van Tuiver's side.

In a last desperate effort, I cried, "Even suppose that I grant your request, even suppose I agree not to tell Sylvia the truth--still the day will come when you will hear from her the point-blank question: 'Is my child blind because of this disease?' And what will you answer?"

He said, in his cold, measured tones, "I will answer that there are a thousand ways in which the disease can be innocently acquired."

For a long time there was silence between us. At last he spoke again, and his voice was as emotionless as if we had just met: "Do I understand you, madam, that if I reject your advice and refuse to tell my wife what you call the truth, it is your intention to tell her yourself?"

"You understand me correctly," I replied.

"And may I ask when you intend to carry out this threat?"

"I will wait," I said, "I will give you every chance to think it over--to consult with the doctors, in case you wish to. I will not take the step without giving you fair notice."

"For that I am obliged to you," he said, with a touch of irony; and that was our last word.

26. Our island was visible in the distance and I was impatient for the time when I should be free from this man's presence. But as we drew nearer, I noticed a boat coming out; it proved to be one of the smaller launches heading directly for us. Neither van Tuiver nor I spoke, but both of us watched it, and he must have been wondering, as I was, what its purpose could be. When it was near enough, I made out that its passengers were Dr. Perrin and Dr. Gibson.

We slowed up, and the other boat did the same, and they lay within a few feet of each other. Dr. Perrin greeted van Tuiver, and after introducing the other man, he said: "We came out to have a talk with you. Would you be so good as to step into this boat?"

"Certainly," was the reply. The two launches were drawn side by side, and the transfer made; the man who was running the smaller launch stepped into ours-- evidently having been instructed in advance.

"You will excuse us please?" said the little doctor to me. The man who had stepped into our launch spoke to the captain of it, and the power was then put on, and we moved away a sufficient distance to be out of hearing. I thought this a strange procedure, but I conjectured that the doctors had become nervous as to what I might have told van Tuiver. So I dismissed the matter from my mind, and spent my time reviewing the exciting adventure I had just passed through.

How much impression had I made? It was hard for me to judge such a man. He would pretend to be less concerned than he actually was. But surely he must see that he was in my power, and would have to give way in the end!

There came a hail from the little vessel, and we moved alongside again. "Would you kindly step in here with us, Mrs. Abbott?" said Dr. Perrin, and when I had done so, he ordered the boatman to move away once more. Van Tuiver said not a word, but I noted a strained look upon his face, and I thought the others seemed agitated also.

As soon as the other vessel was out of hearing, Dr. Perrin turned to me and said: "Mrs. Abbott, we came out to see Mr. van Tuiver, to warn him of a distressing accident which has just happened. Mrs. van Tuiver was asleep in her room, and Miss Lyman and another of the nurses were in the next room. They indiscreetly made some remarks on the subject which we have all been discussing--how much a wife should be told about these matters, and suddenly they discovered Mrs. van Tuiver standing in the doorway of the room."

My gaze had turned to Douglas van Tuiver. "So she **knows!**" I cried.

"We don't think that she knows, but she has a suspicion and is trying to find out. She asked to see you."

"Ah, yes!" I said.

"She declared that she wished to see you as soon as you returned--that she would not see anyone else, not even Mr. van Tuiver. You will understand that this portends trouble for all of us. We judged it necessary to have a consultation about the matter."

I bowed in assent.

"Now, Mrs. Abbot," began the little doctor, solemnly, "there is no longer a question of abstract ideas, but of an immediate emergency. We feel that we, as the physicians in charge of the case, have the right to take control of the matter. We do not see----"

"Dr. Perrin," I said, "let us come to the point. You want me to spin a new web of deception?"

"We are of the opinion, Mrs. Abbott, that in such matters the physicians in charge----"

"Excuse me," I said, quickly, "we have been over all this before, and we know that we disagree. Has Mr. van Tuiver told you of the proposition I have just made?"

"You mean for him to go to his wife----"

"Yes."

"He has told us of this, and has offered to do it. We are of the opinion that it would be a grave mistake."

"It has been three weeks since the birth of the baby," I said. "Surely all danger of fever is past. I will grant you that if it were a question of telling her deliberately, it might be better to put it off for a while. I would have been willing to wait for months, but for the fact that I dreaded something like the present situation. Now that it has happened, surely it is best to use our opportunity while all of us are here and can persuade her to take the kindest attitude towards her husband."

"Madam!" broke in Dr. Gibson. (He was having difficulty in controlling his excitement.) "You are asking us to overstep the bounds of our professional duty. It is not for the physician to decide upon the attitude a wife should take toward her husband."

"Dr. Gibson," I replied, "that is what you propose to do, only you wish to conceal the fact. You would force Mrs. van Tuiver to accept your opinion of what a wife's duty is."

Dr. Perrin took command once more. "Our patient has asked for you, and she looks to you for guidance. You must put aside your own convictions and think of her health. You are the only person who can calm her, and surely it is your duty to do so!"

"I know that I might go in and lie again to my friend, but she knows too much to be deceived for very long. You know what a mind she has--a lawyer's mind! How can I persuade her that the nurses--why, I do not even know what she heard the nurses say!"

"We have that all written down for you," put in Dr. Perrin, quickly.

"You have their recollection of it, no doubt--but suppose they have forgotten some of it? Sylvia has not forgotten, you may be sure--every word is burned with fire into her brain. She has put with this everything she ever heard on the subject--the experience of her friend, Harriet Atkinson-all that I've told her in the past about such things----"

"Ah!" growled Dr. Gibson. "That's it! If you had not meddled in the beginning----"

"Now, now!" said the other, soothingly. "You ask me to relieve you of the embarrassment of this matter. I quite agree with Mrs. Abbott that there is too much ignorance about these things, but she must recognise, I am sure, that this is not the proper moment for enlightening Mrs. van Tuiver."

"I do not recognise it at all," I said. "If her husband will go to her and tell her humbly and truthfully----"

"You are talking madness!" cried the old man, breaking loose again. "She would be hysterical--she would regard him as something loathsome--some kind of criminal----"

"Of course she would be shocked," I said, "but she has the coolest head of anyone I know--I do not think of any man I would trust so fully to take a rational attitude in the end. We can explain to her what extenuating circumstances there are, and she will have to recognise them. She will see that we are considering her rights----"

"Her *rights!*" The old man fairly snorted the words.

"Now, now, Dr. Gibson!" interposed the other. "You asked me----"

"I know! I know! But as the older of the physicians in charge of this case----"

Dr. Perrin managed to frown him down, and went on trying to placate me. But through the argument I could hear the old man muttering in his collar a kind of double bass *pizzicato*: "Suffragettes! Fanatics! Hysteria! Woman's Rights!"

27. The breeze was feeble, and the sun was blazing hot, but nevertheless I made myself listen patiently for a while. They had said it all to me, over and over again; but it seemed that Dr. Perrin could not be satisfied until it had been said in Douglas van Tuiver's presence.

"Dr. Perrin," I exclaimed, "even supposing we make the attempt to deceive her, we have not one plausible statement to make----"

"You are mistaken, Mrs. Abbott," said he. "We have the perfectly well-known fact that this disease is often contracted in ways which involve no moral blame. And in this case I believe I am in position to state how the accident happened."

"What do you mean?"

"I don't know whether you heard that just before Mrs. van Tuiver's confinement, I was called away to one of the other keys to attend a negro-woman. And since this calamity has befallen us, I have realized that I was possibly not as careful in sterilizing my instruments as I might have been. It is of course a dreadful thing for any physician to have to believe----"

He stopped, and there was a long silence. I gazed from one to another of the men. Two of them met my gaze; one did not. "He is going to let you say that?" I whispered, at last.

"Honour and fairness compel me to say it, Mrs. Abbott. I believe----"

But I interrupted him. "Listen to me, Dr. Perrin. You are a chivalrous gentleman, and you think you are helping a man in desperate need. But I say that anyone who would permit you to tell such a tale is a contemptible coward!"

"Madam," cried Dr. Gibson, furiously, "there is a limit even to a woman's rights!"

A silence followed. At last I resumed, in a low voice, "You gentlemen have your code: you protect the husband--you protect him at all hazards. I could understand this, if he were innocent of the offence in question; I could understand it if there were any possibility of his being innocent. But how can you protect him, when you know that he is guilty?"

"There can be no question of such knowledge!" cried the old doctor.

"I have no idea," I said, "how much he has admitted to you; but let me remind you of one circumstance, which is known to Dr. Perrin--that I came to this place with the definite information that symptoms of the disease were to be anticipated. Dr. Perrin knows that I told that to Dr. Overton in New York. Has he informed you of it?"

There was an awkward interval. I glanced at van Tuiver, and I saw that he was leaning forward, staring at me. I thought he was about to speak, when Dr. Gibson broke in, excitedly, "All this is beside the mark! We have a serious emergency to face, and we are not getting anywhere. As the older of the physicians in charge of this case----"

And he went on to give me a lecture on the subject of authority. He talked for five minutes, ten minutes--I lost all track of the time. I had suddenly begun to picture how I would act and what I would say when I went into Sylvia's room. What a state must Sylvia be in, while we sat out here in the blazing mid-day sun, discussing her right to freedom and knowledge!

28. "I have always been positive," Dr. Gibson was saying, "but the present discussion has made me more positive than ever. As the older of the physicians in charge of this case, I say most emphatically that the patient shall not be told!"

I could not stand him any longer. "I am going to tell the patient," I said.

"You shall *not* tell her!"

"But how will you prevent me?"

"You shall not *see* her!"

"But she is determined to see *me!*"

"She will be told that you are not there."

"And how long do you imagine that that will satisfy her?"

There was a pause. They looked at van Tuiver, expecting him to speak. And so I heard once more his cold, deliberate voice. "We have done all we can. There can no longer be any question as to the course to be taken. Mrs. Abbott will not return to my home."

"What?" I cried. I stared at him, aghast. "What do you mean?"

"I mean what I say--that you will not be taken back to the island."

"But where will I be taken?"

"You will be taken to the mainland."

I stared at the others. No one gave a sign. At last I whispered, "You would *dare?*"

"You leave us no other alternative," replied the master.

"You--you will practically kidnap me!" My voice must have been rather wild at that moment.

"You left my home of your own free will. I think I need hardly point out to you that I am not compelled to invite you back to it."

"And what will Sylvia----" I stopped; appalled at the vista the words opened up.

"My wife," said van Tuiver, "will ultimately choose between her husband and her most remarkable acquaintance."

"And you gentlemen?" I turned to the others. "You would give your sanction to this outrageous action?"

"As the older of the physicians in charge of this case----" began Dr. Gibson.

I turned to van Tuiver again. "When your wife finds out what you have done to me--what will you answer?"

"We will deal with that situation when we come to it."

"Of course," I said, "you understand that sooner or later I shall get word to her!"

He answered, "We shall assume from now on that you are a mad woman, and shall take our precautions accordingly."

Again there was a silence.

"The launch will return to the mainland," said van Tuiver at last. "It will remain there until Mrs. Abbott sees fit to go ashore. May I ask if she has sufficient money in her purse to take her to New York?"

I could not help laughing. The thing was so wild--and yet I could see that from their point of view it was the only thing to do. "Mrs. Abbott is not certain that she is going back to New York," I replied. "If she does go, it will not be with Mr. van Tuiver's money."

"One thing more," said Dr. Perrin. It was the first time he had spoken since van Tuiver's incredible announcement. "I trust, Mrs. Abbott, that this unfortunate situation may at all costs be concealed from servants, and from the world in general."

From which I realized how badly I had them frightened. They actually saw me making physical resistance!

"Dr. Perrin," I replied, "I am acting in this matter for my friend. I will add this: that I believe that you are letting yourself be overborne, and that you will regret it some day."

He made no answer. Douglas van Tuiver put an end to the discussion by rising and signalling the other launch. When it had come alongside, he said to the captain, "Mrs. Abbott is going back to the railroad. You will take her at once."

Then he waited; I was malicious enough to give him an anxious moment before I rose. Dr. Perrin offered me his hand; and Dr. Gibson said, with a smile, "Good-bye, Mrs. Abbott. I'm sorry you can't stay with us any longer."

I think it was something to my credit that I was able to play out the game before the boatmen. "I am sorry, too," I countered. "I am hoping I shall be able to return."

And then came the real ordeal. "Good-bye, Mrs. Abbott," said Douglas van Tuiver, with his stateliest bow; and I managed to answer him!

As I took my seat, he beckoned his secretary. There was a whispered consultation for a minute or two, and then the master returned to the smaller launch with the doctors. He gave the word, and the two vessels set out--one to the key, and the other to the railroad. The secretary went in the one with me!

29. And here ends a certain stage of my story. I have described Sylvia as I met her and judged her; and if there be any reader who has been irked by this method, who thinks of me as a crude and pushing person, disposed to meddle in the affairs of others, here is where that reader will have his satisfaction and revenge. For if ever a troublesome puppet was jerked suddenly off the stage--if ever a long-winded orator was effectively snuffed out--I was that puppet and that orator. I stop and think-- shall I describe how I paced up and down the pier, respectfully but emphatically watched by the secretary? And all the melodramatic plots I conceived, the muffled

oars and the midnight visits to my Sylvia? My sense of humour forbids it. For a while now I shall take the hint and stay in the background of this story. I shall tell the experiences of Sylvia as Sylvia herself told them to me long afterwards; saying no more about my own fate--save that I swallowed my humiliation and took the next train to New York, a far sadder and wiser social-reformer!

BOOK III
SYLVIA AS REBEL

1. Long afterwards Sylvia told me about what happened between her husband and herself; how desperately she tried to avoid discussing the issue with him--out of her very sense of fairness to him. But he came to her room, in spite of her protest, and by his implacable persistence he made her hear what he had to say. When he had made up his mind to a certain course of action, he was no more to be resisted than a glacier.

"Sylvia," he said, "I know that you are upset by what has happened. I make every allowance for your condition; but there are some statements that I must be permitted to make, and there are simply no two ways about it--you must get yourself together and hear me."

"Let me see Mary Abbott!" she insisted, again and again. "It may not be what you want--but I demand to see her."

So at last he said, "You cannot see Mrs. Abbott. She has gone back to New York." And then, at her look of consternation: "That is one of the things I have to talk to you about."

"Why has she gone back?" cried Sylvia.

"Because I was unwilling to have her here."

"You mean you sent her away?"

"I mean that she understood she was no longer welcome."

Sylvia drew a quick breath and turned away to the window.

He took advantage of the opportunity to come near, and draw up a chair for her. "Will you not pleased to be seated," he said. And at last she turned, rigidly, and seated herself.

"The time has come," he declared, "when we have to settle this question of Mrs.

Abbott, and her influence upon your life. I have argued with you about such matters, but now what has happened makes further discussion impossible. You were brought up among people of refinement, and it has been incredible to me that you should be willing to admit to your home such a woman as this--not merely of the commonest birth, but without a trace of the refinement to which you have been accustomed. And now you see the consequences of your having brought such a person into our life!"

He paused. She made no sound, and her gaze was riveted upon the window-curtain.

"She happens to be here," he went on, "at a time when a dreadful calamity befalls us--when we are in need of the utmost sympathy and consideration. Here is an obscure and terrible affliction, which has baffled the best physicians in the country; but this ignorant farmer's wife considers that she knows all about it. She proceeds to discuss it with every one--sending your poor aunt almost into hysterics, setting the nurses to gossiping--God knows what else she has done, or what she will do, before she gets through. I don't pretend to know her ultimate purpose--blackmail, possibly----"

"Oh, how can you!" she broke out, involuntarily. "How can you say such a thing about a friend of mine?"

"I might answer with another question--how can you have such a friend? A woman who has cast off every restraint, every consideration of decency--and yet is able to persuade a daughter of the Castlemans to make her an intimate! Possibly she is an honest fanatic. Dr. Perrin tells me she was the wife of a brutal farmer, who mistreated her. No doubt that has embittered her against men, and accounts for her mania. You see that her mind leaped at once to the most obscene and hideous explanation of this misfortune of ours--an explanation which pleased her because it blackened the honour of a man."

He stopped again. Sylvia's eyes had moved back to the window-curtain.

"I am not going to insult your ears," he said, "with discussions of her ideas. The proper person to settle such matters is a physician, and if you wish Dr. Perrin to do so, he will tell you what he knows about the case. But I wish you to realize somehow what this thing has meant to me. I have managed to control myself----" He saw her shut her lips more tightly. "The doctors tell me that I must not excite you.

But picture the situation. I come to my home, bowed down with grief for you and for my child. And this mad woman thrusts herself forward, shoves aside your aunt and your physicians, and comes in the launch to meet me at the station. And then she accuses me of being criminally guilty of the blindness of my child--of having wilfully deceived my wife! Think of it--that is my welcome to my home!"

"Douglas," she cried, wildly, "Mary Abbott would not have done such a thing without reason----"

"I do not purpose to defend myself," he said, coldly. "If you are bent upon filling your mind with such matters, go to Dr. Perrin. He will tell you that he, as a physician, knows that the charge against me is preposterous. He will tell you that even granting that the cause of the blindness is what Mrs. Abbott guesses, there are a thousand ways in which such an infection can be contracted, which are perfectly innocent, involving no guilt on the part of anyone. Every doctor knows that drinking-cups, wash-basins, towels, even food, can be contaminated. He knows that any person can bring the affliction into a home--servants, nurses, even the doctors themselves. Has your mad woman friend told you any of that?"

"She has told me nothing. You know that I have had no opportunity to talk with her. I only know what the nurses believe----"

"They believe what Mrs. Abbott told them. That is absolutely all the reason they have for believing anything!"

She did not take that quite as he expected. "So Mary Abbott *did* tell them!" she cried.

He hurried on: "The poisonous idea of a vulgar Socialist woman--this is the thing upon which you base your suspicions of your husband!"

"Oh!" she whispered, half to herself. "Mary Abbott *did* say it!"

"What if she did?"

"Oh, Douglas, Mary would never have said such a thing to a nurse unless she had been certain of it!"

"Certain?" he broke out. "What certainty could she imagine she had? She is a bitter, frantic woman--a divorced woman--who jumped to the conclusion that pleased her, because it involved the humiliation of a rich man."

He went on, his voice trembling with suppressed passion: "When you know the real truth, the thing becomes a nightmare. You, a delicate woman, lying here helpless--the victim of a cruel misfortune, and with the life of an afflicted infant depending upon your peace of mind. Your physicians planning day and night to keep you quiet, to keep the dreadful, unbearable truth from you----"

"Oh, what truth? That's the terrifying thing--to know that people are keeping things from me! What *was* it they were keeping?"

"First of all, the fact that the baby was blind; and then the cause of it----"

"Then they *do* know the cause?"

"They don't know positively--no one can know positively. But poor Dr. Perrin had a dreadful idea, that he had to hide from you because otherwise he could not bear to continue in your house----"

"Why, Douglas! What do you mean?"

"I mean that a few days before your confinement, he was called away to the case of a negro-woman--you knew that, did you not?"

"Go on."

"He had the torturing suspicion that possibly he was not careful enough in sterilizing his instruments, and that he, your friend and protector, may be the man who is to blame."

"Oh! Oh!" Her voice was a whisper of horror.

"That is one of the secrets your doctors have been trying to hide."

There was silence, while her eyes searched his face. Suddenly she stretched out her hands to him, crying desperately: "Oh, is this true?"

He did not take the outstretched hands. "Since I am upon the witness-stand, I have to be careful of my replies. It is what Dr. Perrin tells me. Whether the explanation he gives is the true one--whether he himself, or the nurse he recommended, may have brought the infection----"

"It couldn't have been the nurse," she said quickly. "She was so careful----"

He did not allow her to finish. "You seem determined," he said, coldly, "to spare everyone but your husband."

"No!" she protested, "I have tried hard to be fair--to be fair to both you and my friend. Of course, if Mary Abbott was mistaken, I have done you a great injustice--"

He saw that she was softening, and that it was safe for him to be a man. "It has been with some difficulty that I have controlled myself throughout this experience," he said, rising to his feet. "If you do not mind, I think I will not carry the discussion any further, as I don't feel that I can trust myself to listen to a defence of that woman from your lips. I will only tell you my decision in the matter. I have never before used my authority as a husband; I hoped I should never have to use it. But the time has come when you will have to choose between Mary Abbott and your husband. I will positively not tolerate your corresponding with her, or having anything further to do with her. I take my stand upon that, and nothing will move me. I will not even permit of any discussion of the subject. And now I hope you will excuse me. Dr. Perrin wishes me to tell you that either he or Dr. Gibson are ready at any time to advise you about these matters, which have been forced upon your mind against their judgment and protests."

2. You can see that it was no easy matter for Sylvia to get at the truth. The nurses, already terrified because of their indiscretion, had been first professionally thrashed, and then carefully drilled as to the answers they were to make. But as a matter of fact they did not have to make any answers at all, because Sylvia was unwilling to reveal to anyone her distrust of her husband.

One of two things was certain: either she had been horribly wronged by her husband, or now she was horribly wronging him. Which was the truth? Was it conceivable that I, Mary Abbott, would leap to a false conclusion about such a matter? She knew that I felt intensely, almost fanatically, on the subject, and also that I had been under great emotional stress. Was it possible that I would have voiced mere suspicions to the nurses? Sylvia could not be sure, for my standards were as strange to her as my Western accent. She knew that I talked freely to everyone about such matters--and would be as apt to select the nurses as the ladies of the house. On the other hand, how was it conceivable that I could know positively? To recognize a disease might be easy; but to specify from what source it had come--that was surely not in my power!

They did not leave her alone for long. Mrs. Tuis came in, with her feminine terrors. "Sylvia, you must know that you are treating your husband dreadfully! He has gone away down the beach by himself, and has not even seen his baby!"

"Aunt Varina--" she began, "won't you please go away?"

But the other rushed on: "Your husband comes here, broken with grief because of this affliction; and you overwhelm him with the most cruel and wicked reproaches with charges you have no way in the world of proving----" And the old lady caught her niece by the hand. "My child! Come, do your duty!"

"My duty?"

"Make yourself fit, and take your husband to see his baby."

"Oh, I can't!" cried Sylvia. "I don't want to be there when he sees her! If I loved him--" Then, seeing her aunt's face of horror, she was seized with a sudden impulse of pity, and caught the poor old lady in her arms. "Aunt Varina," she said, "I am making you suffer, I know--I am making everyone suffer! But if you only knew how I am suffering myself! How can I know what to do."

Mrs. Tuis was weeping; but quickly she got herself together, and answered in a firm voice, "Your old auntie can tell you what to do. You must come to your senses, my child--you must let your reason prevail. Get your face washed, make yourself presentable, and come and take your husband to see your baby. Women have to suffer, dear; we must not shirk our share of life's burdens."

"There is no danger of my shirking," said Sylvia, bitterly.

"Come, dear, come," pleaded Mrs. Tuis. She was trying to lead the girl to the mirror. If only she could be made to see how distraught and disorderly she looked! "Let me help you to dress, dear--you know how much better it always makes you feel."

Sylvia laughed, a trifle wildly--but Mrs. Tuis had dealt with hysteria before. "What would you like to wear?" she demanded. And then, without waiting for an answer, "Let me choose something. One of your pretty frocks."

"A pretty frock, and a seething volcano underneath! That is your idea of a woman's life!"

The other responded very gravely, "A pretty frock, my dear, and a smile--instead of a vulgar scene, and ruin and desolation afterwards."

Sylvia made no reply. Yes, that was the life of woman--her old aunt knew! And her old aunt knew also the psychology of her sex. She did not go on talking about pretty frocks in the abstract; she turned at once to the clothes-closet, and began laying pretty frocks upon the bed!

3. Sylvia emerged upon the "gallery," clad in dainty pink muslin, her beautiful shiny hair arranged under a semi-invalid's cap of pink maline. Her face was pale, and the big red-brown eyes were hollow; but she was quiet, and apparently mis-

tress of herself again. She even humoured Aunt Varina by leaning slightly upon her feeble arm, while the maid hastened to place her chair in a shaded spot.

Her husband came, and the doctors; the tea-things were brought, and Aunt Varina poured tea, a-flutter with excitement. They talked about the comparative temperatures of New York and the Florida Keys, and about hedges of jasmine to shade the gallery from the evening sun. And after a while, Aunt Varina arose, explaining that she would prepare Elaine for her father's visit. In the doorway she stood for a moment, smiling upon the pretty picture; it was all settled now--the outward forms had been observed, and the matter would end, as such matters should end between husband and wife--a few tears, a few reproaches, and then a few kisses.

The baby was made ready, with a new dress, and a fresh silk bandage to cover the pitiful, lifeless eyes. Aunt Varina had found pleasure in making these bandages; she made them soft and pretty--less hygienic, perhaps, but avoiding the suggestion of the hospital.

When Sylvia and her husband came into the room, the faces of both of them were white. Sylvia stopped near the door-way; and poor Aunt Varina fluttered about, in agony of soul. When van Tuiver went to the cradle, she hurried to his side, and sought to awaken the little one with gentle nudges. Quite unexpectedly to her, van Tuiver sought to pick up the infant; she helped him, and he stood, holding it awkwardly, as if afraid it might go to pieces in his arms.

So any man might appear, with his first infant; but to Sylvia it seemed the most tragic sight she had ever seen in her life. She gave a low cry, "Douglas!" and he turned, and she saw his face was working with the feeling he was ashamed for anyone to see. "Oh, Douglas," she whispered, "I'm so *sorry* for you!" At which Aunt Varina decided that it was time for her to make her escape.

4. But the trouble between these two were not such as could be settled by any burst of emotion. The next day they were again in a dispute, for he had come to ask her word of honour that she would never see me again, and would give him my letters to be returned unopened. This last was what she had let her father do in the case of Frank Shirley; and she had become certain in her own mind that she had done wrong.

But he was insistent in his demand; declaring that it should be obvious to her there could be no peace of mind for him so long as my influence continued in her life.

"But surely," protested Sylvia, "to hear Mary Abbott's explanation----"

"There can be no explanation that is not an insult to your husband, and to those who are caring for you. I am speaking in this matter not merely for myself, but for your physicians, who know this woman, heard her menaces and her vulgarity. It is their judgment that you should be protected at all hazards from further contact with her."

"Douglas," she argued, "you must realize that I am in distress of mind about this matter----"

"I certainly realize that."

"And if you are thinking of my welfare, you should choose a course that would set my mind at rest. But when you come to me and ask me that I should not even read a letter from my friend--don't you realize what you suggest to me, that there is something you are afraid for me to know?"

"I do not attempt to deny my fear of this woman. I have seen how she has been able to poison your mind with suspicions----"

"Yes, Douglas--but now that has been done. What else is there to fear from her?"

"I have no idea what. She is a bitter, jealous woman, with a mind full of hatred; and you are an innocent girl, who cannot judge about these matters. What idea have you of the world in which you live, of the slanders to which a man in your husband's position is exposed?"

"I am not quite such a child as that----"

"You have simply no idea, I tell you. I remember your consternation when we first met, and I told you about the woman who had written me a begging letter, and got an interview with me, and then started screaming, and refused to leave the house till I had paid her a lot of money. You had never heard such stories, had you? Yet it is the kind of thing that is happening to rich men continually; it was one of the first rules I was taught, never to let myself be alone with a strange woman, no matter of what age, or under what circumstances."

"But, I assure you, I would not listen to such people----"

"You are asking right now to listen! And you would be influenced by her--you could not help it, any more than you can help being distressed about what she has already said. She intimated to Dr. Perrin that she believed that I had been a man of depraved life, and that my wife and child were now paying the penalty. How can I tell what vile stories concerning me she may not have heard? How could I have any peace of mind while I knew that she was free to pour them into your ear?"

Sylvia sat dumb with questions she would not utter, hovering on the tip of her tongue.

He took her silence for acquiesence, and went on, quickly, "Let me give you an illustration. A friend of mine whom you know well--I might as well tell you his name, it was Freddie Atkins--was at supper with some theatrical women; and one of them, not having any idea that Freddie knew me, proceeded to talk about me, and how she had met me, and where we had been together--about my yacht, and my castle in Scotland, and I don't know what all else. It seems that this woman had been my mistress for several years; she told quite glibly about me and my habits. Freddie got the woman's picture, on some pretext or other, and brought it to me; I had never laid eyes on her in my life. He could hardly believe it, and to prove it to him I offered to meet the woman, under another name. We sat in a restaurant, and she told the tale to Freddie and myself together--until finally he burst out laughing, and told her who I was."

He paused, to let this sink in. "Now, suppose your friend, Mary Abbott, had met that woman! I don't imagine she is particularly careful whom she associates with; and suppose she had come and told you that she knew such a woman--what would you have said? Can you deny that the tale would have made an impression on you? Yet, I've not the least doubt there are scores of women who made such tales about me a part of their stock in trade; there are thousands of women whose fortunes would be made for life if they could cause such a tale to be believed. And imagine how well-informed they would be, if anyone were to ask them concerning my habits, and the reason why our baby is blind! I tell you, when the rumour concerning our child has begun to spread, there will be ten thousand people in New York city who will know of first-hand, personal knowledge exactly how it happened, and how you took it, and everything that I said to you about it. There will be sneers in the society-papers, from New York to San Francisco; and smooth-tongued gentlemen calling, to give us hints that we can stop these sneers by purchasing a de-luxe edition of a history of our ancestors for six thousand dollars. There will be well-meaning and beautiful-souled people who will try to get you to confide in them, and then use their knowledge of your domestic unhappiness to blackmail you; there will be threats of law-suits from people who will claim that they have contracted a disease from you or your child--your laundress, perhaps, or your maid, or one of these nurses----"

"Oh, stop! stop!" she cried.

"I am quite aware," he said, quietly, "that these things are not calculated to preserve the peace of mind of a young mother. You are horrified when I tell you of them--yet you clamour for the right to have Mrs. Abbott tell you of them! I warn you, Sylvia--you have married a rich man, who is exposed to the attacks of cunning and unscrupulous enemies. You, as his wife, are exactly as much exposed--possibly even more so. Therefore when I see you entering into what I know to be a danger-ous intimacy, I must have the right to say to you, This shall stop, and I tell you, there can never be any safety or peace of mind for either of us, so long as you at-tempt to deny me that right."

5. Dr. Gibson took his departure three or four days later; and before he went, he came to give her his final blessing; talking to her, as he phrased it, "like a Dutch uncle." "You must understand," he said, "I am almost old enough to be your grand-father. I have four sons, anyone of whom might have married you, if they had had the good fortune to be in Castleman County at the critical time. So you must let me be frank with you."

Sylvia indicated that she was willing.

"We don't generally talk to women about these matters; because they've no standard by which to judge, and they almost always fly off and have hysterics. Their case seems to them exceptional and horrible, their husbands the blackest criminals in the whole tribe."

He paused for a moment. "Now, Mrs. van Tuiver, the disease which has made your baby blind is probably what we call gonorrhea. When it gets into the eyes, it has very terrible results. But it doesn't often get into the eyes, and for the most part it's a trifling affair, that we don't worry about. I know there are a lot of new-fangled notions, but I'm an old man, with experience of my own, and I have to have things proven to me. I know that with as much of this disease as we doctors see, if it was a deadly disease, there'd be nobody left alive in the world. As I say, I don't like to

discuss it with women; but it was not I who forced the matter upon your atten-
tion----"

"Pray go on, Dr. Gibson," she said. "I really wish to know all that you will tell
me."

"The question has come up, how was this disease brought to your child? Dr.
Perrin suggested that possibly he--you understand his fear; and possibly he is correct. But it seems to me an illustration of the unwisdom of a physician's departing
from his proper duty, which is to cure people. If you wish to find out who brought
a disease, what you need is a detective. I know, of course, that there are people who
can combine the duties of physician and detective--and that without any previous
preparation or study of either profession."

He waited for this irony to sink in; and Sylvia also waited, patiently.

At last he resumed, "The idea has been planted in your mind that your husband
brought the trouble; and that idea is sure to stay there and fester. So it becomes
necessary for someone to talk to you straight. Let me tell you that eight men out of
ten have had this disease at some time in their lives; also that very few of them were
cured of it when they thought they were. You have a cold: and then next month,
you say the cold is gone. So it is, for practical purposes. But if I take a microscope,
I find the germs of the cold still in your membranes, and I know that you can give
a cold, and a bad cold, to some one else who is sensitive. It is true that you may go
through all the rest of your life without ever being entirely rid of that cold. You
understand me?"

"Yes," said Sylvia, in a low voice.

"I say eight out of ten. Estimates would differ. Some doctors would say seven
out of ten--and some actual investigations have shown nine out of ten. And understand me, I don't mean bar-room loafers and roustabouts. I mean your brothers, if
you have any, your cousins, your best friends, the men who came to make love to
you, and whom you thought of marrying. If you had found it out about any one
of them, of course you'd have cut the acquaintance; yet you'd have been doing an
injustice--for if you had done that to all who'd ever had the disease, you might as
well have retired to a nunnery at once."

The old gentleman paused again; then frowning at her under his bushy eye-
brows, he exclaimed, "I tell you, Mrs. van Tuiver, you're doing your husband a

wrong. Your husband loves you, and he's a good man--I've had some talks with him, and I know he's not got nearly so much on his conscience as the average husband. I'm a Southern man, and I know these gay young bloods you've danced and flirted with all your young life. Do you think if you went probing into their secret affairs, you'd have had much pleasure in their company afterwards? I tell you again, you're doing your husband a wrong! You're doing something that very few men would stand, as patiently as he has stood it so far."

All this time Sylvia had given no sign. So the old gentleman began to feel a trifle uneasy. "Mind you," he said, "I'm not saying that men ought to be like that. They deserve a good hiding, most of them--they're very few of them fit to associate with a good woman. I've always said that no man is really good enough for a good woman. But my point is that when you select one to punish, you select not the guiltiest one, but simply the one who's had the misfortune to fall under suspicion. And he knows that's not fair; he'd have to be more than human if deep in his soul he did not bitterly resent it. You understand me?"

"I understand," she replied, in the same repressed voice.

And the doctor rose and laid his hand on her shoulder. "I'm going home," he said--"very probably we'll never meet each other again. I see you making a great mistake, laying up unhappiness for yourself in the future; and I wish to prevent it if I can. I wish to persuade you to face the facts of the world in which we live. So I am going to tell you something that I never expected I should tell to a lady."

He was looking her straight in the eye. "You see me--I'm an old man, and I seem fairly respectable to you. You've laughed at me some, but even so, you've found it possible to get along with me without too great repugnance. Well, I've had this disease; I've had it, and nevertheless I've raised six fine, sturdy children. More than that-- I'm not free to name anybody else, but I happen to know positively that among the men your husband employs on this island there are two who have the disease right now. And the next charming and well-bred gentleman you are introduced to, just reflect that there are at least eight chances in ten that he has had the disease, and perhaps three or four in ten that he has it at the minute he's shaking hands with you. And now you think that over, and stop tormenting your poor husband!"

6. One of the first things I did when I reached New York was to send a little

love-letter to Sylvia. I said nothing that would distress her; I merely assured her that she was in my thoughts, and that I should look to see her in New York, when we could have a good talk. I put this in a plain envelope, with a typewritten address, and registered it in the name of my stenographer. The receipt came back, signed by an unknown hand, probably the secretary's. I found out later that the letter never got to Sylvia.

No doubt it was the occasion of renewed efforts upon her husband's part to obtain from her the promise he desired. He would not be put off with excuses; and at last he got her answer, in the shape of a letter which she told him she intended to mail to me. In this letter she announced her decision that she owed it to her baby to avoid all excitement and nervous strain during the time that she was nursing it. Her husband had sent for the yacht, and they were going to Scotland, and in the winter to the Mediterranean and the Nile. Meantime she would not correspond with me; but she wished me to know that there was to be no break in our friendship, and that she would see me upon her return to New York.

"There is much that has happened that I do not understand," she added. "For the present, however, I shall try to dismiss it from my mind. I am sure you will agree that it is right for me to give a year to being a mother; as I wish you to feel perfectly at peace in the meantime, I mention that it is my intention to be a mother only, and not a wife. I am showing this letter to my husband before I mail it, so that he may know exactly what I am doing, and what I have decided to do in the future."

"Of course," he said, after reading this, "you may send the letter, if you insist-- but you must realize that you are only putting off the issue."

She made no reply; and at last he asked, "You mean you intend to defy me in this matter?"

"I mean," she replied, quietly, "that for the sake of my baby I intend to put off all discussion for a year."

7. I figured that I should hear from Claire Lepage about two days after I reached New York; and sure enough, she called me on the 'phone. "I want to see you at once," she declared; and her voice showed the excitement under which she was labouring.

"Very well," I said, "come down."

She entered my little living-room. It was the first time she had ever visited me, but she did not stop for a glance about her; she did not even stop to sit down. "Why didn't you tell me that you knew Sylvia Castleman?" she cried.

"My dear woman," I replied, "I was not under the least obligation to tell you."

"You have betrayed me!" she exclaimed, wildly.

"Come, Claire," I said, after I had looked her in the eye a bit to calm her. "You know quite well that I was under no bond of secrecy. And, besides, I haven't done you any harm."

"Why did you do it?" I regret to add that she swore.

"I never once mentioned your name, Claire."

"How much good do you imagine that does me? They have managed to find out everything. They caught me in a trap."

I reminded myself that it would not do to show any pity for her. "Sit down, Claire," I said. "Tell me about it."

She cried, in a last burst of anger, "I don't want to talk to you!"

"All right," I answered. "But then, why did you come?"

There was no reply to that. She sat down. "They were too much for me!" she lamented. "If I'd had the least hint, I might have held my own. As it was--I let them make a fool of me."

"You are talking hieroglyphics to me. Who are 'they'?"

"Douglas, and that old fox, Rossiter Torrance."

"Rossiter Torrance?" I repeated the name, and then suddenly remembered. The thin-lipped old family lawyer!

"He sent up his card, and said he'd been sent to see me by Mary Abbot. Of course, I had no suspicion--I fell right into the trap. We talked about you for a while--he even got me to tell him where you lived; and then at last he told me that he hadn't come from you at all, but had merely wanted to find out if I knew you, and how intimate we were. He had been sent by Douglas; and he wanted to know right away how much I had told you about Douglas, and why I had done it. Of course, I denied that I had told anything. Heavens, what a time he gave me!"

Claire paused. "Mary, how could you have played such a trick upon me?"

"I had no thought of doing you any harm," I replied. "I was simply trying to help Sylvia."

"To help her at any expense!"

"Tell me, what will come of it? Are you afraid they'll cut off your allowance?"

"That's the threat."

"But will they carry it out?"

She sat, gazing at me resentfully. "I don't know whether I ought to trust you any more," she said.

"Do what you please about that," I replied. "I don't want to urge you."

She hesitated a bit longer, and then decided to throw herself upon my mercy. They would not dare to carry out their threat, so long as Sylvia had not found out the whole truth. So now she had come to beg me to tell no more than I had already told. She was utterly abject about it. I had pretended to be her friend, I had won her confidence and listened to her confessions; how did I wish to ruin her utterly, to have her cast out on the street?

Poor Claire! I said in the early part of my story that she understood the language of idealism; but I wonder what I have told about her that justifies this. The truth is, she was going down so fast that already she seemed a different person; and she had been frightened by the thin-lipped old family lawyer, so that she was incapable of even a decent pretence.

"Claire," I said, "there is no need for you to go on like this. I have not the slightest intention of telling Sylvia about you. I cannot imagine the circumstances that would make me want to tell her. Even if I should do it, I would tell her in confidence, so that her husband would never have any idea----"

She went almost wild at this. To imagine that a woman would keep such a confidence! As if she would not throw it at her husband's head the first time they quarreled! Besides, if Sylvia knew this truth, she might leave him; and if she left him, Claire's hold on his money would be gone.

Over this money we had a long and lachrymose interview. And at the end of it, there she sat gazing into space, baffled and bewildered. What kind of a woman was I? How had I got to be the friend of Sylvia van Tuiver? What had she seen in me, and what did I expect to get out of her? I answered briefly; and suddenly Claire was overwhelmed by a rush of curiosity--plain human curiosity. What was Sylvia like? Was she as clever as they said? What was the baby like, and how was Sylvia taking the misfortune? Could it really be true that I had been visiting the van Tuivers in Florida, as old Rossiter Torrance had implied?

Needless to say, I did not answer these questions freely. And I really think my visitor was more pained by my uncommunicativeness than she was by my betrayal of her. It was interesting also to notice a subtle difference in her treatment of me. Gone was the slight touch of condescension, gone was most of the familiarity! I had become a personage, a treasurer of high state secrets, an intimate of the great ones! There must be something more to me than Claire had realized before!

Poor Claire! She passes here from this story. For years thereafter I used to catch a glimpse of her now and then, in the haunts of the birds of gorgeous plumage; but I never got a chance to speak to her, nor did she ever call on me again. So I do not know if Douglas van Tuiver still continues her eight thousand a year. All I can say is that when I saw her, her plumage was as gorgeous as ever, and its style duly certified to the world that it had not been held over from a previous season of prosperity. Twice I thought she had been drinking too much; but then--so had many of the other ladies with the little glasses of bright-coloured liquids before them.

8. For the rest of that year I knew nothing about Sylvia except what I read in the "society" column of my newspaper--that she was spending the late summer in her husband's castle in Scotland. I myself was suffering from the strain of what I had been through, and had to take a vacation. I went West; and when I came back in the fall, to plunge again into my work, I read that the van Tuivers, in their yacht, the "Triton," were in the Mediterranean, and were planning to spend the winter in Japan.

And then one day in January, like a bolt from the blue, came a cablegram from Sylvia, dated Cairo: "Sailing for New York, Steamship 'Atlantic,' are you there, answer."

Of course I answered. And I consulted the sailing-lists, and waited, wild with impatience. She sent me a wireless, two days out, and so I was at the pier when the great vessel docked. Yes, there she was, waving her handkerchief to me; and there by her side stood her husband.

It was a long, cold ordeal, while the ship was warped in. We could only gaze at each other across the distance, and stamp our feet and beat our hands. There were other friends waiting for the van Tuivers, I saw, and so I held myself in the background, full of a thousand wild speculations. How incredible that Sylvia, arriving with her husband, should have summoned me to meet her!

At last the gangway was let down, and the stream of passengers began to flow. In time came the van Tuivers, and their friends gathered to welcome them. I waited; and at last Sylvia came to me--outwardly calm--but with her emotions in the pressure of her two hands. "Oh, Mary, Mary!" she murmured. "I'm so glad to see you! I'm so glad to see you!"

"What has happened?" I asked.

Her voice went to a whisper. "I am leaving my husband."

"Leaving your husband!" I stood, dumbfounded.

"Leaving him for ever, Mary."

"But--but----" I could not finish the sentence. My eyes moved to where he stood, calmly chatting with his friends.

"He insisted on coming back with me, to preserve appearances. He is terrified of the gossip. He is going all the way home, and then leave me."

"Sylvia! What does it mean?" I whispered.

"I can't tell you here. I want to come and see you. Are you living at the same place?"

I answered in the affirmative.

"It's a long story," she added. "I must apologise for asking you to come here, where we can't talk. But I did it for an important reason. I can't make my husband really believe that I mean what I say; and you are my Declaration of Independence!" And she laughed, but a trifle wildly, and looking at her suddenly, I realized that she was keyed almost to the breaking point.

"You poor dear!" I murmured.

"I wanted to show him that I meant what I said. I wanted him to see us meet. You see, he's going home, thinking that with the help of my people he can make me change my mind."

"But why do you go home? Why not stay here with me? There's an apartment vacant next to mine."

"And with a baby?"

"There are lots of babies in our tenement," I said. But to tell the truth, I had almost forgotten the baby in the excitement of the moment. "How is she," I asked.

"Come and see," said Sylvia; and when I glanced enquiringly at the tall gentleman who was chatting with his friends, she added, "She's *my* baby, and I have a right to show her."

The nurse, a rosy-cheeked English girl in a blue dress and a bonnet with long streamers, stood apart, holding an armful of white silk and lace. Sylvia turned back the coverings; and again I beheld the vision which had so thrilled me--the comical little miniature of herself--her nose, her lips, her golden hair. But oh, the pitiful little eyes, that did not move! I looked at my friend, uncertain what I should say; I was startled to see her whole being aglow with mother-pride. "Isn't she a dear?" she whispered. "And, Mary, she's learning so fast, and growing--you couldn't believe it!" Oh, the marvel of mother-love, I thought--that is blinder than any child it ever bore!

We turned away; and Sylvia said, "I'll come to you as soon as I've got the baby settled. Our train starts for the South to-night, so I shan't waste any time."

"God bless you, dear," I whispered; and she gave my hand a squeeze, and turned away. I stood for a few moments watching, and saw her approach her husband, and exchange a few smiling words with him in the presence of their friends. I, knowing the agony that was in the hearts of that desperate young couple, marvelled anew at the discipline of caste.

9. She sat in my big arm-chair; and how proud I was of her, and how thrilled by her courage. Above all, however, I was devoured by curiosity. "Tell me!" I exclaimed.

"There's so much," she said.

"Tell me why you are leaving him."

"Mary, because I don't love him. That's the one reason. I have thought it out--I have thought of little else for the last year. I have come to see that it is wrong for a woman to live with a man she does not love. It is the supreme crime a woman can commit."

"Ah, yes!" I said. "If you have got that far!"

"I have got that far. Other things have contributed, but they are not the real things--they might have been forgiven. The fact that he had this disease, and made my child blind----"

"Oh! You found out that?"

"Yes, I found it out."

"How?"

"It came to me little by little. In the end, he grew tired of pretending, I think."
She paused for a moment, then went on, "The trouble was over the question of my
obligations as a wife. You see, I had told him at the outset that I was going to live
for my baby, and for her alone. That was the ground upon which he had persuaded
me not to see you or read any of your letters. I was to ask no questions, and be nice
and bovine--and I agreed. But then, a few months ago, my husband came to me
with the story of his needs. He said that the doctors had given their sanction to our
reunion. Of course, I was stunned. I knew that he had understood me before we left
Florida."

She stopped. "Yes, dear," I said, gently.

"Well, he said now the doctors were agreed there was no danger to either of us.
We could take precautions and not have children. I could only plead that the whole
subject was distressing to me. He had asked me to put off my problems till my baby
was weaned; now I asked him to put off his. But that would not do, it seemed. He
took to arguing with me. It was an unnatural way to live, and he could not endure
it. I was a woman, and I couldn't understand this. It seemed utterly impossible to
make him realize what I felt. I suppose he has always had what he wanted, and
he simply does not know what it is to be denied. It wasn't only a physical thing, I
think; it was an affront to his pride, a denial of his authority." She stopped, and I
saw her shudder.

"I have been through it all," I said.

"He wanted to know how long I expected to withhold myself. I said, 'Until I
have got this disease out of my mind, as well as out of my body; until I know that
there is no possibility of either of us having it, to give to the other.' But then, after I
had taken a little more time to think it over, I said, 'Douglas, I must be honest with
you. I shall never be able to live with you again. It is no longer a question of your
wishes or mine--it is a question of right or wrong. I do not love you. I know now
that it can never under any circumstances be right for a woman to give herself in
the intimacy of the sex-relation without love. When she does it, she is violating the
deepest instinct of her nature, the very voice of God in her soul.'

"His reply was, 'Why didn't you know that before you married?'

"I answered, 'I did not know what marriage meant; and I let myself be persuaded by others.'

"'By your own mother!' he declared.

"I said, 'A mother who permits her daughter to commit such an offence is either a slave-dealer, or else a slave.' Of course, he thought I was out of my mind at that. He argued about the duties of marriage, the preserving of the home, wives submitting themselves to their husbands, and so on. He would not give me any peace----"

And suddenly she started up. I saw in her eyes the light of old battles. "Oh, it was a horror!" she cried, beginning to pace the floor. "It seemed to me that I was living the agony of all the loveless marriages of the world. I felt myself pursued, not merely by the importunate desires of one man--I suffered with all the millions of women who give themselves night after night without love! He came to seem like some monster to me; I could not meet him unexpectedly without starting. I forbade him to mention the subject to me again, and for a long time he obeyed. But several weeks ago he brought it up afresh, and I lost my self-control completely. 'Douglas,' I said, 'I can stand it no longer! It is not only the tragedy of my blind child--it's that you have driven me to hate you. You have crushed all the life and joy and youth out of me! You've been to me like a terrible black cloud, constantly pressing down on me, smothering me. You stalk around me like a grim, sepulchral figure, closing me up in the circle of your narrow ideas. But now I can endure it no longer. I was a proud, high-spirited girl, you've made of me a colourless social automaton, a slave of your stupid worldly traditions. I'm turning into a feeble, complaining, discontented wife! And I refuse to be it. I'm going home--where at least there's some human spontaneity left in people; I'm going back to my father!'--And I went and looked up the next steamer!"

She stopped. She stood before me, with the fire of her wild Southern blood shining in her cheeks and in her eyes.

I sat waiting, and finally she went on, "I won't repeat all his protests. When he found that I was really going, he offered to take me in the yacht, but I wouldn't go in the yacht. I had got to be really afraid of him--sometimes, you know, his obstinacy seems to be abnormal, almost insane. So then he decided he would have to go in the steamer with me to preserve appearances. I had a letter saying that papa was not well, and he said that would serve for an excuse. He is going to Castleman County, and after he has stayed a week or so, he is going off on a hunting-trip, and not return."

"And will he do it?"

"I don't think he expects to do it at present. I feel sure he has the idea of start-ing mamma to quoting the Bible to me, and dragging me down with her tears. But I have done all I can to make clear to him that it will make no difference. I told him I would not say a word about my intentions at home until he had gone away, and that I expected the same silence from him. But, of course--" She stopped abruptly, and after a moment she asked: "What do you think of it, Mary?"

I leaned forward and took her two hands in mine. "Only," I said, "that I'm glad you fought it out alone! I knew it had to come--and I didn't want to have to help you to decide!"

10. She sat for a while absorbed in her own thoughts. Knowing her as I did, I understood what intense emotions were seething within her, what a terrific strug-gle her decision must have represented.

"Dear Friend," she said, suddenly, "don't think I haven't seen his side of the case. I try to tell myself that I dealt with him frankly from the beginning. But then I ask was there ever a man I dealt with frankly? There was coquetry in the very clothes I wore! And now that we are so entangled, now that he loves me, what is my duty? I find I can't respect his love for me. A part of it is because my beauty fas-cinates him, but more of it seems to me just wounded vanity. I was the only woman who ever flouted him, and he has a kind of snobbery that made him think I must be something remarkable because of it. I talked that all out with him--yes, I've dragged him through all that humiliation. I wanted to make him see that he didn't really love me, that he only wanted to conquer me, to force me to admire him and submit to him. I want to be myself, and he wants to be himself--that has always been the issue between us."

"That is the issue in many unhappy marriages," I said.

"I've done a lot of thinking in the last year," she resumed--"about things gen-erally, I mean. We American women think we are so free. That is because our husbands indulge us, give us money, and let us run about. But when it comes to real freedom--freedom of intellect and of character, English women are simply an-other kind of being from us. I met a cabinet minister's wife--he's a Conservative in everything, and she's an ardent suffragist; she not merely gives money, she makes speeches and has a public name. Yet they are friends, and have a happy home-life. Do you suppose my husband would consider such an arrangement?"

"I thought he admired English ways," I said.

"There was the Honorable Betty Annersley--the sister of a chum of his. She was friendly with the militants, and I wanted to talk to her to understand what such women thought. Yet my husband tried to stop me from going to see her. And it's the same way with everything I try to do, that threatens to take me out of his power. He wanted me to accept the authority of the doctors as to any possible danger from venereal disease. When I got the books, and showed him what the doctors admitted about the question--the narrow margin of safety they allowed, the terrible chances they took--he was angry again."

She stopped, seeing a question in my eyes. "I've been reading up on the subject," she explained. "I know it all now--the things I should have known before I married."

"How did you manage that?"

"I tried to get two of the doctors to give me something to read, but they wouldn't hear of it. I'd set myself crazy imagining things, it was no sort of stuff for a woman's mind. So in the end I took the bit in my teeth. I found a medical book store, and I went in and said: 'I am an American physician, and I want to see the latest works on venereal disease.' So the clerk took me to the shelves, and I picked out a couple of volumes."

"You poor child!" I exclaimed.

"When Douglas found that I was reading these books he threatened to burn them. I told him 'There are more copies in the store, and I am determined to be educated on this subject.'"

She paused. "How much like my own experience!" I thought.

"There were chapters on the subject of wives, how much they were not told, and why this was. So very quickly I began to see around my own experience. Douglas must have figured out that this would be so, for the end of the matter was an admission."

"You don't mean he confessed to you!"

She smiled bitterly. "No," she said. "He brought Dr. Perrin to London to do it for him. Dr. Perrin said he had concluded I had best know that my husband had had some symptoms of the disease. He, the doctor, wished to tell me who was to blame for the attempt to deceive me. Douglas had been willing to admit the truth, but all the doctors had forbidden it. I must realise the fearful problem they had, and not blame them, and, above all I must not blame my husband, who had been in their hands in the matter."

"How stupid men are! As if that would excuse him!"

"I'm afraid I showed the little man how poor an impression he had made--both for himself and for his patron. But I had suffered all there was to suffer, and I was tired of pretending. I told him it would have been far better for them if they had told me the truth at the beginning."

"Ah, yes!" I said. "That is what I tried to make them see; but all I got for it was a sentence of deportation!"

11. When Sylvia's train arrived at the station of her home town, the whole family was waiting upon the platform for her, and a good part of the town besides. The news that she had arrived in New York, and was coming home on account of her father's illness, had, of course, been reproduced in all the local papers, with the result that the worthy major had been deluged with telegrams and letters concerning his health. Notwithstanding, he had insisted upon coming to the train to meet his daughter. He was not going to be shut up in a sickroom to please all the gossips of two hemispheres. In his best black broad-cloth, his broad, black hat newly brushed, and his old-fashioned, square-toed shoes newly shined, he paced up and down the station platform for half an hour, and it was to his arms that Sylvia flew when she alighted from the train.

There was "Miss Margaret," who had squeezed her large person and fluttering draperies out of the family automobile, and was waiting to shed tears over her favourite daughter; there was Celeste, radiant with a wonderful piece of news which she alone was to impart to her sister; there were Peggy and Maria, shot up suddenly into two amazingly-gawky girls; there was Master Castleman Lysle, the only son of the house, with his black-eyed and bad-tempered French governess. And finally there was Aunt Varina, palpitating with various agitations, not daring to whisper to anyone else the fears which this sudden home-coming inspired in her. Bishop Chilton and his wife were away, but a delegation of cousins had come; also Uncle Mandeville Castleman had sent a huge bunch of roses, which were in the family automobile, and Uncle Barry Chilton had sent a pair of wild turkeys, which were soon to be in the family.

Behind Sylvia stalked her cold and haughty husband, and behind him tripped the wonderful nursemaid, with her wonderful blue streamers, and her wonderful bundle of ruffles and lace. All the huge family had to fall upon Sylvia and kiss and embrace her rapturously, and shake the hand of the cold and haughty husband, and peer into the wonderful bundle, and go into ecstasies over its contents. Rarely, indeed, did the great ones of this earth condescend to spread so much of their emotional life before the public gaze; and was it any wonder that the town crowded about, and the proprieties were temporarily repealed?

It had never been published, but it was generally known throughout the State that Sylvia's child was blind, and it was whispered that this portended something strange and awful. So there hung about the young mother and the precious bundle an atmosphere of mystery and melancholy. How had she taken her misfortune? How had she taken all the great events that had befallen her--her progress through the courts and camps of Europe? Would she still condescend to know her fellow-townsmen? Many were the hearts that beat high as she bestowed her largess of smiles and friendly words. There were even humble old negroes who went off enraptured to tell the town that "Mi' Sylvia" had actually shaken hands with them. There was almost a cheer from the crowd as the string of automobiles set out for Castleman Hall.

12. There was a grand banquet that evening, at which the turkeys entered the family. Not in years had there been so many people crowded into the big dining-room, nor so many servants treading upon each other's toes in the kitchen.

Such a din of chatter and laughter! Sylvia was her old radiant self, and her husband was quite evidently charmed by the patriarchal scene. He was affable, really genial, and won the hearts of everybody; he told the good major, amid a hush which almost turned his words into a speech, that he was able to understand how they of the South loved their own section so passionately; there was about the life an intangible something--a spell, an elevation of spirit, which set it quite apart by itself. And since this was the thing which they of the South most delighted to believe concerning themselves, they listened enraptured, and set the speaker apart as a rare and discerning spirit.

Afterwards came the voice of Sylvia: "You must beware of Douglas, Papa; he is an inveterate flatterer." She laughed as she said it; and of those present it was Aunt Varina alone who caught the ominous note, and saw the bitter curl of her lips as she spoke. Aunt Varina and her niece were the only persons there who knew Douglas van Tuiver well enough to appreciate the irony of the term "inveterate flatterer."

Sylvia realized at once that her husband was setting out upon a campaign to win her family to his side. He rode about the major's plantations, absorbing information about the bollweevil. He rode back to the house, and exchanged cigars, and listened to stories of the major's boyhood during the war. He went to call upon Bishop Chilton, and sat in his study, with its walls of faded black volumes on theology. Van Tuiver himself had had a Church of England tutor, and was a punctilious high churchman; but he listened respectfully to arguments for a simpler form of church organization, and took away a voluminous exposé of the fallacies of "Apostolic Succession." And then came Aunt Nannie, ambitious and alert as when she had helped the young millionaire to find a wife; and the young millionaire made the suggestion that Aunt Nannie's third daughter should not fail to visit Sylvia at Newport.

There was no limit, apparently, to what he would do. He took Master Castleman Lysle upon his knee, and let him drop a valuable watch upon the floor. He got up early in the morning and went horse-back riding with Peggy and Maria. He took Celeste automobiling, and helped by his attentions to impress the cocksure young man with whom Celeste was in love. He won "Miss Margaret" by these attentions to all her children, and the patience with which he listened to accounts of the ailments which had afflicted the precious ones at various periods of their lives. To Sylvia, watching all these proceedings, it was as if he were binding himself to her with so many knots.

She had come home with a longing to be quiet, to avoid seeing anyone. But this could not be, she discovered. There was gossip about the child's blindness, and the significance thereof; and to have gone into hiding would have meant an admission of the worst. The ladies of the family had prepared a grand "reception," at which all Castleman County was to come and gaze upon the happy mother. And then there was the monthly dance at the Country Club, where everybody would come, in the hope of seeing the royal pair. To Sylvia it was as if her mother and aunts were behind her every minute of the day, pushing her out into the world. "Go on, go on! Show yourself! Do not let people begin to talk!"

13. She bore it for a couple of weeks; then she went to her cousin, Harley Chilton. "Harley," she said, "my husband is anxious to go on a hunting-trip. Will you go with him?"

"When?" asked the boy.

"Right away; to-morrow or the next day."

"I'm game," said Harley.

After which she went to her husband. "Douglas, it is time for you to go."

He sat studying her face. "You still have that idea?" he said, at last.

"I still have it."

"I was hoping that here, among your home-people, your sanity would partially return."

"I know what you have been hoping, Douglas. And I am sorry--but I am quite unchanged."

"Have we not been getting along happily here?" he demanded.

"No, I have not--I have been wretched. And I cannot have any peace until you no longer haunt me. I am sorry for you, but I must be alone--and so long as you are here the entertainments will continue."

"We could make it clear that we did not care for entertainments. We could find some quiet place near your people, where we could live in peace."

"Douglas," she said, "I have spoken to Cousin Harley. He is ready to go hunting with you. Please call him up and make arrangements to start to-morrow. If you are still here the following day, I shall leave for one of Uncle Mandeville's plantations."

There was a long silence. "Sylvia," he said, at last, "how long do you imagine this behaviour of yours can continue?"

"It will continue forever. My mind is made up. It is necessary that you make up yours."

Again he waited, while he made sure of his self-control. "You propose to keep the baby with you?" he asked, at last.

"For the present, yes. The baby cannot get along without me."

"And for the future?"

"We will make a fair arrangement as to that. Give me a little time to get myself together, and then I will come and live somewhere near you in New York, and I will arrange it so that you can see the child as often as you please. I have no desire to take her from you--I only want to take myself from you."

"Sylvia," he said, "have you realized all the unhappiness this course of yours is going to bring to your people?"

"Oh, don't begin that now!" she pleaded.

"I know," he said, "how determined you are to punish me. But I should think you would try to find some way to spare them."

"Douglas," she replied, "I know exactly what you have been doing. I have watched your change of character since you came here. You may be able to make my people so unhappy that I must be unhappy also. You see how deeply I love them, how I yield everything for love of them. But let me make it clear, I will not yield this. It was for their sake I went into this marriage, but I have come to see that it was wrong, and no power on earth can induce me to stay in it. My mind is made up--I will not live with a man I do not love. I will not even pretend to do it. Now do you understand me, Douglas?"

There was a silence, while she waited for some word from him. When none came, she asked, "You will arrange to go to-morrow?"

He answered calmly, "I see no reason why I, your husband, should permit you to pursue this insane course. You propose to leave me; and the reason you give is one that would, if it were valid, break up two-thirds of the homes in the country. Your own family will stand by me in my effort to prevent your ruin."

"What do you expect to do?" she asked in a suppressed voice.

"I have to assume that my wife is insane; and I shall look after her till she comes to her senses."

She sat watching him for a few moments, wondering at him. Then she said, "You are willing to stay on here, day after day, pursuing me in the only refuge I have. Well then, I shall not consider your feelings. I have a work to do here--and I think that when I begin it, you will want to be far away."

"What do you mean?" he asked--and he looked at her as if she were really a maniac.

"You see my sister Celeste is about to marry. That was the wonderful news she had to tell me at the depot. It happens that I have known Roger Peyton all my life, and know he has the reputation of being one of the 'fastest' boys in the town."

"Well?" he asked.

"Just this, Douglas--I do not intend to leave my sister unprotected as I was. I am going to tell her about Elaine. I am going to tell her all that she needs to know. It is bound to mean arguments with the old people, and in the end the whole family will be discussing the subject. I feel sure you will not care to be here under such circumstances."

"And may I ask when this begins?" he inquired, with intense bitterness in his tone.

"Right away," she said. "I have merely been waiting until you should go."

He said not a word, but she knew by the expression on his face that she had carried her point at last. He turned and left the room; and that was the last word she had with him, save for their formal parting in the presence of the family.

14. Roger Peyton was the son and heir of one of the oldest families in Castleman County. I had heard of this family before--in a wonderful story that Sylvia told of the burning of "Rose Briar," their stately mansion, some years previously: how the neighbours had turned out to extinguish the flames, and failing, had danced a last whirl in the ball-room, while the fire roared in the stories overhead. The house had since been rebuilt, more splendid than ever, and the prestige of the family stood undiminished. One of the sons was an old "flame" of Sylvia's, and another was married to one of the Chilton girls. As for Celeste, she had been angling for Roger the past year or two, and she stood now at the apex of happiness.

Sylvia went to her father, to talk with him about the difficult subject of venereal disease. The poor major had never expected to live to hear such a discourse from a daughter of his; however, with the blind child under his roof, he could not find words to stop her. "But, Sylvia," he protested, "what reason have you to suspect such a thing of Roger Peyton?"

"I have the reason of his life. You know that he has the reputation of being 'fast'; you know that he drinks, you know that I once refused to speak to him because he danced with me when he was drunk."

"My child, all the men you know have sowed their wild oats."

"Papa, you must not take advantage of me in such a discussion. I don't claim to know what sins may be included in the phrase 'wild oats.' Let us speak frankly--can you say that you think it unlikely that Roger Peyton has been unchaste?"

The major hesitated and coughed; finally he said: "The boy drinks, Sylvia; further than that I have no knowledge."

"The medical books tell me that the use of alcohol tends to break down self-control, and to make continence impossible. And if that be true, you must admit that we have a right to ask assurances. What do you suppose that Roger and his crowd are doing when they go roistering about the streets at night? What do they do when they go off to Mardi Gras? Or at college--you know that Cousin Clive had to get him out of trouble several times. Go and ask Clive if Roger has ever been exposed to the possibility of these diseases."

"My child," said the major, "Clive would not feel he had the right to tell me such things about his friend."

"Not even when the friend wants to marry his cousin?"

"But such questions are not asked, my daughter."

"Papa, I have thought this matter out carefully, and I hava something definite to propose to you. I have no idea of stopping with what Clive Chilton may or may not see fit to tell about his chum. I want *you* to go to Roger."

Major Castleman's face wore a blank stare.

"If he's going to marry your daughter, you have the right to ask about his past. What I want you to tell him is that you will get the name of a reputable specialist in these diseases, and that before he can have your daughter he must present you with a letter from this man, to the effect that he is fit to marry."

The poor major was all but speechless. "My child, who ever heard of such a proposition?"

"I don't know that any one ever did, papa. But it seems to me time they should begin to hear of it; and I don't see who can have a better right to take the first step than you and I, who have paid such a dreadful price for our neglect."

Sylvia had been prepared for opposition--the instinctive opposition which men manifest to having this embarrassing subject dragged out into the light of day. Even men who have been chaste themselves--good fathers of families like the major--cannot be unaware of the complications incidental to frightening their women-folk, and setting up an impossibly high standard in sons-in-law. But Sylvia stood by her guns; at last she brought her father to his knees by the threat that if he could not bring himself to talk with Roger Peyton, she, Sylvia Castleman, would do it.

15. The young suitor came by appointment the next day, and had a session with the Major in his office. After he had gone, Sylvia went to her father and found him pacing the floor, with an extinct cigar between his lips, and several other ruined cigars lying on the hearth.

"You asked him, papa?"

"I did, Sylvia."

"And what did he say?"

"Why, daughter----" The major flung his cigar from him with desperate energy. "It was most embarrassing!" he exclaimed--"most painful!" His pale old face was crimson with blushes.

"Go on, papa," said Sylvia, gentle but firm.

"The poor boy--naturally, Sylvia, he could not but feel hurt that I should think it necessary to ask such questions. Such things are not done, my child. It seemed to him that I must look upon him as--well, as much worse than other young fellows----"

The old man stopped, and began to walk restlessly up and down. "Yes, papa," said Sylvia. "What else?"

"Well, he said it seemed to him that such a matter might have been left to the honour of a man whom I was willing to think of as a son-in-law. And you see, my child, what an embarrassing position I was in; I could not give him any hint as to my reason for being anxious about these matters--anything, you understand, that might be to the discredit of your husband."

"Go on, papa."

"Well, I gave him a fatherly talking to about his way of life."

"Did you ask him the definite question as to his health?"

"No, Sylvia."

"Did he tell you anything definite?"

"No."

"Then you didn't do what you had set out to do!"

"Yes, I did. I told him that he must see a doctor."

"You made quite clear to him what you wanted?"

"Yes, I did--really, I did."

"And what did he say?" She went to him and took his arm and led him to a couch. "Come, papa, let us get to the facts. You must tell me." They sat down, and the major sighed, lit a fresh cigar, rolled it about in his fingers until it was ruined, and then flung it away.

"Boys don't talk freely to older men," he said. "They really never do. You may doubt this----"

"What did he *say,* papa?"

"Why, he didn't know what to say. He didn't really say anything." And here the major came to a complete halt.

His daughter, after studying his face for a minute, remarked, "In plain words, papa, you think he has something to hide, and he may not be able to give you the evidence you asked?"

The other was silent.

"You fear that is the situation, but you are trying not to believe it." As he still said nothing, Sylvia whispered, "Poor Celeste!"

Suddenly she put her hands upon his shoulders, and looked into his eye. "Papa, can't you see what that means--that Celeste ought to have been told these things long ago?"

"What good would that have done?" he asked, in bewilderment.

"She could have known what kind of man she was choosing; and she might be spared the dreadful unhappiness that is before her now."

"Sylvia! Sylvia!" protested the other. "Surely such things cannot be discussed with innocent young girls!"

"So long as we refuse to do it, we are simply entering into a conspiracy with the man of loose life, so that he may escape the worst penalty of his evil-doing. Take the boys in our own set--why is it they feel safe in running off to the big cities and 'sowing their wild oats'--even sowing them in the obscure parts of their own town? Is it not because they know that their sisters and girl friends are ignorant and help-less; so that when they are ready to pick a wife, they will be at no disadvantage? Here is Celeste; she knows that Roger has been 'wild,' but no one has hinted to her what that means; she thinks of things that are picturesque--that he's high-spirited, and brave, and free with his money."

"But, my daughter," protested the major, "such knowledge would have a terrible effect upon young girls!" He rose and began to pace the floor again. "Daughter, you are letting yourself run wild! The sweetness, the virginal innocence of young and pure women--if you take that from them, there'd be nothing left to keep men from falling to the level of brutes!"

"Papa," said Sylvia, "all that sounds well, but it has no meaning. I have been robbed of my 'innocence,' and I know that it has not debased me. It has only fitted me to deal with the realities of life. And it will do the same for any girl who is taught by earnest and reverent people. Now, as it is, we have to tell Celeste, but we tell her too late."

"But we *won't* have to tell her!" cried the major.

"Dear papa, please explain how we can avoid telling her."

"I will inform her that she must give the young man up. She is a good and dutiful daughter----"

"Yes," replied Sylvia, "but suppose on this one occasion she were to fail to be good and dutiful? Suppose the next day you learn that she had run away and married Roger--what would you do about it then?"

16. That evening Roger was to take his fiancée to one of the young people's dances. And there was Celeste, in a flaming red dress, with a great bunch of flaming roses; she could wear these colours, with her brilliant black hair and gorgeous complexion. Roger was fair, with a frank, boyish face, and they made a pretty couple; but that evening Roger did not come. Sylvia helped to dress her sister, and then watched her wandering restlessly about the hall, while the hour came and went. Later in the evening Major Castleman called up the Peyton home. The boy was not there, and no one seemed to know where he was.

Nor the next day did there come any explanation. At the Peytons it was still declared that no one had heard from Roger, and for another day the mystery continued, to Celeste's distress and mortification. At last, from Clive Chilton, Sylvia managed to extract the truth. Roger was drunk--crazy drunk, and had been taken off by some of the boys to be straightened out.

Of course this rumour soon got to the rest of the family and they had to tell Celeste, because she was frantic with anxiety. There were grave consultations among the Castleman ladies. It was a wanton affront to his fiancée that the boy had committed, and something must be done about it quickly. Then came the news that Roger had escaped from his warders, and got drunker than ever; he had been out at night, smashing the street lamps, and it had required extreme self-control on the part of the town police force to avoid complications.

"Miss Margaret" went to her young daughter, and in a tear-flooded scene informed her of the opinion of the family, that her self-respect required the breaking of the engagement. Celeste went into hysterics. She would *not* have her happiness ruined for life! Roger was "wild," but so were all the other boys--and he would atone for his recklessness. She had the idea that if only she could get hold of him, she could recall him to his senses; the more her mother was scandalised by this proposal, the more frantically Celeste wept. She shut herself up in her room, refusing to appear at meals, and spending her time pacing the floor and wringing her hands.

The family had been through all this with their eldest daughter several years before, but they had not learned to handle it any better. The whole household was in a state of distraction, and the conditions grew worse day by day, as bulletins came in concerning the young man. He seemed to have gone actually insane. He was not to be restrained even by his own father, and if the unfortunate policemen could be believed, he had violently attacked them. Apparently he was trying to break down the unwritten law that the sons of the "best families" are not arrested.

Poor Celeste, with pale, tear-drenched face, sent for her elder sister, to make one last appeal. Could Sylvia not somehow get hold of Roger and bring him to his senses? Could she not interview some of the other boys, and find out what he meant by his conduct?

So Sylvia went to her cousin Clive, and had a talk with him--assuredly the most remarkable talk that that young man had ever had in his life. She told him that she wanted to know the truth about Roger Peyton, and after a cross-examination that would have made the reputation of a criminal lawyer, she got what she wanted. All the young men in town, it seemed, knew the true state of affairs, and were in a panic concerning it; that Major Castleman had sent for Roger and informed him that he could not marry his daughter, until he produced a certain kind of medical certificate. No, he couldn't produce it! Was there a fellow in town who could produce it? What was there for him to do but to get drunk and stay drunk, until Celeste had cast him off?

It was Clive's turn then to do some plain speaking. "Look here, Sylvia," he said, "since you have made me talk about this----"

"Yes, Clive?"

"Do you know what people are saying--I mean the reason the Major made this proposition to Roger?"

She answered, in a quiet voice: "I suppose, Clive, it has something to do with Elaine."

"Yes, exactly!" exclaimed Clive. "They say--" But then he stopped. He could not repeat it. "Surely you don't want that kind of talk, Sylvia?"

"Naturally, Clive, I'd prefer to escape that kind of talk, but my fear of it will not make me neglect the protection of my sister."

"But Sylvia," cried the boy, "you don't understand about this! A woman *can't* understand about these things----"

"You are mistaken, my dear cousin," said Sylvia--and her voice was firm and decisive. "I *do* understand."

"All right!" cried Clive, with sudden exasperation. "But let me tell you this--Celeste is going to have a hard time getting any other man to propose to her!"

"You mean, Clive, because so many of them are----?"

"Yes, if you must put it that way," he said.

There was a pause, then Sylvia went on: "Let us discuss the practical problem, Clive. Don't you think it would have been better if Roger, instead of going off and getting drunk, had set about getting himself cured?"

The other looked at her, with evident surprise. "You mean in that case Celeste might marry him?"

"You say the boys are all alike, Clive; and we can't turn our girls into nuns. Why didn't some of you fellows point that out to Roger?"

"The truth is," said Clive, "we tried to." There was a little more cordiality in his manner, since Sylvia had shown such a unexpected amount of intelligence.

"Well?" she asked. "What then?"

"Why, he wouldn't listen to anything."

"You mean--because he was drunk?"

"No, we had him nearly sober. But you see--" And Clive paused for a moment, painfully embarrassed. "The truth is, Roger had been to a doctor, and been told it might take him a year or two to get cured."

"Clive!" she cried. "Clive! And you mean that in the face of that, he proposed to go on and marry?"

"Well, Sylvia, you see--" And the young man hesitated still longer. He was crimson with embarrassment, and suddenly he blurted out: "The truth is, the doctor told him to marry. That was the only way he'd ever get cured."

Sylvia was almost speechless. "Oh! Oh!" she cried, "I can't believe you!"

"That's what the doctors tell you, Sylvia. You don't understand--it's just as I told you, a woman can't understand. It's a question of a man's nature----"

"But Clive--what about the wife and her health? Has the wife no rights whatever?"

"The truth is, Sylvia, people don't take this disease with such desperate seriousness. You understand, it isn't the one that everybody knows is dangerous. It doesn't do any real harm----"

"Look at Elaine! Don't you call that real harm?"

"Yes, but that doesn't happen often, and they say there are ways it can be prevented. Anyway, fellows just can't help it! God knows we'd help it if we could."

Sylvia thought for a moment, and then came back to the immediate question. "It's evident what Roger could do in this case. He is young, and Celeste is still younger. They might wait a couple of years and Roger might take care of himself, and in time it might be properly arranged."

But Clive did not seem too warm to the proposition, and Sylvia, who knew Roger Peyton, was not long in making out the reason. "You mean you don't think he has character enough to keep straight for a year or two?"

"To tell you the honest truth, we talked it out with him, and he wouldn't make any promises."

To which Sylvia answered: "Very well, Clive--that settles it. You can help me find some man for Celeste who loves her a little more than that!"

17. That afternoon came Aunt Nannie, the Bishop's wife, in shining chestnut-coloured silk to match a pair of shining chestnut-coloured horses. Other people, it appeared, had been making inquiries into Roger Peyton's story, and other people besides Clive Chilton had been telling the truth. Aunt Nannie gathered the ladies of the family in a hurried conference, and Sylvia was summoned to appear before

it--quite as in the days of her affair with Frank Shirley.

"Miss Margaret" and Aunt Varina were solemn and frightened, as of old; and, as of old, Aunt Nannie did the talking. "Sylvia, do you know what people are saying about you?"

"Yes, Aunt Nannie" said Sylvia.

"Oh, you do know?"

"Yes, of course. And I knew in advance that they would say it."

Something about the seraphic face of Sylvia, chastened by terrible suffering, must have suggested to Mrs. Chilton the idea of caution. "Have you thought of the humiliation this must inflict upon your relatives?"

"I have found, Aunt Nannie," said Sylvia, "that there are worse afflictions than being talked about."

"I am not sure," declared the other, "that anything could be worse than to be the object of the kind of gossip that is now seething around our family. It has been the tradition of our people to bear their afflictions in silence."

"In this case, Aunt Nannie, it is obvious that silence would have meant more afflictions, many more. I have thought of my sister--and of all the other girls in our family, who may be led to sacrifice by the ambitions of their relatives." Sylvia paused a moment, so that her words might have effect.

Said the bishop's wife: "Sylvia, we cannot undertake to save the world from the results of its sins. God has his own ways of punishing men."

"Perhaps so, but surely God does not wish the punishment to fall upon innocent young girls. For instance, Aunt Nannie, think of your own daughters----"

"My daughters!" broke out Mrs. Chilton. And then, mastering her excitement: "At least, you will permit me to look after my own children."

"I noticed, my dear aunt, that Lucy May turned colour when Tom Aldrich came into the room last night. Have you noticed anything?"

"Yes--what of it?"

"It means that Lucy May is falling in love with Tom."

"Why should she not? I certainly consider him an eligible man."

"And yet you know, Aunt Nannie, that he is one of Roger Peyton's set. You know that he goes about town getting drunk with the gayest of them, and you let Lucy May go on and fall in love with him! You have taken no steps to find out about him--you have not warned your daughter--"

Mrs. Chilton was crimson with agitation. "Warned my daughter! Who ever heard of such a thing?"

Said Sylvia, quietly: "I can believe that you never heard of it--but you will hear soon. The other day I had a talk with Lucy May--"

"Sylvia Castleman!" And then it seemed Mrs. Chilton reminded herself that she was dealing with a dangerous lunatic. "Sylvia," she said, in a suppressed voice, "you mean to tell me that you have been poisoning my young daughter's mind--"

"You have brought her up well," said Sylvia, as her aunt stopped for lack of words. "She did not want to listen to me. She said that young girls ought not to know about such matters. But I pointed out Elaine, and then she changed her mind--just as you will have to change yours in the end, Aunt Nannie."

Mrs. Chilton sat glaring at her niece, her bosom heaving. Then suddenly she turned her indignant eyes upon Mrs. Castleman. "Margaret, cannot you stop this shocking business? I demand that the tongues of gossip shall no longer clatter around the family of which I am a member! My husband is the bishop of this diocese, and if our ancient and untarnished name is of no importance to Sylvia van Tuiver, then, perhaps the dignity and authority of the church may have some weight----"

"Aunt Nannie," interrupted Sylvia, "it will do no good to drag Uncle Basil into this matter. I fear you will have to face the fact that from this time on your authority in our family is to be diminished. You had more to do than any other person with driving me into the marriage that has wrecked my life, and now you want to go on and do the same thing for my sister and for your own daughters--to marry them with no thought of anything save the social position of the man. And in the same way you are saving up your sons to find rich girls. You know that you kept Clive from marrying a poor girl in this town a couple of years ago--and meantime it seems to be nothing to you that he's going with men like Roger Peyton and Tom Aldrich, learning all the vices the women in the brothels have to teach him----"

Poor "Miss Margaret" had several times made futile efforts to check her daughter's outburst. Now she and Aunt Varina started up at the same time. "Sylvia! Sylvia! You must not talk like that to your aunt!"

And Sylvia turned and gazed at them with her sad eyes. "From now on," she said, "that is the way I am going to talk. You are a lot of ignorant children. I was one too, but now I know. And I say to you: Look at Elaine! Look at my little one, and see what the worship of Mammon has done to one of the daughters of your family!"

18. After this, Sylvia had her people reduced to a state of terror. She was an avenging angel, sent by the Lord to punish them for their sins. How could one rebuke the unconventionality of an avenging angel? On the other hand, of course, one could not help being in agony, and letting the angel see it in one's face. Outside, there were the tongues of gossip clattering, as Aunt Nannie had said; quite literally everyone in Castleman County was talking about the blindness of Mrs. Douglas van Tuiver's baby, and how, because of it, the mother was setting out on a campaign to destroy the modesty of the State. The excitement, the curiosity, the obscene delight of the world came rolling back into Castleman Hall in great waves, that picked up the unfortunate inmates and buffeted them about.

Family consultations were restricted, because it was impossible for the ladies of the family to talk to the gentlemen about these horrible things; but the ladies talked to the ladies, and the gentlemen talked to the gentlemen, and each came separately to Sylvia with their distress. Poor, helpless "Miss Margaret" would come wringing her hands, and looking as if she had buried all her children. "Sylvia! Sylvia! Do you realise that you are being DISCUSSED?" That was the worst calamity that could befal a woman in Castleman County--it summed up all possible calamities that could befal her--to be "discussed." "They were discussing you once when you wanted to marry Frank Shirley! And now--oh, now they will never stop discussing you!"

Then would come the dear major. He loved his eldest daughter as he loved nothing else in the world, and he was a just man at heart. He could not meet her arguments--yes, she was right, she was right. But then he would go away, and the waves of scandal and shame would come rolling.

"My child," he pleaded, "have you thought what this thing is doing to your husband? Do you realise that while you talk about protecting other people, you are putting upon Douglas a brand that will follow him through life?"

Uncle Mandeville came up from New Orleans to see his favourite niece; and the wave smote him as he alighted from the train, and he became so much excited that he went to the club and got drunk, and then could not see his niece, but had to be carried off upstairs and given forcible hypodermics. Cousin Clive told Sylvia about it afterwards--how Uncle Mandeville refused to believe the truth, and swore that he would shoot some of these fellows if they didn't stop talking about his niece. Said Clive, with a grim laugh: "I told him: 'If Sylvia had her way, you'd shoot a good part of the men in the town.'" He answered: "Well, by God, I'll do it--it would serve the scoundrels right!" And he tried to get out of bed and get his pants and his pistols--so that in the end it was necessary to telephone for the major, and then for Barry Chilton and two of his gigantic sons from their plantation.

Sylvia had her way, and talked things out with the agonised Celeste. And the next day came Aunt Varina, hardly able to contain herself. "Oh, Sylvia, such a horrible thing! To hear such words coming from your little sister's lips--like the toads and snakes in the fairy story! To think of these ideas festering in a young girl's brain!" And then again: "Sylvia, your sister declares she will never go to a party again! You are teaching her to hate men! You will make her a STRONG-MINDED woman!"--that was another phrase they had summing up a whole universe of horrors. Sylvia could not recall a time when she had not heard that warning. "Be careful, dear, when you express an opinion, always end it with a question: 'Don't you think so?' or something like that, otherwise, men may get the idea that you are 'STRONG-MINDED'!"

Sylvia, in her girlhood, had heard vague hints and rumours which now she was able to interpret in the light of her experience. In her courtship days she had met a man who always wore gloves, even in the hottest weather, and she had heard that this was because of some affliction of the skin. Now, talking with the young matrons of her own set, she learned that this man had married, and had since had to take to a wheel-chair, while his wife had borne a child with a monstrous deformed head, and had died of the ordeal and the shock.

Oh, the stories that one uncovered--right in one's own town, among one's own set--like foul sewers underneath the pavements! The succession of deceased generations, of imbeciles, epileptics, paralytics! The innocent children born to a lifetime of torment; the women hiding their secret agonies from the world! Sometimes women went all through life without knowing the truth about themselves. There was poor Mrs. Valens, for example, who reclined all day upon the gallery of one of the most beautiful homes in the county, and showed her friends the palms of her hands, all covered with callouses and scales, exclaiming: "What in the world do you suppose can be the matter with me?" She had been a beautiful woman, a "belle" of "Miss Margaret's" day; she had married a man who was rich and handsome and witty--and a rake. Now he was drunk all the time, and two of his children had died in hospital, and another had arms that came out of joint, and had to be put in plaster of Paris for months at a time. His wife, the one-time darling of society, would lie on her couch and read the Book of Job until she knew it by heart.

And could you believe it, when Sylvia came home, ablaze with excitement over the story, she found that the only thing that her relatives were able to see in it was the Book of Job! Under the burden of her afflictions the woman had become devout; and how could anyone fail to see in this the deep purposes of Providence revealed? "Verily," said "Miss Margaret," "'whom the Lord loveth, He chasteneth.' We are told in the Lord's Word that 'the sins of the fathers shall be visited upon the children, even unto the third and fourth generations,' and do you suppose the Lord would have told us that, if He had not known there would be such children?"

19. I cannot pass over this part of my story without bringing forward Mrs. Armistead, the town cynic, who constituted herself one of Sylvia's sources of information in the crisis. Mrs. Sallie Ann Armistead was the mother of two boys with whom Sylvia, as a child, had insisted upon playing, in spite of the protests of the family. "Wha' fo' you go wi' dem Armistead chillun, Mi' Sylvia?" would cry Aunt Mandy, the cook. "Doan' you know they granddaddy done pick cottin in de fiel' 'long o' me?" But while her father was picking cotton, Sallie Ann had looked after her complexion and her figure, and had married a rising young merchant. Now he was the wealthy proprietor of a chain of "nigger stores," and his wife was the possessor of the most dreaded tongue in Castleman County.

She was a person who, if she had been born a duchess, would have made a reputation in history; the one woman in the county who had a mind and was not afraid to have it known. She used all the tricks of a duchess--lorgnettes, for example, with which she stared people into a state of fright. She did not dare try anything like that on the Castlemans, of course, but woe to the little people who crossed her path! She had an eye that sought out every human weakness, and such a wit that even her victims were fascinated. One of the legends about her told how her dearest foe, a dashing young matron, had died, and all the friends had gathered with their floral tributes. Sallie Ann went in to review the remains, and when she came out a sentimental voice inquired: "And how does our poor Ruth look?"

"Oh," was the answer, "as old and grey as ever!"

Now Mrs. Armistead stopped Sylvia in the street: "My dear, how goes the eugenics campaign?"

And while Sylvia gazed, dumbfounded, the other went on as if she were chatting about the weather: "You can't realise what a stir you are making in our little frog pond. Come, see me, and let me tell you the gossip! Do you know you've enriched our vocabulary?"

"I have made someone look up the meaning of eugenics, at least," answered Sylvia--having got herself together in haste.

"Oh, not only that, my dear. You have made a new medical term--the 'van Tuiver disease.' Isn't that interesting?"

For a moment Sylvia shrivelled before this flame from hell. But then, being the only person who had ever been able to chain this devil, she said: "Indeed? I hope that with so fashionable a name the disease does not become an epidemic!"

Mrs. Armistead gazed at her, and then, in a burst of enthusiasm, she exclaimed: "Sylvia Castleman, I have always insisted that one of the most interesting women in the world was spoiled by the taint of goodness in you."

She took Sylvia to her bosom, as it were. "Let us sit on the fence and enjoy this spectacle! My dear, you can have no idea what an uproar you are making! The young married women gather in their boudoirs and whisper ghastly secrets to each other; some of them are sure they have it, and some of them say they can trust their husbands--as if any man could be trusted as far as you can throw a bull by the horns! Did you hear about poor Mrs. Pattie Peyton, she has the measles, but she sent for a specialist, and vowed she had something else--she had read about it, and knew all the symptoms, and insisted on having elaborate blood-tests! And little Mrs. Stanley Pendleton has left her husband, and everybody says that's the reason. The men are simply shivering in their boots--they steal into the doctor's offices by the back-doors, and a whole car-load of the boys have been shipped off to Hot Springs to be boiled--" And so on, while Mrs. Armistead revelled in the sensation of strolling down Main Street with Mrs. Douglas van Tuiver!

Then Sylvia would go home, and get the newest reactions of the family to these horrors. Aunt Nannie, it seemed, made the discovery that Basil, junr., her fifth son, was carrying on an intrigue with a mulatto girl in the town; and she forbade him to go to Castleman Hall, for fear lest Sylvia should worm the secret out of him; also she shipped Lucy May off to visit a friend, and came and tried to persuade Mrs. Chilton to do the same with Peggy and Maria, lest Sylvia should somehow corrupt these children.

The bishop came, having been ordered to preach religion to his wayward niece. Poor dear Uncle Basil--he had tried preaching religion to Sylvia many years ago, and never could do it because he loved her so well that with all his Seventeenth Century theology he could not deny her chance of salvation. Now the first sight that met his eyes when he came to see her was his little blind grand-niece. And also he had in his secret heart the knowledge that he, a rich and gay young planter before he became converted to Methodism, had played with the fire of vice, and been badly burned. So Sylvia did not find him at all the Voice of Authority, but just a poor, hen-pecked, unhappy husband of a tyrannous Castleman woman.

The next thing was that "Miss Margaret" took up the notion that a time such as this was not one for Sylvia's husband to be away from her. What if people were to say that they had separated? There were family consultations, and in the midst of them there came word that van Tuiver was called North upon business. When the family delegations came to Sylvia, to insist that she go with him, the answer they got was that if they could not let her stay quietly at home without asking her any questions, she would go off to New York and live with a divorced woman Social-ist!

"Of course, they gave up," she wrote me. "And half an hour ago poor dear mamma came to my room and said: 'Sylvia, dear, we will let you do what you want, but won't you please do one small favour for me?' I got ready for trouble, and asked what she wanted. Her answer was: 'Won't you go with Celeste to the Young Ma-trons' Cotillion tomorrow night, so that people won't think there's anything the matter?'"

20. Roger Peyton had gone off to Hot Springs, and Douglas van Tuiver was in New York; so little by little the storms about Castleman Hall began to abate in violence. Sylvia was absorbed with her baby, and beginning to fit her life into that of her people. She found many ways in which she could serve them--entertaining Uncle Mandeville to keep him sober; checking the extravagance of Celeste; nurs-ing Castleman Lysle through green apple convulsions. That was to be her life for

the future, she told herself, and she was making herself really happy in it--when suddenly, like a bolt from the blue, came an event that swept her poor little plans into chaos.

It was an afternoon in March, the sun was shining brightly and the Southern springtime was in full tide, and Sylvia had had the old family carriage made ready, with two of the oldest and gentlest family horses, and took the girls upon a shopping expedition to town. In the front seat sat Celeste, driving, with two of her friends, and in the rear seat was Sylvia, with Peggy and Maria. When an assemblage of allurements such as this stopped on the streets of the town, the young men would come out of the banks and the offices and gather round to chat. There would be a halt before an ice-cream parlour, and a big tray of ices would be brought out, and the girls would sit in the carriage and eat, and the boys would stand on the curb and eat--undismayed by the fact that they had welcomed half a dozen such parties during the afternoon. The statistics proved that this was a thriving town, with rapidly increasing business, but there was never so much business as to interfere with gallantries like these.

Sylvia enjoyed the scene; it took her back to happy days, before black care had taken his seat behind her. She sat in a kind of dream, only half hearing the merriment of the young people, and only half tasting her ice. How she loved this old town, with its streets deep in black spring mud, its mud-plastered "buck-boards" and saddle horses hitched at every telegraph pole! Its banks and stores and law offices seemed shabbier after one had made the "grand tour," but they were none the less dear to her for that. She would spend the rest of her days in Castleman County, and the sunshine and peace would gradually enfold her.

Such were her thoughts when the unforeseen event befel. A man on horseback rode down a side-street, crossing Main Street a little way in front of her; a man dressed in khaki, with a khaki riding hat pulled low over his face. He rode rapidly--appearing and vanishing, so that Sylvia scarcely saw him--really did not see him with her conscious mind at all. Her thoughts were still busy with dreams, and the clatter of boys and girls; but deep within her had begun a tumult--a trembling, a pounding of the heart, a clamouring under the floors of her consciousness.

And slowly this excitement mounted. What was the matter, what had happened? A man had ridden by, but why should a man--. Surely it could not have been--no. There were hundreds of men in Castleman County who wore khaki and rode horse-back, and had sturdy, thick-set figures! But then, how could she make a mistake? How could her instinct have betrayed her so? It was that same view of him as he sat on a horse that had first thrilled her during the hunting party years ago!

He had gone West, and had said that he would never return. He had not been heard from in years. What an amazing thing, that a mere glimpse of a man who looked and dressed and rode like him should be able to set her whole being into such a panic! How futile became her dreams of peace!

She heard the sound of a vehicle close beside her carriage, and turned and found herself looking into the sharp eyes of Mrs. Armistead. It happened that Sylvia was on the side away from the curb, and there was no one talking to her; so Mrs. Armistead ran her electric alongside, and had the stirring occasion to herself. Sylvia looked into her face, so full of malice, and knew two things in a flash: First, it really had been Frank Shirley riding by; and second, Mrs. Armistead had seen him!

"Another candidate for your eugenics class!" said the lady.

Sylvia glanced at the young people and made sure they were paying no attention. She might have made some remark that would have brought them into the conversation, and delivered her from the torments of this devil. But no, she had never quailed from Mrs. Armistead in her life, and she would not now give her the satisfaction of driving off to tell the town that Sylvia van Tuiver had seen Frank Shirley, and had been overcome by it, and had taken refuge behind the skirts of her little sisters!

"You can see I have my carriage full of pupils" she said, smilingly.

"How happy it must make you, Sylvia--coming home and meeting all your old friends! It must set you trembling with ecstasy--angels singing in the sky above you--little golden bells ringing all over you!"

Sylvia recognised these phrases. They were part of an effort she had made to describe the raptures of young love to her bosom friend, Harriet Atkinson. And so Harriet had passed them on to the town! And they had been cherished all these years.

She could not afford to recognise these illegitimate children of romance. "Mrs. Armistead," she said, "I had no idea you had so much poetry in you!"

"I am simply improvising, my dear--upon the colour in your cheeks at present!"

There was no way save to be bold. "You couldn't expect me not to be excited, Mrs. Armistead. You see, I had no idea he had come back from the West."

"They say he left a wife there." remarked the lady, innocently.

"Ah!" said Sylvia. "Then he will not be staying long, presumably."

There was a pause; all at once Mrs. Armistead's voice became gentle and sympathetic. "Sylvia," she said, "don't imagine that I fail to appreciate what is going on in your heart. I know a true romance when I see one. If only you could have known in those days what you know now, there might have been one beautiful love story that did not end as a tragedy."

You would have thought the lady's better self had suddenly been touched. But Sylvia knew her; too many times she had seen this huntress trying to lure a victim out of his refuge.

"Yes, Mrs. Armistead," she said, gently. "But I have the consolation at least of being a martyr to science."

"In what way?"

"Have you forgotten the new medical term that I have given to the world?"

And Mrs. Armistead looked at her for a moment aghast. "My God, Sylvia!" she whispered; and then--an honest tribute: "You certainly can take care of yourself!"

"Yes," said Sylvia. "Tell that to my other friends in town." And so, at last, Mrs. Armistead started her machine, and this battle of hell-cats came to an end.

21. Sylvia rode home in a daze, answering without hearing the prattle of the children. She was appalled at the emotions that possessed her--that the sight of Frank Shirley riding down the street could have affected her so! She forgot Mrs. Armistead, she forgot the whole world, in her dismay over her own state of mind. Having dismissed Frank from her life and her thoughts forever, it seemed to her preposterous that she should be at the mercy of such an excitement.

She found herself wondering about her family. Did they know that Frank Shirley had returned? Would they have failed to mention it to her? For a moment she told herself it would not have occurred to them she could have any interest in the subject. But no--they were not so *naive*--the Castleman women--as their sense of propriety made them pretend to be! But how stupid of them not to give her warning! Suppose she had happened to meet Frank face to face, and in the presence of others! She must certainly have betrayed her excitement; and just at this time, when the world had the Castleman family under the microscope!

She told herself that she would avoid such difficulty in future; she would stay at home until Frank had gone away. If he had a wife in the West, presumably he had merely come for a visit to his mother and sisters. And then Sylvia found herself in an argument with herself. What possible difference could it make that Frank Shirley had a wife? So long as she, Sylvia, had a husband, what else mattered? Yet she could not deny it--it brought her a separate and additional pang that Frank Shirley should have married. What sort of wife could he have found--he, a stranger in the far West? And why had he not brought his wife home to his people?

When she stepped out of the carriage, it was with her mind made up that she would stay at home until all danger was past. But the next afternoon a neighbour called up to ask Sylvia and Celeste to come and play cards in the evening. It was not a party, Mrs. Witherspoon explained to "Miss Margaret," who answered the 'phone; just a few friends and a good time, and she did so hope that Sylvia was not going to refuse. The mere hint of the fear that Sylvia might refuse was enough to excite Mrs. Castleman. Why should Sylvia refuse? So she accepted the invitation, and then came to plead with her daughter--for Celeste's sake, and for the sake of all her family, so that the world might see that she was not crushed by misfortune!

There were reasons why the invitation was a difficult one to decline. Mrs. Virginia Witherspoon was the daughter of a Confederate general whose name you read in every history-book; and she had a famous old home in the country which was falling about her ears--her husband being seldom sober enough to know what was happening. She had also three blossoming daughters, whom she must manage to get out of the home before the plastering of the drawing-room fell upon the heads of their suitors; so that the ardour of her husband-hunting was one of the jokes of the State. Naturally, under such circumstances, the Witherspoons had to be treated with consideration by the Castlemans. One might snub rich Yankees, and chasten the suddenly-prosperous; but a family with an ancient house in ruins, and with faded uniforms and battle-scarred sabres in the cedar-chests in its attic--such a family can with difficulty overdraw its social bank account.

Dolly Witherspoon, the oldest daughter, had been Sylvia's rival for the palm as the most beautiful girl in Castleman County. And Sylvia had triumphed, and Dolly had failed. So, in her secret heart she hated Sylvia, and the mother hated her; and yet--such was the social game--they had to invite Sylvia and her sister to their card-parties, and Sylvia and her sister had to go. They had to go and be the most striking figures there: Celeste, slim and pale from sorrow, virginal, in clinging white chiffon; and Sylvia, regal and splendid, shimmering like a mermaid in a gown of emerald green.

The mermaid imagined that she noticed a slight agitation underneath the cordiality of her hostess. The next person to greet her was Mrs. Armistead; and Sylvia was sure that she did not imagine the suppressed excitement in that lady's manner. But even while she was speculating and suspecting, she was led toward the drawing-room. It was late, her hostess explained; the other guests were waiting, so if they did not mind, the play would start at once. Celeste was to sit at that table over there, with Mr. Witherspoon's crippled brother, and old Mr. Perkins, who was deaf; and Sylvia was to come this way--the table in the corner. Sylvia moved toward it, and Dolly Witherspoon and her sister, Emma, greeted her cordially, and then stepped out of the way to let her to her seat; and Sylvia gave one glance--and found herself face to face with Frank Shirley!

22. Frank's face was scarlet; and Sylvia had a moment of blind terror, when she wanted to turn and fly. But there about her was the circle of her enemies; a whole roomful of people, breathless with curiosity, drinking in with eyes and ears every hint of distress that she might give. And the next morning the whole town would, in imagination, attend the scene!

"Good-evening, Julia," said Sylvia, to Mrs. Witherspoon's youngest daughter, the other lady at the table. "Good-evening, Malcolm"--to Malcolm McCallum, an old "beau" of hers. And then, taking the seat which Malcolm sprang to move out for her, "How do you do, Frank?"

Frank's eyes had fallen to his lap. "How do you do?" he murmured. The sound of his voice, low and trembling, full of pain, was like the sound of some old funeral bell to Sylvia; it sent the blood leaping in torrents to her forehead. Oh, horrible, horrible!

For a moment her eyes fell like his, and she shuddered, and was beaten. But there was the roomful of people, watching; there was Mrs. Armistead, there were the Witherspoon women gloating. She forced a tortured smile to her lips, and asked,

"What are we playing?"

"Oh, didn't you know that?" said Julia. "Progressive whist."

"Thank-you," said Sylvia. "When do we begin?" And she looked about--anywhere but at Frank Shirley, with his face grown so old in four years.

No one said anything, no one made a move. Was everybody in the room conspiring to break her down? "I thought we were late," she said, desperately; and then, with another effort--"Shall I cut?" she asked, of Julia.

"If you please," said the girl; but she did not make a motion to pass the cards. Her manner seemed to say, You may cut all night, but it won't help you to rob me of this satisfaction.

Sylvia made a still more determined effort. If the game was to be postponed indefinitely, so that people might watch her and Frank--well, she would have to find something to talk about.

"It is a surprise to see you again, Frank Shirley!" she exclaimed.

"Yes," he said. His voice was a mumble, and he did not lift his eyes.

"You have been in the West, I understand?"

"Yes," again; but still he did not lift his eyes.

Sylvia managed to lift hers as far as his cravat; and she saw in it an old piece of imitation jewelry which she had picked up once on the street, and had handed to him in jest. He had worn it all these years! He had not thrown it away--not even when she had thrown him away!

Again came a surge of emotion; and out of the mist she looked about her and saw the faces of tormenting demons, leering. "Well," she demanded, "are we going to play?"

"We were waiting for you to cut," said Julia, graciously; and Sylvia's fury helped to restore her self-posession. She cut the cards; and fate was kind, sparing both her and Frank the task of dealing.

But then a new difficulty arose. Julia dealt, and thirteen cards lay in front of Frank Shirley; but he did not seem to know that he ought to pick them up. And when the opposing lady called him to time, in what seemed an unnecessarily penetrating voice, he found that he was physically unable to get the cards from the table. And when with his fumbling efforts he got them into a bunch, he could not straighten them out--to say nothing of the labour of sorting them according to suit, which all whist-players know to be an indispensable preliminary to the game. When the opposing lady prodded him again, Frank's face changed from vivid scarlet to a dark and alarming purple.

Miss Julia led the tray of clubs; and Frank, whose turn came next, spilled three cards upon the table, and finally selected from them the king of hearts to play--hearts being trumps. "But you have a club there, Mr. Shirley," said his opponent; something that was pardonable, inasmuch as the nine of clubs lay face up where he had shoved it aside.

"Oh--I beg pardon," he stammered, and took back his king, and reached into his hand and pulled out the six of clubs, and a diamond with it.

It was evident that this could not go on. Sylvia might be equal to the emergency, but Frank was not. He was too much of a human being and too little of a social automaton. Something must be done.

"Don't they play whist out West, Mr. Shirley," asked Julia, still smiling benevolently.

And Sylvia lowered her cards. "Surely, my dear, you must understand," she said, gently. "Mr. Shirley is too much embarrassed to think about cards."

"Oh!" said the other, taken aback. (*L'audace, touljours l'audace!* runs the formula!)

"You see," continued Sylvia, "this is the first time that Frank has seen me in more than three years. And when two people have been as much in love as he and I were, they are naturally disturbed when they meet, and cannot put their minds upon a game of cards."

Julia was speechless. And Sylvia let her glance wander casually about the room. She saw her hostess and her daughters standing watching; and near the wall at the other side of the room stood the head-devil, who had planned this torment.

"Mrs. Armistead," Sylvia called, "aren't you going to play to-night?" Of course everybody in the room heard this; and after it, anyone could have heard a pin drop.

"I'm to keep score," said Mrs. Armistead.

"But it doesn't need four to keep score," objected Sylvia--and looked at the three Witherspoon ladies.

"Dolly and Emma are staying out," said Mrs. Witherspoon. "Two of our guests did not come."

"Well," Sylvia exclaimed, "that just makes it right! Please let them take the place of Mr. Shirley and myself. You see, we haven't seen each other for three or four years, and it's hard for us to get interested into a game of cards."

The whole room caught its breath at once; and here and there one heard a little squeak of hysteria, cut short by some one who was not sure whether it was a joke or a scandal. "Why--Sylvia!" stammered Mrs. Witherspoon, completely staggered.

Then Sylvia perceived that she was mistress of the scene. There came the old rapture of conquest, that made her social genius. "We have so much that we want to talk about," she said, in her most winning voice. "Let Dolly and Emma take our places, and we will sit on the sofa in the other room and chat. You and Mrs. Armistead come and chaperone us. Won't you do that, please?"

"Why--why----" gasped the bewildered lady.

"I'm sure that you will both be interested to hear what we have to say to each other; and you can tell everybody about it afterwards--and that will be so much better than having the card-game delayed any more."

And with this side-swipe Sylvia arose. She stood and waited, to make sure that her ex-fiancé was not too paralysed to follow. She led him out through the tangle of card-tables; and in the door-way she stopped and waited for Mrs. Armistead and Mrs. Witherspoon, and literally forced these two ladies to come with her out of the room.

23. Do you care to hear the details of the punishment which Sylvia administered to the two conspirators? She took them to the sofa, and made Frank draw up chairs for them, and when she had got comfortably seated, she proceeded to talk to Frank just as gently and sincerely and touchingly as she would have talked if there had been nobody present. She asked about all that had befallen him, and when she discovered that he was still not able to chat, she told him about herself, about her baby, who was beautiful and dear, even if she was blind, and about all the interesting things she had seen in Europe. When presently the old ladies showed signs of growing restless, she put hand cuffs on them and chained them to their chairs.

"You see," she said, "it would never do for Mr. Shirley and myself to talk without a chaperon. You got me into this situation, you know, and papa and mamma would never forgive you."

"You are mistaken, Sylvia!" cried Mrs. Witherspoon. "Mr. Shirley so seldom goes out, and he had said he didn't think he would come!"

"I am willing to accept that explanation," said Sylvia, politely, "but you must help me out now that the embarrassing accident has happened."

Nor did it avail Mrs. Witherspoon to plead her guests and their score. "You may be sure they don't care about the score," said Sylvia. "They'd much prefer you stayed here, so that you can tell them how Frank and I behaved."

And then, while Mrs. Witherspoon was getting herself together, Sylvia turned upon the other conspirator. "We will now hold one of my eugenics classes," she said, and added, to Frank, "Mrs. Armistead told me that you wanted to join my class."

"I don't understand," replied Frank, at a loss.

"I will explain," said Sylvia. "It is not a very refined joke they have in the town. Mrs. Armistead meant to say that she credits a disgraceful story that was circulated about you when we were engaged, and which my people made use of to make me break our engagement. I am glad to have a chance to tell you that I have investigated and satisfied myself that the story was not true. I want to apologise to you for ever having believed it; and I am sure that Mrs. Armistead may be glad of this opportunity to apologise for having said that she believed it."

"I never said that I believed it!" cried Sallie Ann.

"No, you didn't, Mrs. Armistead--you would not be so crude as to say it directly. You merely dropped a hint, which would lead everybody to understand that you believed it."

Sylvia paused, just long enough to let the wicked lady suffer, but not long enough to let her find a reply. "When you tell your friends about this scene," she continued, "please make clear that I did not drop hints about anything, but said exactly what I meant--that the story is false, so far as it implies any evil done by Mr. Shirley, and that I am deeply ashamed of myself for having ever believed it. It is all in the past now, of course--we are both us married, and we shall probably never meet again. But it will be a help to us in future to have had this little talk--will it not, Frank?"

There was a pause, while Sallie Ann Armistead recovered from her dismay, and got back a little of her fighting power. Suddenly she rose: "Virginia," she said, firmly, "you are neglecting your guests."

"I don't think you ought to go until Frank has got himself together," said Sylvia. "Frank, can you sort your cards now?"

"Virginia!" commanded Sallie Ann, imperiously. "Come!"

Mrs. Witherspoon rose, and so did Sylvia. "We can't stay here alone," said she. "Frank, will you take Mrs. Witherspoon in?" And she gently but firmly took Mrs. Armistead's arm, and so they marched back into the drawing-room.

Dolly and Emma had progressed to separate tables, it developed, so that the ordeal of Frank and Sylvia was over. Through the remainder of the evening Sylvia chatted and played, and later partook of refreshments with Malcolm McCallum, and mildly teased that inconsolable bachelor, quite as in the old days. Now and then she stole a glance at Frank Shirley, and saw that he was holding up his end; but he kept away from her, and she never even caught his eye.

At last the company broke up, and Sylvia thanked her hostess for a most enjoyable evening. She stepped into the motor with Celeste, and sat with compressed lips, answering in monosyllables her "little sister's" flood of excited questions--"Oh, Sylvia, didn't you feel perfectly *terrible?* Oh, sister, I felt *thrills* running up and down my back! Sister, what *did* you say to him? Sister, do you know old Mr. Perkins kept leaning over me and asking what was happening; and how could I shout into his deaf ear that everybody was stopping to hear what you were saying to Frank Shirley?"

At the end of the ride, there was Aunt Varina waiting up as usual--to renew her own youth in the story of the evening, what this person had worn and what that person had said. But Sylvia left her sister to tell the story, and fled to her room and locked the door, and flung herself upon the bed and gave way to a torrent of weeping.

Half an hour later Celeste went up, and finding that the door between her room and Sylvia's was unlocked, opened it softly, and stood listening. Finally she stole to her sister's side and put her arm about her. "Never mind, sister dear," she whispered, solemnly, "I know how it is! We women all have to suffer!"

The Codes Of Hammurabi And Moses
W. W. Davies

QTY

The discovery of the Hammurabi Code is one of the greatest achievements of archaeology, and is of paramount interest, not only to the student of the Bible, but also to all those interested in ancient history...

Religion   **ISBN:** *1-59462-338-4*   **Pages:132**
                                                MSRP $12.95

The Theory of Moral Sentiments
Adam Smith

QTY

This work from 1749. contains original theories of conscience amd moral judgment and it is the foundation for systemof morals.

Philosophy **ISBN:** *1-59462-777-0*   **Pages:536**
                                                MSRP $19.95

Jessica's First Prayer
Hesba Stretton

QTY

In a screened and secluded corner of one of the many railway-bridges which span the streets of London there could be seen a few years ago, from five o'clock every morning until half past eight, a tidily set-out coffee-stall, consisting of a trestle and board, upon which stood two large tin cans, with a small fire of charcoal burning under each so as to keep the coffee boiling during the early hours of the morning when the work-people were thronging into the city on their way to their daily toil...

                                                Pages:84
Childrens   **ISBN:** *1-59462-373-2*   *MSRP $9.95*

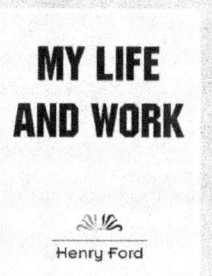

My Life and Work
Henry Ford

QTY

Henry Ford revolutionized the world with his implementation of mass production for the Model T automobile. Gain valuable business insight into his life and work with his own auto-biography... "We have only started on our development of our country we have not as yet, with all our talk of wonderful progress, done more than scratch the surface. The progress has been wonderful enough but..."

                                                Pages:300
Biographies/ **ISBN:** *1-59462-198-5*   *MSRP $21.95*

QTY

The Art of Cross-Examination
Francis Wellman

I presume it is the experience of every author, after his first book is published upon an important subject, to be almost overwhelmed with a wealth of ideas and illustrations which could readily have been included in his book, and which to his own mind, at least, seem to make a second edition inevitable. Such certainly was the case with me; and when the first edition had reached its sixth impression in five months, I rejoiced to learn that it seemed to my publishers that the book had met with a sufficiently favorable reception to justify a second and considerably enlarged edition. ...

Pages:412

Reference   **ISBN: *1-59462-647-2***   *MSRP $19.95*

QTY

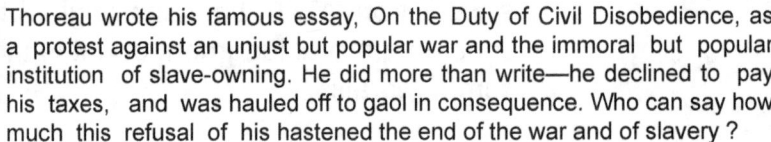

On the Duty of Civil Disobedience
Henry David Thoreau

Thoreau wrote his famous essay, On the Duty of Civil Disobedience, as a protest against an unjust but popular war and the immoral but popular institution of slave-owning. He did more than write—he declined to pay his taxes, and was hauled off to gaol in consequence. Who can say how much this refusal of his hastened the end of the war and of slavery ?

Law   **ISBN: *1-59462-747-9***   **Pages:48**

MSRP $7.45

Dream Psychology Psychoanalysis for Beginners   QTY
Sigmund Freud

Sigmund Freud, born Sigismund Schlomo Freud (May 6, 1856 - September 23, 1939), was a Jewish-Austrian neurologist and psychiatrist who co-founded the psychoanalytic school of psychology. Freud is best known for his theories of the unconscious mind, especially involving the mechanism of repression; his redefinition of sexual desire as mobile and directed towards a wide variety of objects; and his therapeutic techniques, especially his understanding of transference in the therapeutic relationship and the presumed value of dreams as sources of insight into unconscious desires.

Pages:196

Psychology   **ISBN: *1-59462-905-6***   *MSRP $15.45*

QTY

The Miracle of Right Thought
Orison Swett Marden

Believe with all of your heart that you will do what you were made to do. When the mind has once formed the habit of holding cheerful, happy, prosperous pictures, it will not be easy to form the opposite habit. It does not matter how improbable or how far away this realization may see, or how dark the prospects may be, if we visualize them as best we can, as vividly as possible, hold tenaciously to them and vigorously struggle to attain them, they will gradually become actualized, realized in the life. But a desire, a longing without endeavor, a yearning abandoned or held indifferently will vanish without realization.

Pages:360

Self Help   **ISBN: *1-59462-644-8***   *MSRP $25.45*

QTY

The Rosicrucian Cosmo-Conception Mystic Christianity *by Max Heindel*   ISBN: *1-59462-188-8*   **$38.95**
The Rosicrucian Cosmo-conception is not dogmatic, neither does it appeal to any other authority than the reason of the student. It is: not controversial, but is: sent forth in the, hope that it may help to clear...   New Age/Religion Pages 646

Abandonment To Divine Providence *by Jean-Pierre de Caussade*   ISBN: *1-59462-228-0*   **$25.95**
"The Rev. Jean Pierre de Caussade was one of the most remarkable spiritual writers of the Society of Jesus in France in the 18th Century. His death took place at Toulouse in 1751. His works have gone through many editions and have been republished...   Inspirational/Religion Pages 400

Mental Chemistry *by Charles Haanel*   ISBN: *1-59462-192-6*   **$23.95**
Mental Chemistry allows the change of material conditions by combining and appropriately utilizing the power of the mind. Much like applied chemistry creates something new and unique out of careful combinations of chemicals the mastery of mental chemistry...   New Age Pages 354

The Letters of Robert Browning and Elizabeth Barret Barrett 1845-1846 vol II   ISBN: *1-59462-193-4*   **$35.95**
by Robert Browning and Elizabeth Barrett   Biographies Pages 596

Gleanings In Genesis (volume I) *by Arthur W. Pink*   ISBN: *1-59462-130-6*   **$27.45**
Appropriately has Genesis been termed "the seed plot of the Bible" for in it we have, in germ form, almost all of the great doctrines which are afterwards fully developed in the books of Scripture which follow...   Religion/Inspirational Pages 420

The Master Key *by L. W. de Laurence*   ISBN: *1-59462-001-6*   **$30.95**
In no branch of human knowledge has there been a more lively increase of the spirit of research during the past few years than in the study of Psychology, Concentration and Mental Discipline. The requests for authentic lessons in Thought Control, Mental Discipline and...   New Age/Business Pages 422

The Lesser Key Of Solomon Goetia *by L. W. de Laurence*   ISBN: *1-59462-092-X*   **$9.95**
This translation of the first book of the "Lemegton" which is now for the first time made accessible to students of Talismanic Magic was done, after careful collation and edition, from numerous Ancient Manuscripts in Hebrew, Latin, and French...   New Age/Occult Pages 92

Rubaiyat Of Omar Khayyam *by Edward Fitzgerald*   ISBN:*1-59462-332-5*   **$13.95**
Edward Fitzgerald, whom the world has already learned, in spite of his own efforts to remain within the shadow of anonymity, to look upon as one of the rarest poets of the century, was born at Bredfield, in Suffolk, on the 31st of March, 1809. He was the third son of John Purcell...   Music Pages 172

Ancient Law *by Henry Maine*   ISBN: *1-59462-128-4*   **$29.95**
The chief object of the following pages is to indicate some of the earliest ideas of mankind, as they are reflected in Ancient Law, and to point out the relation of those ideas to modern thought.   Religion/History Pages 452

Far-Away Stories *by William J. Locke*   ISBN: *1-59462-129-2*   **$19.45**
"Good wine needs no bush, but a collection of mixed vintages does. And this book is just such a collection. Some of the stories I do not want to remain buried for ever in the files of dead magazine-numbers an author's not unpardonable vanity..."   Fiction Pages 272

Life of David Crockett *by David Crockett*   ISBN: *1-59462-250-7*   **$27.45**
"Colonel David Crockett was one of the most remarkable men of the times in which he lived. Born in humble life, but gifted with a strong will, an indomitable courage, and unremitting perseverance...   Biographies/New Age Pages 424

Lip-Reading *by Edward Nitchie*   ISBN: *1-59462-206-X*   **$25.95**
Edward B. Nitchie, founder of the New York School for the Hard of Hearing, now the Nitchie School of Lip-Reading, Inc, wrote "LIP-READING Principles and Practice". The development and perfecting of this meritorious work on lip-reading was an undertaking...   How-to Pages 400

A Handbook of Suggestive Therapeutics, Applied Hypnotism, Psychic Science   ISBN: *1-59462-214-0*   **$24.95**
by Henry Munro   Health/New Age/Health/Self-help Pages 376

A Doll's House: and Two Other Plays *by Henrik Ibsen*   ISBN: *1-59462-112-8*   **$19.95**
Henrik Ibsen created this classic when in revolutionary 1848 Rome. Introducing some striking concepts in playwriting for the realist genre, this play has been studied the world over.   Fiction/Classics/Plays 308

The Light of Asia *by sir Edwin Arnold*   ISBN: *1-59462-204-3*   **$13.95**
In this poetic masterpiece, Edwin Arnold describes the life and teachings of Buddha. The man who was to become known as Buddha to the world was born as Prince Gautama of India but he rejected the worldly riches and abandoned the reigns of power when...   Religion/History/Biographies Pages 170

The Complete Works of Guy de Maupassant *by Guy de Maupassant*   ISBN: *1-59462-157-8*   **$16.95**
"For days and days, nights and nights, I had dreamed of that first kiss which was to consecrate our engagement, and I knew not on what spot I should put my lips..."   Fiction/Classics Pages 240

The Art of Cross-Examination *by Francis L. Wellman*   ISBN: *1-59462-309-0*   **$26.95**
Written by a renowned trial lawyer, Wellman imparts his experience and uses case studies to explain how to use psychology to extract desired information through questioning.   How-to/Science/Reference Pages 408

Answered or Unanswered? *by Louisa Vaughan*   ISBN: *1-59462-248-5*   **$10.95**
Miracles of Faith in China   Religion Pages 112

The Edinburgh Lectures on Mental Science (1909) *by Thomas*   ISBN: *1-59462-008-3*   **$11.95**
This book contains the substance of a course of lectures recently given by the writer in the Queen Street Hall, Edinburgh. Its purpose is to indicate the Natural Principles governing the relation between Mental Action and Material Conditions...   New Age/Psychology Pages 148

Ayesha *by H. Rider Haggard*   ISBN: *1-59462-301-5*   **$24.95**
Verily and indeed it is the unexpected that happens! Probably if there was one person upon the earth from whom the Editor of this, and of a certain previous history, did not expect to hear again...   Classics Pages 380

Ayala's Angel *by Anthony Trollope*   ISBN: *1-59462-352-X*   **$29.95**
The two girls were both pretty, but Lucy who was twenty-one who supposed to be simple and comparatively unattractive, whereas Ayala was credited, as her Bombwhat romantic name might show, with poetic charm and a taste for romance. Ayala when her father died was nineteen...   Fiction Pages 484

The American Commonwealth *by James Bryce*   ISBN: *1-59462-286-8*   **$34.45**
An interpretation of American democratic political theory. It examines political mechanics and society from the perspective of Scotsman James Bryce   Politics Pages 572

Stories of the Pilgrims *by Margaret P. Pumphrey*   ISBN: *1-59462-116-0*   **$17.95**
This book explores pilgrims religious oppression in England as well as their escape to Holland and eventual crossing to America on the Mayflower, and their early days in New England...   History Pages 268

www.bookjungle.com *email: sales@bookjungle.com fax: 630-214-0564 mail: Book Jungle PO Box 2226 Champaign, IL 61825*

QTY

The Fasting Cure *by Sinclair Upton*
ISBN: *1-59462-222-1* **$13.95**
In the Cosmopolitan Magazine for May, 1910, and in the Contemporary Review (London) for April, 1910, I published an article dealing with my experiences in fasting. I have written a great many magazine articles, but never one which attracted so much attention... New Age/Self Help/Health Pages 164

Hebrew Astrology *by Sepharial*
ISBN: *1-59462-308-2* **$13.45**
In these days of advanced thinking it is a matter of common observation that we have left many of the old landmarks behind and that we are now pressing forward to greater heights and to a wider horizon than that which represented the mind-content of our progenitors... Astrology Pages 144

Thought Vibration or The Law of Attraction in the Thought World
ISBN: *1-59462-127-6* **$12.95**
by William Walker Atkinson
Psychology/Religion Pages 144

Optimism *by Helen Keller*
ISBN: *1-59462-108-X* **$15.95**
Helen Keller was blind, deaf, and mute since 19 months old, yet famously learned how to overcome these handicaps, communicate with the world, and spread her lectures promoting optimism. An inspiring read for everyone... Biographies/Inspirational Pages 84

Sara Crewe *by Frances Burnett*
ISBN: *1-59462-360-0* **$9.45**
In the first place, Miss Minchin lived in London. Her home was a large, dull, tall one, in a large, dull square, where all the houses were alike, and all the sparrows were alike, and where all the door-knockers made the same heavy sound... Childrens/Classic Pages 88

The Autobiography of Benjamin Franklin *by Benjamin Franklin*
ISBN: *1-59462-135-7* **$24.95**
The Autobiography of Benjamin Franklin has probably been more extensively read than any other American historical work, and no other book of its kind has had such ups and downs of fortune. Franklin lived for many years in England, where he was agent... Biographies/History Pages 332

Name	
Email	
Telephone	
Address	
City, State ZIP	

☐ **Credit Card**   ☐ **Check / Money Order**

Credit Card Number	
Expiration Date	
Signature	

Please Mail to: Book Jungle
PO Box 2226
Champaign, IL 61825
or Fax to: 630-214-0564

ORDERING INFORMATION
web*: www.bookjungle.com*
email*: sales@bookjungle.com*
fax*: 630-214-0564*
mail*: Book Jungle PO Box 2226 Champaign, IL 61825*
or PayPal *to sales@bookjungle.com*

Please contact us for bulk discounts

DIRECT-ORDER TERMS

**20% Discount if You Order
Two or More Books**
Free Domestic Shipping!
Accepted: Master Card, Visa,
Discover, American Express

www.ingramcontent.com/pod-product-compliance
Lightning Source LLC
Chambersburg PA
CBHW080730020726
47503CB00010B/2857